ABERDEEN CITY LIBRARIES

MURDER AT COLDITZ

MURDER AT COLDITZ

Leo Kessler

Severn House Large Print
London & New York

This first large print edition published in Great Britain 2003 by
SEVERN HOUSE LARGE PRINT BOOKS LTD of
9-15 High Street, Sutton, Surrey, SM1 1DF.
First world regular print edition published 2002 by
Severn House Publishers, London and New York.
This first large print edition published in the USA 2003 by
SEVERN HOUSE PUBLISHERS INC., of
595 Madison Avenue, New York, NY 10022

British Library Cataloguing in Publication Data

Kessler, Leo, 1926 -
Murder at Colditz. - Large print ed.
1. Hitler, Adolf, 1889-1945 - Assassination attempts - Fiction
2. Intelligence officers - Great Britain - Fiction
3. World War, 1939-1945 - Secret service - Great Britain - Fiction
4. World War, 1939-1945 - Prisoners and prisons, German - Fiction
5. War stories
6. Large type books
I. Title
823.9'14 [F]

ISBN 0-7278-7315-6

Printed and bound in Great Britain by
MPG Books Ltd, Bodmin, Cornwall.

For Irma
from Leo Kessler
and all the Old Gang

He, the trained spy, had walked into the trap
For a bogus guide, seduced with the old tricks.

W.H. Auden

THE VENLO KIDNAPPING

'The British Secret Service has a great tradition. Germany possesses nothing comparable to it. The cunning and perfidy of the British Secret Service is known throughout the world.'

Adolf Hitler, 1939

It was Thursday, 9 November 1939.

To the east where the German frontier with Holland lay, there hung ominous black curtains of rain. The dawn air had grown colder too. The middle-aged captain in Britain's Secret Intelligence Service told himself it wasn't going to be a nice day. How bad it would be in reality, Captain Best didn't yet know. This Thursday his whole life would change – for the worse.

He gave a little sigh, stared at his face in the shaving mirror through the monocle he affected in the British upper-class fashion and continued to lather his face from the shaving mug. As he did so, he was overcome with a strange sense of apprehension. He shuddered a little and told himself that he was seeing ghosts or the like.

All the same, he couldn't shake off the mood of foreboding. He felt he was being followed and, with a quarter of a century of the war in the shadows of Intelligence behind him, he felt he knew when something was wrong. How did he explain the fat man who had appeared to be listening yesterday when they had gone up to the frontier to talk to the Huns? Or the fact that twice he had caught a glimpse of field glasses glittering in the weak winter sun as they had driven away from the preliminary talks with the German traitors, who were preparing to betray their Führer? All very strange, very strange indeed.

'Get a grip of yourself, you silly bugger,' he snapped at himself in the mirror. 'Behaving like a bloody old woman.' He started to scrape his taut skin with the cut-throat razor. In the old war he had been on secret ops like this on the Dutch–German frontier scores of times. Why, once he had even been captured by the Huns and had saved his life by breaking away, with bullets plucking at his flying heels, and diving into an icy canal. In those days he had really run risks. Now these new-fangled Huns, all German Army officers, were traitors to the man. They were only too eager to do away with their bloody Führer, who looked like Charlie Chaplin without the baggy suit. What danger could they present? He calmed himself and got on with his shave. Down the street, the man in the shabby raincoat leaning against the lamppost looked at his cheap watch yet once again...

His wife, fat, Dutch, and connected with some of the best families in Holland, was still in bed. She was reading the morning paper and enjoying her usual breakfast plate of cold meats and sausage, washed down with many cups of strong Dutch coffee. '*De Koffie ist klaar*,' she said.

He nodded and told her that he might well be home late for dinner. If she had invited guests, she shouldn't wait later than seven thirty. Even upper-class Dutch people ate at the same time as the working class. Best asked himself for the umpteenth time why he had stuck it so long in Holland. After all, the Dutch were a dull, boring folk, lacking any kind of style or sophistication.

But Frau Best did not notice his expression – she never did. Instead she urged him, 'Don't hurry back. You drive much too fast as it is. It makes me nervous. I'm having a bridge party this afternoon. No guests tonight. So there's no hurry. Have dinner out somewhere. I shall be much happier if I know that you are driving carefully.'

He nodded, kissed his wife dutifully and said, '*Tot ziens*.' But already she was busy chewing her roll and cheese and reading the death announcements in the paper. He sighed and departed from the headquarters of the Secret Service in Holland. At the corner, the man in the dirty raincoat stubbed out his cheap cigarette and followed hastily. As he did so, he winced. His pistol had banged painfully against his hip...

Major Stevens, dark, foreign-looking and

inexperienced in European Intelligence work – he had spent most of his career in India – was waiting for Best when he arrived in his chauffeur-driven Buick, the pride of his life. They exchanged a few words. Stevens mentioned they were still waiting for Lieutenant Klop, their Dutch escorting officer, to arrive. Although the Dutch were neutral, they were eager to bring about this final meeting between the German plotters and the British. Perhaps in this way, the war might be brought to a quick end with Hitler out of the way, as the German plotters had promised; Holland would be saved from the threatening German invasion.

Then Stevens did something which surprised the 'old hand' Best greatly. He opened the door of his desk to reveal a number of Browning automatics. 'Take one, old chap,' he said with apparent carelessness. 'You never know with the Hun.'

Best didn't comment but again his fears were aroused. Suddenly he was apprehensive again as he had been while shaving. Were they walking into a bloody trap?

Expertly he picked one of the automatics, checked the magazine and just in case pocketed another spare mag, saying, 'God, it's like being in the last show, getting ready to go over the top.'

Stevens forced a smile. 'I don't think there's much likelihood of that, old bean.

The Huns are Huns, as I well know. But this lot seem genuine enough. Like us they don't want this bloody silly war to continue any further than necessary. They're well aware that the great danger facing both our countries is from the East – from the Reds.'

Let's hope you're right, Best told himself. But aloud he said, 'That's Lieutenant Klop's car arriving outside. Let's get on with it.' But even as he turned and prepared to meet their completely bald Dutch conducting officer, he felt the energy drain from his body, as if someone had opened an invisible tap. Suddenly, startlingly, Best, not the most imaginative of men, sensed everything was going to go wrong – *bloody wrong!*

The rugged-looking tough in the shabby overlong Dutch raincoat touched the rim of his battered trilby and, turning to his colleague, said, 'Major, Old Baldy–' he meant Klop – 'has arrived. His nibs and Best are ready to go, sir.'

'Thanks, Mac,' Major Dalby of the Secret Field Intelligence Police responded. His voice sounded weary, even despondent. It was as if all this tailing of the two foolish, gullible Secret Service agents had become too much for him. Staff Sergeant Mackenzie understood why. They had been operating illegally and out of their own territory for over a month now ever since 'Old Winnie', the new First Lord of the Admiralty, had recruited them through 'channels' that didn't bear looking at too closely.

Dalby, his face lined and his eyes red-rimmed, took another sip from the silver flask of whisky which he carried with him all the time these days. Mackenzie knew it had saved his life on the first day of the Somme, back on 1 July 1916; but it wasn't for sentimental reasons he carried it with him all the time. The Major needed the support that the fierce spirit gave him. He offered the flask to the younger man.

Mackenzie shook his head and said, 'They're going to go through with it then, the bloody fools.' It was a rhetorical question for he continued immediately with, 'God Almighty, don't they know that they could be shot for treachery – parleying with the enemy – SS at that – in wartime?' He sighed.

Mackenzie ceased his outburst, knowing, even as he spoke, he was upsetting the Major. Dalby was old school. He saw things in black and white. In wartime you didn't deal with the enemy, however good your reason was for doing so. Now at the command of someone very high up in Britain, probably someone in the Chamberlain government, Best and Stevens were trying to arrange the assassination of Hitler supposedly by his own generals so that a peace could be concluded between the two warring countries.

But he and Dalby had already found out the two SIS officers weren't negotiating with Wehrmacht officers. The head of the German team was a young, cunning scar-faced officer, named Walter Schellenberg – and Schellenberg was the blue-eyed boy of no less a person than General der SS Reinhard Heydrich, the most fanatical Nazi of them all. Would such a man be plotting to remove the Führer by assassination and then make peace with the British?

Both Dalby and he knew that simply wasn't the case. 'The Man with the Iron Heart', as the ruthless SS General was known within the Reich – even Hitler was supposed to be scared of him – was the last man who would want to make peace with Britain. The new war had already advanced Heydrich's career greatly. They knew that Heydrich wanted it to continue in order to achieve high office in a victorious Germany. There were rumours that SS General Heydrich hoped one day to be the Nazi viceroy of Britain, ruling in the place of those Whitehall plotters, who foolishly believed currently that they could 'do business', as they phrased it, with 'Germany's New Order'.

'All right, Mac.' Dalby cut into the heavy brooding silence. He took a last sip of the Scotch and reluctantly slipped the flask into the pocket of his heavy civilian overcoat. 'We'd better get on with the bloody rotten business.'

'Orders, sir?' asked Mackenzie in his new military style as if he had been a Regular Army NCO for years instead of a recent recruit who up to August 1939 was a PhD student at the German University of Hamburg, writing a thesis on the causes of the Thirty Years' War.

'Shadow them at a respectable distance. We don't want to blow our cover, Mac. It might cause awkward questions to be asked in the House.' Dalby sighed and abruptly looked very old. 'You see, if this ever came out in London, that in the middle of a war we were treating with the enemy, hell's teeth, it might well bring down the government and then there'd be all hell to pay.'

'And if the Jerries start to act up, sir, what then? After all they'll be watching the road to Venlo as well, sir.'

But Major Dalby didn't seem to hear the question. Perhaps he didn't want, to...

'Noch ein Schnaps,' Schellenberg barked. *'Dalli, Mensch,'* he ordered the Dutch waiter in his rusty black suit. Next to him, his fellow plotter, also in civilian clothes, asked for the same.

While they waited in the little red-brick Café Bacchus, they stared out of the window of the little border establishment. The road outside was packed, it seemed, with civilians, mostly on bicycles. Schellenberg, scar-faced like his boss, Heydrich, didn't find the cyclists strange. It was to be expected in a country where the cycle was the most popular mode of transport. But who were the Dutch civilians a little way off, accompanied by what were obviously trained police dogs, straining at their metal chains? What game were they playing?

The clever young ex-lawyer, who was now one of the most feared men in Nazi Germany, concluded they were Dutch cops in civilian clothes. Obviously the British agents and their running dog, Klop, had convinced the Dutch authorities to take precautions. Schellenberg gave a thin, cruel smile. But with all the security precautions in the world, he told himself, nothing would save Best and Stevens this grey November day.

Time passed leadenly. He ordered more of the fiery Dutch *genever* schnapps. He and his companion were hardly aware of the fact that they were drinking far too much and that they were both now chain-smoking – the ashtrays in front of them were piled high with cigarette butts. It was the tension. Schellenberg felt a vein in his temple begin to tick nervously. He tried to stop it. To no avail. He ordered another round of drinks from the old waiter in his rusty black tail-coat. Even he had begun to look apprehensively out of the café's big picture window now. Though, Schellenberg told himself, what the sway-backed old Dutchman expected to see there, God only knew. Then he returned mentally to his immediate problem. Where in three devils' names were the two shit-Englishmen? *Scheissenglander*.

In fact, Best's big Buick, his pride and joy, had made excellent time on the road to Venlo. Now the two agents and Klop paused for a few minutes in a roadside café, while they talked in anxious tones about the latest rumour that Germany was about to invade Holland, neutral now for almost a hundred years. Just before they finished their coffee and broke off the conversation, Stevens did a surprising thing for a spymaster, which he was, being in charge of the whole of the SIS's Continental agent network. He took out a scrap of paper and calmly set about preparing a list of people – agents, informants and the like – who would have to get out of Holland in a hurry if the Germans *did* invade.

Best, the more experienced of the two, could hardly believe the evidence of his own eyes. He barked, 'For God's sake, Stevens, you'd better destroy that list before we get to the frontier. If that thing ever fell into the hands of the Boche it would mean a death sentence for all your chaps.' He paused and added in a worried undertone so that Lieutenant Klop couldn't hear, 'I have an awful feeling, old chap, that something's going to go wrong ... just can't chuck it off. Can you?'

'I'll get rid of it,' Stevens promised, 'if something goes wrong, don't worry.'

Best nodded his approval. He could see now that Stevens, not the sharpest of types, in his opinion, was getting worried too.

Five minutes later they were on their way, the gloomy, grey November sky noticeably greyer and gloomier, as if Nature itself was warning them to go no further; there was danger ahead. But duty-conscious as the two upper-class Englishmen were (with their monocles and receding chins looking the very caricature of their type), they pretended not to notice.

They came close to the frontier. They saw at a glance that the Dutch had redoubled their security arrangements; they were taking the German threat seriously. There were sandbagged gun positions and new roadblocks everywhere. Time and time again they were stopped to have their papers examined by hard-faced Dutch NCOs in full battle gear. Even Klop's presence couldn't speed up their progress.

Once, an officious Dutch sergeant stopped the big American car and took away their papers to be examined by an officer. Silently Best prayed he'd come back and inform them they could go no further. But that wasn't to be. A few minutes later he returned and waved them on. Best sighed and let what was to happen happen.

Finally they stopped at the last Dutch border post. Best, on the alert now, peered through his monocle at the little scene. The Dutch here seemed more relaxed than their comrades on the road to the meeting. Everything appeared to be quite normal, save for one thing. The red-and-white striped border post on the other side of the frontier was open. That was surprising. The Huns usually kept the pole down. Suddenly he realized that there was nothing between them and the enemy. One wrong move and he and Stevens could be in the hands of the Huns: British spies in wartime who faced an automatic sentence of death. Still there was no sign of the Germans save for a fat, bored frontier official, leaning against his wooden cabin, smoking a cigar fitfully.

Next to the driver, Klop said, 'Go ahead, driver ... everything is all right. We'll park over there...'

Dalby lowered his glasses and bit his bottom lip, his mind in a turmoil. The bloody silly fools were walking right into a trap. For he had spotted the big black Mercedes parked out of sight just beyond the border post; and there was no mistaking the beefy toughs standing around the car for what they were – Gestapo or SS thugs of the worst kind.

Next to him Mackenzie, who had seen the trap being prepared for the unsuspecting SIS agents, asked, 'What now, sir? Do we warn them?'

'How?' Dalby asked. 'You see there's only a matter of a few yards between their car and the German frontier. By the time we reached them, the Boche would have spotted us and the balloon would have gone up.'

Mackenzie nodded his understanding and said, 'But we can't just stand here and let the Germans take them like that, sir. Fools they may be, but they're our own people.'

'You're right,' Dalby said, new vigour in his voice, as his mind raced electrically, trying to work out some sort of rescue plan while there was still time. 'We'll approach as close as we can to the Boche coming in to the back of that outhouse—' He broke off abruptly.

Down below, the motor of the big Mercedes had suddenly roared into noisy life. The thugs were springing on to the running boards on both sides of the powerful automobile. The Germans were going into action.

'Christ Almighty,' Mackenzie yelled above

the sudden roar. 'The ruddy balloon's gone up, sir.'

It had. The Mercedes had lurched forward, the thugs hanging on for their lives, as they drew their pistols. Heavy as it was, the German automobile began to gather speed rapidly, heading for the German pole barrier and Holland beyond. There, still unaware of what was in store for them, the two SIS officers were directing their driver to turn off the main road into the parking lot at the side of Café Bacchus. Here Schellenberg had knocked over his drink and in abrupt confusion, perhaps through the alcohol, wondered what he should do next, the carefully worked-out German plan totally forgotten.

But if the SS general couldn't make up his mind what to do, Major Dalby did. 'All right, Mackenzie, let's try to stop the bloody fools before it's too late.'

'Sir.' Mackenzie reacted immediately. He pulled out his own Browning. Before the Major could stop him, he doubled forward on to the cobbled frontier road. Now the German Mercedes was swinging round the corner on the German side of the border, going all out.

At the Dutch frontier post, the Dutch soldiers on guard gaped at the Mercedes in open-mouthed amazement. They simply stood there like a bunch of gawping village yokels, not even attempting to use their weapons.

Doubling after the younger man, Dalby gasped in Dutch, 'Use your rifles, *Gottverdamme*! ... *Idioten* ... *Open fire!*'

But still the guards remained motionless.

Not the Germans, however. On the running board, the thugs spotted the running Mackenzie. They saw the pistol in his hand and guessed he was going to attempt to stop them carrying out their plan. Almost immediately wild firing broke out as, tyres screeching shrilly, the Mercedes rushed for the stalled Buick.

Mackenzie zig-zagged expertly. For a former academic who had been in the British Army only a matter of months, Dalby thought he was performing excellently in his first combat mission. All the same, he wished the younger man wasn't so damned daring. But for a moment or two, Mackenzie seemed to bear a charmed life. Slugs ripped the air to both sides of the running figures. The bullets struck angry red-blue sparks on the cobbles at his flying feet. But still he wasn't hit.

In a final burst of speed, the big Mercedes hurtled towards the Buick. The big bald-headed Dutch lieutenant sprang from the car. His pistol was out in a flash. Standing upright, one arm behind his back, as if he were back on the range, he pumped three shots at the Mercedes. Its windscreen shattered to a glistening spider's web. Blinded, the driver braked to a shuddering halt.

'Bloody good show,' Dalby gasped in the very same instant that Mackenzie yelled, staggered, faltered, ran a few paces more and then collapsed on one knee, blood spurting in a bright red arc from a shattered shoulder. The German who had shot, a typical Gestapo thug in his ankle-length leather coat, gave a cry of triumph.

It died in a scream of absolute agony, as Dalby shot him in the face. Suddenly his features started to drip down on to his chest like molten red wax. He fell to the ground, dead before he slammed into the cobbles.

Dalby stumbled on. He had to save Mackenzie. Everything else didn't matter now. Even as the firing continued and the Mercedes with the shattered windscreen swung round and blocked the Buick, Dalby knew the two SIS men had had it. They hadn't a chance in hell of escaping now.

Next moment the death of Klop proved Dalby correct. Abruptly German bullets stitched a series of blood-red buttonholes across the Dutchman's broad chest. His knees buckled weakly beneath him like those of a newly born foal. He sank to the blood-stained cobbles and died there quietly and without a murmur of pain.

Dalby reached Mackenzie, who was

gasping for breath like someone who had run a long, hard race. 'Got you, Sergeant!' he cried above the angry snap-and-crack of the small-arms fire. 'Put yer arm around me, son.'

'Yessir,' Mackenzie said a little weakly. 'I'm all right. You—' He broke off as the pain stabbed his shoulder like a jab from a red-hot poker. Tamely, he allowed Dalby to support him, as the latter backed off towards where their car was hidden, automatic clenched in his fist ready for immediate use.

To their front, Best and Stevens had stepped out of their car, its engine still beating steadily like a mechanical heart. They had raised their hands in surrender for they were now surrounded by the angry, flushed Germans, all armed with pistols.

Best tried to reason with the Germans in his fluent German, snorting that they were British civilians on neutral ground and that this was an outrage that they were being assaulted in this manner. '*Ich werde Berlin unterrichten und ein Protest ein*—' His protest ended in a groan of pain as one of the thugs landed a hefty kick on his shin with his cruelly nailed boot. Next minute, both of them were seized in an armlock. Their feet raised so that they appeared to be carried by their kidnappers, they were rushed to the German frontier, while Schellenberg turned over Klop's body with the toe of his elegant shoe. The Dutch officer would never report to his Intelligence bosses in the Hague any more. He was very dead. He dismissed the Dutchman and turned to the big hulking bully boy who had driven the Mercedes. 'All right, Naujocks,' he commanded. 'Let's get the hell out of it before those slow-witted cheeseheads–' he meant the Dutch – 'wake up to what has just happened.'

'*Jawhol, Brigadeführer*,' Naujocks snapped happily. Again he had survived one of Heydrich's highly dangerous undercover missions with his skin intact. He was only too eager to get away from the scene of the crime. Besides he could hear the Dutch finally beginning to react. There were angry shouts, hurried orders and the first wild shots from their side of the border as their soldiers slowly began to realize what had just happened. One of their officers had been mortally wounded in a gun battle and two civilians with him had been abducted under their very noses by a handful of cheeky *moppen*.

Hurriedly Schellenberg and the big bully boy Naujocks, pistols in their hands pointed at the Dutch who were appearing cautiously from their pillboxes and bunkers, backed off to the safety of their own country. Watching them go, while he tried to stem the flow of blood from the young staff sergeant's shoulders, Dalby said half-aloud, as if to himself, 'God only knows, but we're not going to hear the end of this affair for a bloody long time to come...'

Dalby was right, though he couldn't possibly have known that November day just how long it would take. The kidnapping of Captain Best and Major Stevens in 1939 would have reverberations years after Major Dalby had been murdered. Indeed, in some quarters, they would go on right into the second decade of the twenty-first century...*

*The Public Records Office will not release the full details of the Venlo Kidnap until the year 2015. *Translator.*

BOOK ONE:

A MURDER IS ARRANGED

'My experience is that the gentlemen who seem the best behaved and most sleek are those who are doing the mischief. We cannot be sure of anybody.'

Field Marshal Lord Ironside,
Chief of the British General Staff, 1940

One

The SOE* staff officer was full of enthusiasm for his new recruit. His fresh young face gleamed excitedly, as he babbled on about the man in the dirty Wehrmacht uniform they were watching through the two-way mirror. 'Ideal candidate ... ready to do anything, sir ... knows Berchtesgaden and Berlin, too, like the back of his hand ... member of the *Leibstandarte* ... and to cap it all, sir, as a member of his race he's got the best of all motives to want revenge...' The SOE staff officer paused for breath, his chest heaving with the effort of trying to convince the Army officer next to him that they couldn't have found a better man for the SOE's bold new plan.

In the inner room behind the two-way mirror, the 'whites', as the anti-Nazi German POWs were categorized, chattered in low voices among themselves as they waited

**Special Operations Executive: a wartime British Intelligence organization.*

their turn to be interrogated by their British captors at this special Intelligence camp. Most of them were clean and shaven, but their skinny faces still bore the haunting traces of the battlefield on which they had been taken prisoner only days before. They smoked in quick nervous puffs and when they struck a match, their hands trembled.

'Has he been circumcised?'

'Yes, apparently his father, a non-Jew, didn't object and his mother insisted. Though,' the SOE officer said with an attempt at humour, 'if she'd have known what was to come in Germany under Hitler, undoubtedly she would have stopped the rabbi working on the poor devil's John Thomas.'

The Major wasn't impressed by the puerile humour. He ignored it. 'So you're telling me that a circumcised half-Jew was able to join the premier regiment of the SS, Hitler's own bodyguard, the *Leibstandarte*, where once they wouldn't take a recruit if he had fillings in his teeth. Didn't any of their medics notice that his foreskin was missing?'

The SOE officer had been expecting the question. He was ready to answer it in a flash. 'Naturally he had to be very careful not to display his ... penis–' he said the word as if it were dirty – 'too often. And the rabbi hadn't done too good a job on him. With practice and a lot of pain, so he informs me, he had managed to pull some of the remaining skin down and make a kind of makeshift cover for the end of his John Thomas.'

'Ingenious bugger, what,' the Major said, as if to himself. 'But it won't work, Captain, I'm afraid.'

The SOE captain looked crestfallen. 'How do you mean, sir?'

Through the mirror the Major looked at the would-be candidate for the assassination of Adolf Hitler either at Berlin or his mountain retreat at Berchtesgaden. Hagemann's face showed no emotion. Unlike the other 'whites' he seemed perfectly contained. He smoked the English cigarettes they had been given as a special concession, too, but his hands were perfectly steady. Obviously he was at ease with himself – too much so, the Major told himself. That was always the sign of the trained agent.

The Major reached into the battered leather briefcase which he had bought in Germany so long ago in what seemed now another age and brought out the colour photograph. 'Have a look at that,' he commanded, thrusting it at the surprised captain. 'I had it taken by one of our medical experts yesterday afternoon while you were up in the Smoke.'

The SOE man looked puzzled. It showed the lower half of a man's body in excellent detail: a tangle of black pubic hair and a penis, hanging there limply, but with red marks and arrows pencilled in, pointing at the lower end of the male organ. 'I don't understand—' he stuttered.

'It's your chap.' The Major cut him short almost brutally, as if he were now bored with the whole matter and wanted it concluded as soon as possible. 'His John Thomas to be precise.'

'I see,' the other man said, but in truth he didn't see at all.

'You see the red ink marks?'

The other man nodded.

'Well, they indicate stitches. To put it crudely, Captain, Hagemann, if that's his real name, has had his dick docked – *recently*.'

'*Recently*?'

'Yes, it must have been damned painful for a grown man. But as the medics inform me, the sutures are of a recent origin. Your man has been circumcised in the last year or so.' He peered over the tops of his steel-rimmed Army-issue glasses challengingly at the other man.

'But why, sir?' the SOE officer stuttered. 'What was the purpose...?'

'He's a plant, that's the reason why. The *Abwehr*, if that's the organization he belongs to – and I think he does – is desperate to find out what our plans are vis-à-vis the

Fatherland. They'd go to any lengths to find them out and there's always plenty of supposed mugs in this crazy game of ours who are prepared to carry them out, cost what it may. Look at him, obviously very pleased with himself, smoking and smirking as if he hasn't a care in the world, believing he's got himself through and fooled us with this Jewish thing. He simply doesn't realize that he's expendable – a stupid pawn in a game of chess played by a master who doesn't care a twopenny fuck about him.' There was a sudden venom in the Major's voice that startled the young SOE staff officer. Abruptly he recalled the older man's reputation for being the most ruthless spy-catcher in the kingdom. No one escaped, so they maintained in hushed whispers, once Mackenzie got his claws into them; he pursued his quarry without mercy till the kill.

'What's the drill now, sir?' he asked in a suddenly tired voice, knowing that his grandiose plans for this supposed Jewish turncoat had come to nothing. 'What do we do with his nibs?'

Mackenzie appeared bored. He said, without taking those cold blue eyes behind the spectacles off Hagemann. 'Bring him in here – without escort. I don't want any unnecessary witnesses—'

'But it's customary to have—'

'I said *without an escort, Captain.*' Mackenzie cut him short brutally. 'Let's get on with it. We'll prove he's a spy, just for the record and then we'll deal with him, that is if he's not prepared to play ball with us and allow himself to be turned, which I suspect he won't. He looks the stupid type, the big oaf.'

A few minutes later, Hagemann was pushed through the door by the big burly Redcap in charge of the 'whites'. 'Shall I stand by, sir?' he rapped.

'No, I don't think we'll have any trouble with his nibs,' Mackenzie answered. He gave Hagemann a fake smile as if all was well with the world and a benevolent God was beaming down at them from his heaven. Hagemann smiled back. 'Yes, stand down now, Sergeant. Go and get yourself a cup of char at the Sergeants' Mess – you deserve it.'

Smartly the big NCO clicked to attention and saluted. He was off like a shot and it was obvious to the two officers it wasn't a mug of char that he was hurrying off to, but something stronger.

'*Na, Soldat Hagemann, oder sollte ich sagen, "Oberjager Hagemann"*?' Mackenzie commenced in his fluent German.

Hagemann became more relaxed than ever. '*Oberjager*,' he said, and then in heavily accented English: 'But I am speaking English with no difficulty, sir.'

Again Mackenzie gave him that fake smile and next to him, the SOE officer waited for the explosion to come; for he had taken the measure of the spymaster, young and inexperienced as he was. Mackenzie was one of these officers who had managed to survive the years of war somehow or other. All the same the war had had an effect upon them which they'd never lose now. Calm and controlled as they seemed on the surface, beneath it there raged constantly a bitter hatred that could burst out with a murderous force at any time. The slightest thing could trigger off an outburst; and at the moment, the SOE officer could see, Hagemann was doing all the wrong things. He tensed and waited.

'So, you are speaking English with no difficulty, eh,' Mackenzie echoed. 'Then perhaps you'll understand – *without difficulty* – what I shall now say to you?'

Irony was wasted in Hagemann. 'Yes, I am understanding everything, sir.'

'Good. Then get this, Hagemann. You're not a bloody Jew. No' – Mackenzie's thin face flushed an angry red suddenly – 'you're a bloody German spy! Now what do you say to that?'

Hagemann's face blanched. He reeled back, as if he had just been struck. 'What ... what do you say?' he managed to stutter. 'I am telling the truth – *die ganze Wahrheit*,

Herr Major—'

'Leck mich am Arsch!' Mackenzie yelled in fury, eyes blazing. 'You're lying. You're a plant. You're damned to all hell, do you understand that, Hagemann? If you don't confess now, you won't live beyond tomorrow. Have you understood – with your perfect bloody English?' He hammered out sentence after sentence, as if he were striking nails into Hagemann's coffin. Which, in reality, he was. For by now the younger officer had realized that Mackenzie would stop at nothing. That was how he got his results. With him the gloves were always off. And his victims knew it – mostly.

But Hagemann, still smug and still believing that no one would disguise himself like he had done as a circumcised Jew and not be believed, attempted to bluster it out. But by now he was speaking German, making sure that his blazing accuser understood perfectly. 'But it's true, Herr Major. Why should I – a Jew – work for the Nazis—' His plea ended in a shocked gasp, as Mackenzie lashed out and struck him right across the cheek with his officer's stick. *'Du lügst, du Scheisskerl,'* he bellowed.

A shocked SOE officer said, 'Steady on, Major, sir. You can't strike prisoners like that, sir. *Please*.'

Mackenzie turned on him slowly. Despite that savage blow which had left a crimson weal across Hagemann's pale face, his eyes were now very calm, all anger vanished; and the SOE officer realized that this, too, was part of the spy-catcher's act. Perhaps the rage was artificial too. 'Captain,' Mackenzie said slowly, 'I can do exactly what I like.' The words sounded like an act of faith. 'I have been in this bloody game far too long now to give a tuppenny damn about what anyone cares about my actions. I simply want results.'

And he had them now. Hagemann had broken down. The smug look had vanished from his suddenly ashen face and it was clear that his spirit was broken. In half a minute he'd be singing like the good old yellow canary. Even the new boy from the staff of the Special Operations Executive knew that.

Taking out a battered silver cigarette case, Mackenzie pulled out and lit one of the Turkish cigarettes, the only ones obtainable off ration. He said carelessly, as if he had lost all interest in Hagemann, 'He's all yours, Captain. Try him as a double. But I doubt if he'd be much good.' He shrugged. 'If he doesn't play ball, have him shot in the Tower like the rest of them.'

The SOE officer looked at him aghast. Mackenzie noted the look, but pretended not to. What did it matter to him now what people thought of him? He had long given up caring about such matters. Besides, since the death of his wife during the first V-1 campaign the previous summer, he had acted on instinct, going through the motions as duty demanded. But in reality he didn't care anymore whether he lived or died. What was there to live for anyway?

But his words had had a definite impact on Hagemann. Despite the coldness of the unheated interrogation room, he was sweating hard, his forehead greased with perspiration as if oil had been rubbed on it. '*Ich werde Ihnen alles erzahlen ... alles. Ich wollte es nicht machen...*' Now his dark eyes were bulging from his head like those of a man close to madness. His whole body seemed to be trembling. '*Aber* ... die *haben mich gezwungen...*'

Mackenzie laughed cynically to himself, while the POW babbled on. They all said that in the end: 'I didn't want to do it, but they forced me to.' He picked up his cap and put it on his head at an angle that certainly wouldn't have passed 'King's Regulations'. But once again he didn't care. He could do without the British Army. But the British Army couldn't do without him, at least till the war with Germany was over.

He nodded to a perplexed SOE officer, who was obviously at a loss as to how to stop Hagemann's frantic babbling, and went out into the winter morning. Sergeant

Campbell 175 was waiting for him next to the little utility van, its heater going full blast. He grinned as he saw the look on his superior's face. He took the battered briefcase from Mackenzie and said, mouth twisted to one side in that knowing fashion of his, 'They have to call in us Scots when they need a bit of real Intelligence work, sir.' His accent was markedly un-Scottish. 'You cracked him, sir?'

Mackenzie nodded. To the east over 'the Smoke', the air-raid sirens were sounding their warning yet again. The 'doodle-bugs' were coming back to commence another day of terror in the hard-pressed capital. 'Yes, *we Scots*, did it again, Campbell.'

Campbell 175 grinned and opened the door for his boss.

Mackenzie returned the grin. 'We Scots' was a private joke, shared only between the two of them. 'Scottish Campbell 175' – the number was to distinguish him from all the other Campbells in the British Army – was in reality Heino Hirschmann, formerly of Hirschmann und Sohne of Cologne. Heino had seen the way things were going in the 'New Germany' of Adolf Hitler early on. He had fled over the border into nearby Belgium, taking what he could find in the family vault with him (his father, now vanished, had never believed that Hitler would carry out his threats against the Jews

– Heino had).

In 1939 the Jewish emigrant had been interned on the Isle of Man in response to Churchill's command to 'collar the lot', Jews, Nazis, fellow travellers – anyone who had possessed German nationality.

One year later Heino had managed to obtain his release by volunteering for the Pioneer Corps, transferring as soon as possible to the Highland Light Infantry where he had been given the name and paybook of one Hector Campbell, just in case he was captured by his former countryman. But the L/Corporal had not been captured. Instead, fighting with his regiment in the 51st Highland Division he had been badly wounded at the Battle of El Alamein and been returned to the United Kingdom. Downgraded to category C-3 so that he could not be sent to the front again, he had dodged a return to the 'shit and shovel brigade', as he had called the Pioneer Corps contemptuously, by volunteering yet once again – this time for the Intelligence Corps.

Thus he had come to serve as Mackenzie's aide, batman, driver and, above all, the Major's 'second opinion', as the former called him. For Hirschmann, now known as Campbell, had that easy Continental Jewish ability to sum up people in a matter of minutes: that gift to see through pretensions, poses, fake personalities that had made the Hirschmanns such successful businessmen in an anti-Semitic world ever since they had escaped the Trier ghetto at the same time as that terrible communist bogeyman, Karl Marx, senior.

Now, as the flak to the east opened up in yet another vain attempt to stop Hitler's latest secret weapon penetrating the capital's defences, peppering the sky with useless puffballs of black smoke and shell fragments, Campbell said, 'There was a signal for you, sir. Pretty important. They even sent it by dispatch rider,' he corrected himself swiftly, '–by DR, sir.' As always Campbell wanted to get the terminology correct.

'What was it?' Mackenzie asked without much interest, watching one of the new supercharged Spitfires streaking across the pale-blue winter sky, cannon spurting white shell fire at a V-1. But the flying bomb, containing one ton of high explosive plodded on steadily, trailing its fiery tail behind it, sounding like an old-fashioned two-stroke motorbike. Mackenzie knew that if the Spitfire pilot failed to blast it out of the sky before it reached the area of high-density council houses ahead, he'd risk his own life by coming under the bomb. There he'd try to slip one wing underneath the thing and attempt to tilt it off course. With a bit of luck, he'd force it to dive downwards and explode harmlessly before it reached the council houses. If he fluffed the dangerous manoeuvre, he might well be blown up himself. Mackenzie sighed and wondered again at the bravery of all these young men, fliers, sailors and soldiers who had given their lives and continued to give them in this war for the sake of an Empire that the damned politicians had already patently lost.

'I'd just started to decode when you came out, sir,' Campbell 175 answered. 'I didn't get too far...'

Mackenzie took his eyes momentarily off the Spitfire zooming in at well over four hundred miles an hour. The pilot had ceased firing now. He obviously knew he couldn't down the flying bomb that way. Instead he was racing towards the bomb to carry out that death-defying manoeuvre which might well cost him his own life. 'Did you get anything at all ... Give me a clue – *quick!*'

'Two things, sir,' Campbell 175 replied, sensing the tremendous urgency of this moment. 'First the signal came from the War Office itself. Top level stuff—'

'Cut the cackle!' Mackenzie interrupted harshly.

'And the second, sir...'

Now the Spitfire was almost underneath and flying at top speed parallel with the deadly flying bomb. In a moment the pilot would try the suicidal flick of his port wing. Mackenzie tensed, his teeth gritted hard.

'It concerned a Major ... Dalby—'

'What?'

'I said, sir—'

Campbell 175 stopped short suddenly. He groaned, the signal forgotten. The Spitfire pilot wasn't going to do it. The V-1 had abruptly changed course. They were going to crash. Instinctively he hit the brake. The little camouflaged van shuddered to a stop. In that same instant, the Spitfire's nose struck the V-1's study right wing. A blinding flash of violet light. A great ball of white as the V-1 exploded. Next moment the Spitfire had vanished together with the flying bomb. Debris rained downwards, one solitary wing whirling round and round, as it followed more slowly, like some great metallic leaf. *'Heaven, arse and cloudburst!'* Campbell 175 cursed in the language he hated, German, his dark, clever face abruptly drained of colour.

But even as he swore, Campbell could see out of the corner of his eye that Major Mackenzie had not seemed even to have noticed the tragedy, which had taken the life of yet another brave RAF pilot. He stared through the windscreen at some far horizon known only to himself, oblivious to what was happening outside.

It was only a few moments later, when they had started again, threading their way carefully through the tiny fires started by the red-hot debris and spilled fuel from the crash, that Major Mackenzie spoke. 'Dalby, did you say?' he asked in a toneless voice.

'Yessir.'

Mackenzie nodded, as if in confirmation of some unspoken question. 'God,' he continued in that same unemotional toneless manner, 'I'd imagined he'd been dead these many years...' Thereafter he relapsed into a brooding silence which lasted the rest of their journey to London.

Two

'It won't be long now, Sergeant,' Dalby, the veteran of the Old War, said easily. 'The Huns can't be that stupid or sleepy.'

Mackenzie mumbled something as the broad V of the landing craft surged towards the cliffs which fringed Dieppe on both sides. His whole attention was focused on the French port, which so far had not reacted to the fact that nearly a whole Canadian infantry division, plus the British commandos, were heading straight for it, the Canadians, in particular, lusting for blood and guts.

It was not yet dawn, of course, though the sky to the east was already streaked with the ugly white of the false dawn. But Sergeant Mackenzie (now minus his stripes as Dalby was without his major's crown) couldn't imagine how the garrison's radar had not yet picked up the assault force of destroyers, gunboats and landing craft. Were they just waiting for the damned Tommies to come within comfortable range before opening up with their big coastal guns, as some of Dalby's colleagues back in Intelligence thought? For many of the more senior officers felt the assault on Dieppe had already been compromised by being cancelled once and by the loose talk of the Canadian division which was soon going to be slaughtered on those shingle beaches ahead (though the brave young novices, volunteers to a man, didn't know that yet).

Major Dalby, too, was not very sanguine about the success of Canada's first contribution to the shooting war. Nor their own strange part in it. 'I simply can't understand how we got landed with this stumer,' he had exploded to Mackenzie when he had told him the news that they were 'actually going to take part in a bloody commando raid'. 'We're spy-catchers, working from the comfort of a bloody office in the War House. We're supposed to be too precious and know too bloody much to go and have our tails shot off in some derring-do, foolish adventure in Occupied Europe. Can't bloody understand it at all, Mackenzie, I can't that.' And he had shaken his greying head like a man who was being sorely tried.

In essence, as Dalby had told it in that summer of 1942, in what now seemed another age to Mackenzie, the two of them were to penetrate with the commandos on the left flank to Dieppe HQ of the local Gestapo. There they were to crack the

Gestapo's safe – 'Crack a bloody safe, I ask you.' Mackenzie had snorted, Who the hell do they think we are – Bill bloody Sykes!' – and take out papers relating to the Gestapo's dealings with local traitors, in particular an English SOE agent, who was working with the Germans and was betraying his fellow SOE spies parachuted into France to train the *Resistance*. 'Hell's bells and balls of blazing fire,' Dalby had concluded his briefing, face suddenly flushed purple with anger at the people who had assigned this impossible mission to them, 'I've never heard anything like it in all my born days!'

Mackenzie hadn't either. But he didn't tell his boss that. Instead he set about trying to find out who in the intricate bureaucracy of the War House had assigned this strange mission to them. But he had been unable to do so. At the lower levels their colleagues and friends were just as puzzled as they were. At the higher ones, no one was talking, though one thing did become clear. Whoever had given the order to send them off on this crazy commando raid was right at the top. As Mackenzie confessed to his boss, Dalby, as they joined the happy-go-lucky Canadians at Dieppe, young men already doomed once they stepped on to the crowded landing craft that would take them to France, 'Major, sir, it has to be a civvie.'

'What makes you say that, Mac?' Dalby had queried, checking his .38 pistol yet again, before placing a metal shaving mirror in the left pocket of his battledress – 'just in case'.*

'Well, sir–' Mackenzie felt himself blushing slightly – 'I have my sources.' He had. A buxom ATS, who 'obliged' him every so often when she was drunk on his spirits ration and who worked as a secretary to the top brass. 'They say that none of the brass hats had anything to do with this mission. The order came from elsewhere in Whitehall.'

'You mean from one of the civvie ministries?'

'Yessir.'

Dalby stroked his chin, now covered with black and green camouflage paint. 'Now that's bloody interesting, Mackenzie...' He smiled, his whole face lighting up for a moment. 'What would I do without you, Mac, eh? Now let me ask you from which ministry—'

But before he could really pose that particular, overwhelming question, the ships' sirens had started to wail and, to the accompaniment of cheers from the watching 'dockies and off-watch sailors, the invasion fleet had begun to set sail for their date

* To protect his heart: an old soldier's trick.

with destiny.

Now the commandos' landing craft commenced to separate from the main fleet. Still the Germans had not opened fire, though both Intelligence men, packed in the steel box of a landing craft with the green-bereted commandos, were sure that the enemy had spotted them. Still they were getting ever closer to a fold in the white cliffs which was their landing place. Once there they'd make a tough target for any German heavy guns, though the 'Boche might well be on the top of the cliff,' as Dalby put it, 'and they'll be able to lob grenades right down on top of us.' To which Mackenzie said nothing; it was a possibility he didn't want to think about.

They got closer and closer. Overhead the first of the RAF bomber squadrons flew towards the port. It was their job to flatten the defences the best they could. In the main convoy, the Canadians' main assault weapon, Britain's new heavy tanks, the Churchills, started up their engines. They'd lead the assault up the shingle beach. Abruptly all was controlled chaos – hectic activity. Now Mackenzie knew it could be only a matter of moments before the Germans commenced firing. He was not wrong.

Just as the sun began to flush the dawn sky a blood-red, the heavens were ripped apart.

It was like a huge piece of canvas being torn in two. Smoke browned the shoreline. With a banshee howl, the first shells came hurtling out of the sky to explode in huge geysers of whirling white water around the destroyers. The battle for Dieppe had commenced!

Sweating hard, the Intelligence men followed the commandos up the fold in the cliff, fighting the barbed wire and brambles which were everywhere, cursing and tugging themselves free in almost panic-stricken fury. The commandos, trained as they were, took it all in their stride. 'Come on, mates,' they urged the other two repeatedly, 'there are worse things at sea ... Up yer go, lads – before Old Fritz spots us!'

But 'Old Fritz' didn't spot them. To the surprise of the two panting Intelligence men they managed to clear the fold without a single shot being fired. On the top of the cliff, it was different, however. Almost immediately they reached the top and started advancing with the four commandos allotted to them as a bodyguard, a Spandau machine gun opened up to their right with a high-pitched hysterical hiss. Tracer zipped towards the little group of commandos in white fury. Hastily Mackenzie and the Major hit the *pavé*. Not the commandos. The biggest of the group heaved a grenade in the direction of the building from which the machine-gun fire was coming. In the same instant that it exploded in a ball of violent red, they rushed forward, firing from the hip. The Spandau stuttered off a few more rounds. There was a series of blood-curdling screams and shrieks as the commandos slit the throats of the machine-gun crew and then the big commando was shouting cheerfully across the road, 'All aboard for the *Skylark!* ... This way, gents ... Yer won't get yer feet wet, I promise you!'

Hurriedly the Intelligence men crossed the road, already aware of the heavy firing down on the beach to their right, where one after another the new Churchill tanks were bogging down, unable to cross the shingle, leaving the Canadian infantry naked and open to the merciless slaughter soon to come. But their commando bodyguard had no time for the plight of the Canadian infantry. They had been trained to move fast; that way they avoided casualties. Now with the two Intelligence men in the centre of the rough diamond they had formed, they advanced down the cliff road towards the building near the Casino which had been taken over by the Gestapo back in 1940.

Snipers were everywhere. But that didn't seem to worry the commandos. Under the command of the tallest man, who was a sergeant, already sporting two golden wound stripes on his left sleeve, they advanced purposefully, blasting away at every window along their advance. Here and there German sailors and soldiers in coal-scuttle helmets fell from their hidden perches, slamming into the cobbles below like sacks of wet cement, dead before they hit the rough *pavé*.

Mackenzie, head tucked inside his collar, body tensed for the first sharp *thwack* of a slug hitting it, could see the Canucks down below were getting hell. Neat lines of khaki-clad bodies were now littering the beach. The Canadians had been wiped out before they had been able to fire a shot in their own defence. Here and there groups of armed men under brave and defiant officers and noncoms were still advancing through murderous fire. But others were without helmets and boots, bleeding from their wounds, cowering in the sheltered depressions or behind stalled Churchills until they too were cut down one by one and rolled down the slope to the blood-red sea.

Still the highly trained commandos advanced. It was almost as if they were on an exercise back in the UK. Everything they did was purposeful and thought out well in advance. Once, it seemed they were going to be stopped by a small mortar being operated by a couple of German marines from a garden behind a house to their immediate right. They weren't. From somewhere they produced smoke grenades. As one the four men heaved the bombs. In a flash the Germans were blinded by a thick white fog of smoke. The commandos didn't give them a chance to run for it. The smallest of the group dashed forward, a round pack bouncing up and down on his back. He paused. Legs spread apart like some western gunslinger in a Hollywood movie, he pressed the trigger of his terrible weapon. Angry snarling flame spurted from it. It slapped the building, curled round, turning everything in its path a smoking burning black, and struck the stalled, blinded mortar crew.

Screaming frantically, burning an evil blue as they ran into the street, there to stagger a few more paces before collapsing in pools of burning oil, they were transformed into charred pygmies before Mackenzie's horrified gaze.

'Here we are, gents,' the big commando sergeant announced, sweeping out a paw like a small steam shovel and indicating the bullet-pocked house which supposedly housed the local German Secret State Police. 'The Jerries have done a bunk. All yours.' Without waiting for the two Intelligence men to react, he turned to his little squad and started issuing urgent orders: 'All right, you, Jenkins, up on the roof with the Bren ... You, Slackarse, take the back. If they come in force, give us the wire, but don't open fire till I tell yer...'

Dalby nudged Mackenzie. 'Come on, Sergeant, we can't let these splendid chaps risk their lives a moment longer than necessary.'

Mackenzie agreed. The commandos were really top-rate troops. Together, with their revolvers drawn, they entered the house, which smelt of strong drink, garlic – and fear, abject fear.

Paper was strewn everywhere. Here little fires burned fitfully, as if the Gestapo torturers had attempted to destroy some of their secret documents this way before they had fled. They ignored the litter, which included for some unfathomable reason a pair of black sheer silk woman's knickers. Cautiously they proceeded deeper into the house of torture. They passed a rogues' gallery of Gestapo bosses – Heydrich, Himmler and one portrait they guessed was that of 'Gestapo' Muller, the virtually unknown real head of that feared organization. But they had no eyes for the pictures. Their time was limited. They had to find the safe and its incriminating documents – *fast*. Every minute was precious now. For they could hear the German counter-attack getting ever closer and the Canadian fire becoming weaker by the instant.

They passed into a large study, the door hanging off by one hinge, the window shattered with the blast. On the sofa to one side, a half-naked woman lay, as if she were sleeping gently. But her naked breasts, which lolled to one side of her rib cage, did not move and Dalby said, 'She's dead.' He shrugged. 'A patriot – a whore, who knows? Doesn't matter now—'

'Sir,' Mackenzie interrupted him as a flight of RAF medium bombers swept in low, roaring to some target further inland, but even as they did, the sergeant guessed they weren't going to make much impact on the raid now. It was already clearly a failure. 'Over there – behind the portrait of old Adolf – the safe!'

Dalby didn't waste any time. 'Sergeant,' he called out to the commando leader who was eyeing the dead woman's naked breasts with some interest, 'can you crack it?'

He took his eyes off those breasts which would never be fondled and give sexual pleasure again. 'In a brace of shakes, sir.' Swiftly he pulled out a string of what looked like plasticine and which smelled of bitter almonds from inside his blouse, explaining, 'Plastic explosive, sir. Brand new.' Without saying more, he stuck a time pencil into it and attached the combination to the outer edge of the safe. He pulled the string of the time pencil and ordered urgently, 'Stand back. We've got one minute.'

Hurriedly they obeyed.

'One ... two ... three ... four ... six ... seven ... nine ... TEN!' Steadily he counted off the ten second intervals. At exactly one minute, as he had predicted, the plastic explosive detonated. There was a cloud of smoke. The rending of metal. And the door of the safe sprang open, to reveal ... *nothing!*

For what seemed an age Dalby and Mackenzie stared at each other in total bewilderment. Outside, the battle raged furiously, with the clatter of tanks approaching indicating that the Germans were bringing up their own armour for the final counter-attack on the retreating Canadian survivors.

Dalby croaked, as if he were terribly parched, 'But it's empty. We've come here ... for nothing.'

Mackenzie and the commando sergeant reacted more quickly. Both snapped the same phrase at the same time. 'For Chrissake, let's get out of here before it's too late, sir!'

Bewildered, Dalby let himself be pulled away from the safe. Under the commando sergeant's guidance, they didn't take the same way out they had entered. 'Snipers,' he gasped. 'The buggers will be waiting for us to come out that way. Well, let the Jerry sods wait.' With the butt of his tommy gun, he smashed open a side window and whistled shrilly. 'Abandon ship, lads!' he yelled above the furious snap-and-crack of the small-arms battle outside.

His men needed no urging. One by one they followed him through the window, while he crouched there, tommy gun at his hip, looking like a kids' toy in those big capable hands of his. 'All right,' he cried when they were through, 'follow me, lads.'

They wasted no time moving off. Down below the commandos were holding a small bridge, despite the chaos elsewhere. Mackenzie flashed a glance at the Canadian beach, which was now under heavy attack. It was brutal and terrible. There were piles of dead, stacked like logs, everywhere. Suddenly he was overwhelmed with a feeling of utter hopelessness, as a young Canadian below, crawling on all fours, trailing blood behind him on the shingle, was hit yet again by a vicious burst of tracer in the same instant that he cried to encourage comrades who were already dead: 'Christ, we've gotta beat them ... we've gotta!' Then he was dead himself.

'Come on,' Dalby barked sharply. 'Stop looking like a fart in a trance, Mac.' The coarseness was unusual in him. But later Mackenzie guessed he had used the crude expression to make him snap out of his mood of black despair.

'Sir,' he said and followed the rest at the commando dogtrot.

They passed a burning tobacco factory.

Everywhere on the Esplanade lay the Canadian dead sprawled out in the extravagant unnatural poses of those done violently to death. At times they couldn't even avoid treading on their corpses. But now it was clear it was every man for himself. The beach organization had broken down completely. No one was in command. But on the beaches the ratings of the Royal Navy did their best, nudging their way through the debris and drifting corpses, ignoring the concentrated enemy small-arms fire trying to get off as many survivors as they could before it was too late.

Now even the commando party's progress started to slow down. There seemed to be Germans everywhere. Twice they almost collided with squat black enemy tanks as they nosed their way through the back streets like primeval monsters, swinging their cannon from left to right in search of victims.

Still the big commando sergeant kept the party going the best he could. He led right from the front, seemingly oblivious to his own safety, snapping off quick powerful bursts from his tommy gun immediately he spotted a German-manned obstruction and straight thereafter doubling off in a different direction. As he gasped once in a brief pause: 'Never give 'em time to throw the shit at yer ... Just keep frigging moving.'

Then luck took a hand in this deadly game of hide-and-seek. Out of the fog of war below, a support craft appeared, firing all out as it did so. Red tracer shells from its Oerlikon cannon splattered the top of the cliff just above the gully leading to the beach that they were heading for.

Immediately the Germans defending the top took to the ground, unable to withstand that murderous blazing scarlet fire. It was like a wall of red death. Those who failed to duck in time were reduced to red-tattered shreds in moments.

'Come on, lads!' the commando sergeant yelled above the ear-splitting racket. It was the window out that he had been looking for ever since the abortive attack on the Gestapo headquarters. They needed no urging. They knew it was now or never. Ducked low, they sped forward, risking 'shorts' from the Oerlikon out at sea. For it was their only chance.

Here and there a German risked his neck in an attempt to stop them. He was unlucky. The commandos all seemed crack shots. A sighting and the unfortunate German was riddled with slugs the next instant. Mackenzie felt his confidence begin to grow again. With these men, he and the Major would make it. The commandos seemed unstoppable. God Almighty, they even appeared to *enjoy* these constant brushes with instant death.

They crossed the road at the double. Slugs whined everywhere, bouncing up from the cobbles in vivid little sparking flashes. Still their luck held out. They reached the fold in the cliff that led to the beach and the waiting barges below. It wasn't the one they had ascended. Here the strands of barbed wire running back and forth for a depth of at least twenty yards had not been cut. It didn't appear to deter the commandos. The big sergeant, dark red blood now trickling down the side of his smoke-begrimed face, said, 'Not to worry. We'll make it ... You–' he pointed to Mackenzie – 'you go first. Imagine yer going down a series of prickly steps. Keep moving fast and you won't notice the pricks, if you'll excuse my French.' He guffawed at what he supposed was a joke.

Mackenzie looked at the dizzy descent and the strand after strand of rusting barbed wire and forced a smile. 'You follow me, sir,' he yelled to Dalby.

The latter nodded. His face was pale and strained and, veteran of the trenches that he was, it was clear that he was getting too old for this kind of thing. Still he didn't complain.

'All right,' the sergeant boomed. 'Off we go. They'll have rum and bacon and eggs waiting for us on the galley down there.'

Mackenzie gulped. That prospect didn't excite him one bit; his stomach was churning crazily as it was. He grabbed the first strand. He felt the barbs bite painfully into his palms and bit back his moan just in time. He moved on quickly, the blood already beginning to well up. Behind him, Major Dalby followed more slowly.

Now the Oerlikon had ceased firing. It would have been too dangerous for it to continue; its shells might have struck its own men. The Germans on the cliff top reacted immediately. They rose at once from their hiding places. Tracer started to bounce off and chip flurries of chalk from the cliff wall. Grenades followed. The 'potato mashers' began to explode all around the escapers. They were showered with fragments of stone and metal. More than once Mackenzie yelped with pain as he was hit and felt the hot blood begin to well up from the jagged lacerations on his flesh. Still he and the rest continued their descent doggedly. It was the only means of escape left to them. Even if they attempted to raise their hands in surrender, Mackenzie knew the Germans would not accept it. Their blood was up. They'd gun them down even as they stood there.

Then it happened. A stick grenade exploded directly below Major Dalby. He yelled in agony, as he disappeared momentarily in a cloud of fire and bright white smoke to reappear the next moment five or six feet further down the wire, cruelly impaled on the barbs, his face an ashen white, a bright arc of scarlet blood jetting from his right leg. He appeared to be unconscious.

'Don't stop,' the commando sergeant yelled urgently. 'You know the drill. No stopping for casualties.'

But Mackenzie wasn't listening. He remembered that shoot-out at Venlo and the way the old Major had stood by him when *he* had been wounded. He wasn't going to abandon Major Dalby now. He let go and dropped downwards. He grasped the wire next to where Dalby lay, conscious once more and moaning softly. Ignoring the blood pouring from his torn and lacerated hands, he took a firm grip of Dalby's thigh above the great wound, the bone gleaming like polished ivory inside the gory scarlet pit. He pressed hard. The jet of bright blood diminished a little, but not altogether.

Dropping next to him, the commando sergeant peered at the gaping wound. 'No good, soldier. He needs proper medical attention. He'll have snuffed it before we reach Blighty under present conditions.'

'But we can't just leave him,' Mackenzie protested, as up above the first of their German pursuers ventured on to the wire.

'The Jerries don't shoot wounded,' the

commando sergeant reassured. 'They'll look after him OK. Come on. We'd better bugger off.'

'Do as the sergeant says, Mac.' Dalby's eyelids flickered weakly, as he spoke in a barely audible voice. 'I've had it. Get on off home.'

'But sir—'

'No buts.' Dalby cut him off with surprising firmness for his weak condition bordering on unconsciousness.

'You're needed back there ... you've got a message—' He coughed thickly and his face grew even paler. His eyeballs started to roll upwards and Mackenzie could see that he was about to relapse into unconsciousness once more.

'Needed?'

'Yes, Mac. We were set up ... this whole Gestapo safe business...'

'Come on,' the commando sergeant urged. This time he refrained from firing at the advancing Germans. He was risking being hit himself in order to give the wounded man a chance when the enemy picked him up. 'We ain't got no more time left, mate.'

Mackenzie looked at him and then back to Dalby in utter confusion, his mind racing electrically, as he wondered what he should do.

'Someone back there' – weakly with his head he indicated the west, where the country he would never see again lay – 'wanted us killed ... Mac, watch ... your back, old friend.' Weakly he touched Mackenzie's hand for a moment. Then his head lolled to one side and he was unconscious once more and they were dropping to the waiting boats, the ratings gunning the engines impatiently, as the victorious Germans got ever closer. Minutes later the survivors were moving off, defeated and despondent, with the Germans on the beach now not finding them worthy of wasting another bullet on.

Three

'Watch your back, old friend ...' Those long-forgotten words with their strange warning echoed and re-echoed down the vortex of Mackenzie's brain, as those ghostly, blood-dripping figures of two years rushed silently to their doom on that dread beach. 'But why,' he heard himself say to the fading Major, as the commando sergeant cursed and tugged at his arm, 'what have I to watch? ... Please tell me, Major Dalby...' In his voice, it seemed to him as he listened to it in his sleep, there was a note of almost childish petulance – that of a spoiled kid who can't bear any frustration of his wishes.' *Why...?*

'Sir ... sir ... we're nearly there now, sir.'

He woke with difficulty like a man trying to fight off a drugged sleep. It was Campbell 175 tugging at his sleeve, as he slumped next to the NCO, head resting on the other's shoulder almost. He blinked a couple of times and the grey morning scene came into focus.

It had snowed during the night in the

capital; and as yet it was too early for the morning traffic, what there was of it in wartime, to have turned its pristine sparkling whiteness into the normal dreary slush of a big city. They started to turn into Southampton Row and head for the Thames and their destination. Outside Euston Station a draft was beginning to form up. The draft would obviously march across the capital to Victoria where they would entrain again, bound for France and the new battles of the German frontier.

While they waited for the lights, Mackenzie eyed them, his problem with Dalby forgotten for a moment. The boys, six abreast, each laden with a heavy pack and one grey blanket neatly rolled about it, looked no more than eighteen. Obviously the Army was scraping the barrel for manpower. Recently Churchill had called up the 45-year-olds for the infantry. The country was running out of men. Now these boys were to continue the fight. For a moment or two, he wondered how many of them would survive what was soon to come on the other side of Channel. Not many of them, for they were infantry, he guessed. They were too ill-trained, callow, unwise to the ways of the battlefield. He sighed again and told himself that the bloody war had gone on just too long. The country and its people were simply worn out.

'All right,' the elderly sergeant-major in charge of the draft commanded, a dewdrop hanging at the end of his long red nose, his voice thin and reedy. 'Bags o' swank now ... Remember who yer are ... By the right, then – *quick march!*'

The draft stepped off. There was no spirit in their marching. Laden like beasts of burden, they moved through the snow, heads bowed under the weight like condemned men being led to the gallows. Even the few onlookers, waiting for their buses outside the station, turned away. The draft didn't inspire anybody. 'Left ... left, I had a good job – an' I left,' the elderly sergeant-major attempted. But no one joined in. He gave up, too, face glum.

'Poor sods,' Campbell 175 murmured as he engaged third gear and skirted the long column, attempting not to splash them with the fresh wet snow. 'Cannon fodder – the lot of 'em.'

Mackenzie didn't comment. Of course the smart little Jew masquerading as a hairy-assed braw Highlander was right. But this morning he was in no mood to comment on the state of the nation in this fifth year of the war. Instead he concentrated the best he could on this new problem which had appeared from the past so unexpectedly: one that he had almost forgotten about under the pressures and excitements of the months and years since that disastrous raid on Dieppe, where to his eternal shame he had been forced to abandon Major Dalby. 'Yes, he probably saved your life at Venlo and then you went and did the dirt on him when you might have saved him,' a harsh, accusing voice rasped at the back of his mind.

He forced himself to dismiss that particularly unpleasant thought as Campbell 175 steered the little van closer to the 'War House'. Five minutes later he was sitting in a miserably heated little office with pen-and-ink sketches of long-dead nineteenth-century officers on the drab walls, facing a young brigadier who was totally unknown to him. There hadn't even been a name plate on the door outside and the brigadier had made no attempt either to shake his hand or introduce himself. It was something that puzzled Mackenzie even more. First the unexpected summons to the War Office and now a brigadier without even a medal ribbon on the breast of his immaculate service dress complete with Sam Browne.

Finally after the ex-soldier had brought in the customary mug of tea – 'No sugar today, sir, ration's run out–' the strange brigadier mustered Mackenzie in a manner that the latter thought was damned cheeky and said, 'You can call me Clive, if you wish, Mackenzie.'

'Thank you – *sir*,' Mackenzie said, emphasizing the 'sir'; he had no intention of calling the pompous prick 'Clive'. He had long stopped playing the silly games that Intelligence staff officers were wont to get up to. He waited.

'Clive' finally spoke. Obviously he was that kind of individual who thought by letting subordinates wait he exerted his authority. Now he said, 'We've got a problem with your former chief Major Dalby.' He paused. Deliberately Mackenzie didn't fill in the sudden silence.

'He's dead, you know.'

Mackenzie said, 'I didn't know.' His mind raced though at the information. Suddenly he was eager to find out why he had been summoned here like this and why the authorities thought it important for him to be informed. He sensed that something was going on that sooner or later would involve him. But in what capacity? After all, he had left Dalby behind in German hands. If he had died recently, he would have done so in Germany, probably in some Hun cage once he had recovered from his wounds. And why should this strange brigadier with his overlong hair and cold grey eyes be interested by an ageing major in Intelligence who had been out of circulation for over two years now? Lots of questions and so far no answers.

'After Major Dalby recovered from his wounds, he became something of a thorn in the Germans' side, it appears,' 'Clive' continued. 'Clive' smiled carefully, as if he had taught himself to do so, knowing that 'nice' people smiled, though, in fact, he knew nothing of niceness. On the contrary. 'Despite his age and the long-term problems with his wounds, he escaped from the *Oflag* at Brunswick and then another one at Sagan in Poland ... Anyway, to cut a long story short, the Huns had had enough of him and they ended up by sending him to Colditz. You've heard of Colditz, I presume?'

Mackenzie had, naturally. He knew virtually everything about POW camps, British and enemy. He even knew something of the appalling escape rate of German and Italian POWs from US prisoner-of-war camps, and how the POWs made full use of easy-going Yankee women to help them in their escapes. But he wasn't going out of his way to help 'Clive' in the slightest manner. So he said, 'I hear it's one of the enemy's top security prisons.'

'It is. The bad boys' POW camp, our chaps call it apparently. The Huns send only the worse types there, the inveterate escapers.' 'Clive' seemed to warm to the subject of Colditz, that is if such a cold personality could warm to anything. 'It's a medieval castle in Saxony. It contains Poles, Frogs, a handful ofYanks and a lot of our own chaps, who've escaped time and time again. The Germans thought it was escape-proof until our chaps arrived, then they had to think again. Again 'Clive' gave Mackenzie that careful, self-taught smile of his.

This time Mackenzie's impatience got the better of him. He didn't care if 'Clive' thought he had got one up on him or not, he had to ask that overwhelming question. 'How sir, did Major Dalby die there at this place ... Colditz?'

Now 'Clive's' smile vanished. 'He was shot,' he said without preamble.

'By the Huns?'

'No, there was no doubt, he *wasn't* escaping. He had been weakened by the escape from Sagan and before they sent him to Colditz, the Huns knocked him about quite a bit. No, he was—'

'Well, who shot him?' Mackenzie interrupted harshly. He was in no mood to play any more games.

'If not the Huns, it had to be someone else.'

'And?'

'Frankly, we don't know, Major.' The use of Mackenzie's rank was a quiet warning that he was, after all, talking to a brigadier, his superior by several ranks.

Mackenzie didn't notice. 'What do you mean – we don't know?' he demanded.

'What I say, Mackenzie. You see, the camp in the castle has a secret radio. Most of them do.'

The other man nodded his understanding.

'The radio is only to be used in a dire emergency, such as to relay top-class information. You see, we're expecting the fanatical Nazis to use the quarter of a million allied POWs in their possession as some kind of a trading measure when things get desperate for them – which will be soon. However, the SBO* at Colditz decided Dalby's death warranted radio silence being broken. The result? We got a short transmission indicating that Dalby had been shot...'

At the word 'shot', Mackenzie, surprised at he was by it, was tempted to demand more. But just in time, he decided not to. He'd let 'Clive' tell the story the way he wanted to. It might be better that way.

'But not by the Huns. Eggers, the German officer in the camp in our pay, insisted, according to the radio signal, that the commandant had nothing to do with the shooting. Nor had any of his guards, either deliberately or accidentally. You know, one of them going berserk because of the loss of his family in our bombing raids – something like that. In essence, the Germans in

* *Senior British Officer*

the Colditz camp had nothing to do with the shooting of Major Dalby.'

'But they would say that, wouldn't they?' Mackenzie objected.

'With the war just about lost, they're not going to get blood on their hands, knowing that we'll do our damnedest to bring the criminal to justice.'

'Agreed. But we've checked. The Huns are telling the truth for once. The SBO confirms that. No, my dear Mackenzie, your old boss – and *friend*–' 'Clive' emphasized the word 'friend' for some reason known only to himself – 'was deliberately murdered by someone other than a Hun.'

For what seemed a long time there was silence in the cheerless, cold office, with the few coals flickering fitfully in the black-leaded grate. Outside, the usual air-raid sirens were sounding to the east in the distance. Not that anyone took any notice. People had either got used to the flying bombs or had become resigned to them, knowing there was nothing they or the defences could do about them.

Finally Mackenzie cleared his throat and asked carefully, perhaps too carefully in view of his temperament, 'Sir, admittedly I knew and admired Major Dalby and I am certainly very sorry that he should die now with the war already won, but–' he raised his voice – 'what has this affair got to do with me? I'm here and poor Dalby's over there in enemy hands and probably buried by now, sir?'

For the first time since they had met, 'Clive' showed some agitation. He pursed his lips, cocking his head to one side, as if he were giving the matter a great deal of thought. Mackenzie knew he wasn't. He was prepared for the question; he had already guessed that. 'Clive' was just wondering, he was sure, how he might answer it in a way that was convincing enough for someone like Mackenzie, well known throughout British Army Intelligence for his astute manner. 'Well...' he commenced slowly.

Up above there was the familiar putt-putt of a V-1 motor. In the corridors the ancient porters were croaking the usual request: 'Please, gentlemen, it is advisable now to proceed to the air-raid shelters in the basement as quickly as possible ... Please, gentlemen...'

Mackenzie waited impatiently, wondering what exactly this 'Clive's' game was.

'Clive' decided that he should explain. 'You see, Mackenzie,' he said, sounding more confident of himself than the first time, 'we think there is something very fishy going on at Colditz. If the Huns didn't kill Major Dalby, who did and how the devil did a third party manage to penetrate the place's security? More importantly, what was this unknown person's motive in killing Dalby under such strange circumstances, two years or so since he had been taken prisoner by the Boche?'

Mackenzie lost patience suddenly with 'Clive' and his long-winded explanations. Severely he snapped, 'I asked a simple question, sir. How do I fit into this business?'

Overhead the flying bomb's engine cut out abruptly. 'Clive' tensed. 'You see, Mackenzie ... we thought that, as a friend of Dalby, you might have some idea who would have wanted him dead. Perhaps he knew something that could compromise someone...? If you could unearth the story, then it could prove invaluable intelligence – what's more, when this war is over, you could make sure that whatever it is that someone wants covered up is brought to light. Put before parliament, the press, that sort of thing ... After all, don't you owe it to Dalby?'

Suddenly, startlingly, the phone on the desk in front of him started to ring. Both he and Mackenzie jumped slightly at the strange noise when they had been half-expecting something more dramatic. Instinctively, 'Clive' reached for the phone. A polite man – at times – Mackenzie turned his head while 'Clive' spoke. It was a bad mistake. If he had kept his gaze on the other man, he would have recognized immediately by the surprising change in 'Clive's' expression what kind of a man he really was.

Instead he gazed out of the window at the V-1 diving down some half a mile away to bring fresh death and destruction to some hard-pressed Londoners, aware only of 'Clive' saying hurriedly, 'Yes, I understand completely ... I take your point ... I'll get on to it ... now ... well, soon as possible ... you understand my position of course. Thank you. Goodbye.' There was a click. The phone went dead and Mackenzie turned his gaze back to the other man.

'Clive' had already risen to his feet. Hurriedly he grabbed for his hat and it was only later – too late – that Mackenzie realized that it didn't have the customary red band of a staff brigadier. He said, 'Bit of a flap on back at HQ.' Which headquarters he didn't indicate. 'Got to get back at once. My chaps are doing their nuts.' He allowed himself a careful smile at the slang expression, but there was no answering light in his cold grey eyes. 'I'm handing you over to MI9, you know.'

Mackenzie nodded. That was the secret Intelligence organization, dealing with the escape and evasion of British prisoners-of-war in German hands.

'They'll fill you in. Now must fly.' He thrust out a hand.

Mackenzie didn't take it. Instead he clicked to attention.

'Clive' flushed. But he had no time, it appeared, to comment on the deliberate insult. 'Carry on the good work. Must fly ... See you in due course, Mackenzie.'

But the latter would never see Brigadier 'Clive', if that was his true rank and name, again.

'Cheeribye.' With that he was gone, clattering down the stone steps, as if the very Devil himself was after him, leaving Mackenzie to stare puzzled at the plume of black smoke rising from the site of the V-1 explosion. What, he asked himself almost angrily, was bloody well going on?

Mackenzie was frankly puzzled. So far everything connected with poor old Dalby's apparent murder was confusing. The only clear area that he could see was that someone had been out to get Dalby because he had known too much about that bloody disgraceful Venlo business. Of course there was one obvious suspect, but it was the bizarre behaviour of this 'Clive' which filled Mackenzie with doubt.

As they walked down Whitehall, empty due to the raid, their footsteps echoing in that deserted stone canyon, he said, 'I don't know, but it's a real bugger.'

Campbell forced a grin and proud of his knowledge of colloquial English, joked, 'And so are you, my son.' He smiled.

Mackenzie didn't respond. His mind was

too full of questions seemingly without answers.

They walked on. Somewhere an ambulance bell was jingling urgently. He frowned. Obviously there had been more civvie casualties. God, what a beating London was taking. But now he was taking in another sound. A car racing at speed.

'Somebody's got black-market petrol to waste,' Campbell 175 said, as a low sports car swung round the corner in a screech and squall of protesting rubber. 'Look at that mad sod!'

Mackenzie looked. It was a pre-war Aston Martin that had obviously seen better days. Its dark green British racing colour was scabbed with rust and the bonnet was so battered that he couldn't make out its licence plate. Behind the wheel, a dark figure crouched, hunched low, collar up and a grey trilby pulled well down over his forehead. 'Wonder if he can see—' He broke off suddenly. 'Look out, Campbell. The silly devil's—'

Up in the second floor window 'Poxie', alias 'Brigadier Clive', held his breath. The telephone call had worked splendidly. 'Gelly', once the best gelignite safe-blower in the business until he lost part of his fingers in a premature explosion, was right on time. Now he was hurriedly driving straight down at the two lone figures.

Mackenzie saw the danger immediately. He gave a surprised Campbell 175 a great push. Caught completely off guard, the younger man yelped and, arms whirling wildly, he tumbled into the bomb crater to his left. Next moment, Mackenzie sprang in after him, landing heavily on the brick rubble and broken beams.

Crazily the Aston Martin careered from side to side. Almost before the two men sprawled out in the comb crater realized what had happened, the big sports car had swung round the far corner with a monstrous howl of its engine and was gone, leaving Mackenzie to realize slowly that the real trouble had commenced...

Four

It had been a day like any other in Colditz: a grey day in the grey late years of a grey war with a leaden sky hanging over the narrow rectangle of the cobbled castle courtyard which the prisoners used for their recreation and their duty parades.

Now, however, this early December day with a biting wind coming in straight from Siberia it was recreation time for those who dared to face the icy wind and had the strength on their limited prison diet to brave the elements. But there were always some who would do so, even in the depths of the Saxon winter. There were the 'hearties' who trotted remorsely round and round, beet-root-red and puffing hard in their skimpy sports kit, made of Army issue vests and long woollen underpants. There were the 'doolally types', who wandered all over the place, playing home-made reed flutes, recit-ing poetry, occasionally leaping into the air on some crazy impulse: mixed with the 'cunning buggers', who were trying 'to work their ticket' and hoped to be sent home via the Swedish SS *Gripsholm** as mentally unstable. And there were 'hard men', unrepentant types, whose eyes were here, there and everywhere, looking for yet another means of escape, though over the years since 1939 virtually every avenue to do so had been attempted – more than once.

Major Dalby, so it was reported later after his murder, was none of the above. He was what the Senior British Officer would characterize in his secret radio report to MI9 as 'bloody-minded ... a loner ... who'd do everything to annoy the Hun, even at the risk of his own life'. A loner he was and, by the standards of Colditz, too old and too unfit to even dream of escaping and it was for these reasons that the Germans had left him alone and virtually unwatched ever since he had been admitted to Colditz. They reasoned that the veteran of the 'Old War', with his cane and bad limp, wasn't too much of a risk in comparison with the men half his age who were constantly dreaming up new schemes of escape. After all, they had enough on their hands with them; and the guards available to watch the POWs were getting older and more unfit by the

**A Swedish ship that carried the POWs of both sides back to their own countries when the International Swiss Red Cross judged that the POW was too sick or mad to be kept imprisoned any longer.*

month as the insatiable Russian front ate up ever more young German soldiers.

On this day, those who remembered seeing him (for Dalby had a way of disappearing into the background even in the overcrowded *Oflag*), he seemed to be preoccupied with some problem or other as he followed his usual circuit, puffing hard at his tobaccoless pipe, face set in a look of concentration. When MI9 signalled via that secret radio contact to ask if there was any reason for this seeming concentration on his own thoughts, the Senior British Officer signalled back, 'I haven't a clue ... Dalby keeps his thoughts to himself.' But those who shared the major's mess in the main part of that old Saxon castle did mention that he had recently received a letter from a non-British source – they thought that the stamp on the envelope bore the red cross and recumbent lion of neutral Switzerland. Dalby had been observed, thereafter, reading it several times in the semi-privacy of his bunk. One thing that all the observers did think strange about this letter was that it hadn't apparently been censored by the German authorities and Dalby hadn't offered to share its contents with his mess mates. For it was customary that the officers shared any news with each other; they were all starved of information, however trivial. But that was about all that the SBO could report was in any way unusual.

Towards mid-morning, as most of the 'kriegies'* had returned to the relative warmth of their quarters, but with Dalby still stomping around his circuit, the first soft flakes of snow had begun to drift down. Gently, almost imperceptibly, they floated from the heavens and the freezing guards in the towers told themselves, 'The sky hung full of violins,' as the soldiers' expression had it; they were in for a lot of snow. Thus as the snowfall gathered strength, the sentries retreated to the cover the towers offered, telling themselves that even the crazy, buck-teethed Tommies wouldn't try any of their schoolboyish attempts at escape in this weather. *'Die Englander sind nicht alle verruckt.'*

Thus it was that Major Dalby spent his last moments on this earth unobserved, moving silently around like some grey ghost, forgotten by comrades and captors alike. Later, when Mackenzie knew more of the facts, he would ask himself, what had his old boss being thinking in his last minutes on this earth? Was it about the days of his youth – that carefree young infantry officer who had first gone 'over the top' in 1914 armed only with an ashplant, his 'chaps'

**Slang name for POWs, a corruption of the German word 'Kriegsgefangener' (Transl.)*

kicking a soccer ball as they followed, ready for 'a bit of a match with Old Fritz'? Or had he recalled his dead wife and the morning he found her in the rubble of their London flat, totally naked and not a mark on her, yet cold and stone dead all the same? Or had he remained the professional Intelligence man to the very end; was he considering something – perhaps that letter from neutral Switzerland – which might have caused his mysterious death in the middle of an enemy jail?

Mackenzie would never know and in due course he would conclude in one of those blue moods that seemed to afflict him more often these days that one never knew what people thought in those last minutes before death; perhaps it was for the better...

The killer found it almost too easy to enter the castle. Naturally he was coming in from the German side and who would attempt to stop an SS *Hauptsturmführer*, complete with Knight's Cross hanging at his throat, who stalked by the sentries towards the officers *Kasino* with typical SS arrogance so that they simply were too scared to ask for his pass. Which was fortunate, for he didn't have the special authorization needed to enter Oflag Colditz.

None of them, mostly older men or a few cripples from the *Ostfront*, bothered to even look at the strange narrow case he was carrying in his gloved hand. To the man, the sentries, even the NCO guard commanders, kept their eyes to their front and remained rigidly to attention as he swept by in his fur-collared cloak. No one, even decorated and wounded veterans of the Russian front, would have had the temerity to stop an SS officer, especially now in this fifth year of the war when SS officers shot their own soldiers without trial.

So the killer entered, followed the map of the place he had in his mind (for he had been well briefed for the task ahead), and after passing the last of the guards, mounted the battlements overlooking the courtyard where the prisoners exercised. It was snowing hard now. He knew it would make his task more difficult. At the same time, it would ensure that he had less chance of being interrupted. There'd be fewer prisoners about and the guards in the towers would be preoccupied with keeping warm. Of one thing he was certain: the man he had come to kill would be present below, snowstorm or not. The letter would ensure that.

Now taking up his position at the spot prescribed for him by the others, he opened the strange-looking case. Expertly, despite the freezing cold, he assembled the sniper's rifle. He would have preferred a German weapon, even a Swiss one. But they had not approved his choice. It had to be a British sniper's rifle. There were plenty of them in German hands.

He chuckled slightly – it wasn't a pleasant sound – as he fixed the scope and checked it was sitting correctly. The whole business was strange. 'They'll have one helluva headache sorting this one out,' he said to himself, talking aloud in the fashion of lonely men. He chuckled again. But the one who'd have the worst headache, a permanent one, would be the victim down there somewhere in the white murk of flying snowflakes.

He stuffed his right glove in the pocket of his cloak and replaced it with a thin silk one. It would keep his hand warm enough, but at the same time give him the 'feel' of the rifle which every good rifleman, firing his weapon under these conditions, needed. He hefted the gun, was satisfied with the balance and finally twisted on the silencer. He was ready.

He settled himself more comfortably, shaking the cloak about him to keep as warm as possible. He drew a few deep breaths of the icy air to calm himself. Then he peered through the scope, shielding the sight with his free hand for a moment to keep the snowflakes off.

The courtyard below leapt into focus. Suddenly the area in front of him was not just a white blur. He could make out individual objects – the trough the prisoners used for water for their plants in summer, the raised spots where the NCOs stood when they took the morning and evening roll call and the like. Carefully, systematically, he started to search the snow-heavy yard for his victim, sweeping the rifle from the left to the right, feeling once more an almost sexual excitement at the power at his command. He had done this often enough. All the same he could never quite conquer that mounting sensation of power – the feeling that he was about to kill. It had been like this ever since the *Abwehr* had hired him in Chicago as an eighteen-year-old German-American kid to carry out their political assassinations and it had never changed in the intervening years when he had killed and assassinated everywhere from the Urals to the English Channel.

With a sudden slight gasp, he stopped short. There he was, sheltering under the overhanging arch of the medieval wall, exactly where the coded letter had told him to be. The killer gave a cold smile. What fools human beings were. They hoped, even the most intelligent of them like this Tommy was supposed to be, to the very end. Didn't they realize when their 'case' (he always liked to use that word; it gave the bloody business a sort of professional, official tone) had reached the stage where there was no hope and no way out, save death. Now the time had come to bring the case to an end.

He breathed on his trigger finger. Despite the silk of the glove, it was getting cold and he knew, just like a woman's cunt, his trigger needed to be felt by something that was sensitive and warm. He smirked at the comparison. Tonight undoubtedly they would reward him with a big fat juicy whore. He wouldn't need a warm finger to excite her professional cunt.

Ready, he raised the rifle once more. He grunted. He hadn't judged the distance quite correctly. Carefully he adjusted it to the correct thirty metres. Now he peered through the circle of calibrated glass at the foresight, making sure there was no darkness in the tube. *Perfect!*

Down below, the unsuspecting Tommy waited patiently. His head was bent slightly. All the same the killer could still get a decent fix on his right temple. It was almost as if the Englishman realized he had long been picked out as a victim, someone who had to be killed, and who was now waiting for the inevitable like a dumb animal submitting tamely to the slaughter about to come.

The killer was not given to such fantasies. He was concerned solely with doing a good job of work, getting it over with and being on his way. He wanted no fuss. No problems. The intended victim was acting just as he liked his victims to act. He hated those face-to-face confrontations of the past where there had been screams, protests, pleas for mercy and that damned emotionalism. This middle-aged Tommy, isolated in the raging snowstorm below, was just the kind of target he dreamed of. Perfect.

He curled his finger around the rifle's trigger. He took his time. He remembered to control his breathing. At such moments even experienced killers tended to breathe harder and faster than normal. That was bad for the aim. He took first pressure. In that circle of deadly glass, his victim still remained perfectly still. He took one last look at the living man crouched there like some damned long-haired Yid in front of his damned wailing wall. He took full pressure.

There was a soft *phut*. The butt of the rifle slammed against his right shoulder. A puff of snow. In the circle of bright, calibrated glass, the victim threw up his hands. It was a gesture of overwhelming final despair. Slowly, very slowly, the Tommy started to sink to the snow, blood from his shattered skull dripping in bright red gobs into the whiteness.

The killer smiled with satisfaction, baring those wolfish teeth of his. He had done it – and in the whole of Colditz prisoner-of-war camp not a soul was the wiser. He touched his lucky brass class ring with its American eagle design. Like most of his kind, especially those who were trained as snipers – that lonely, mean job of killing by stealth – he was superstitious; he had to have a lucky charm. That done, he started to strip the rifle. He noticed with satisfaction that his hands did not tremble in the slightest. Down below, Major Dalby died quietly in the snow.

But the killer was not going to escape that easily. Even in his secret, over-planned life, things sometimes went wrong. Now something did...

Colditz contained all types. Yet within this very varied group of officers of different nations, there were some groupings which were even more eccentric or, at least, different in the eyes of the great majority, who constantly cocked a snook at their German captors.

There were 'loonies', as we have seen: those 'doolally types', too unpredictable even for the wildest dreamer among the other officers. There were the 'pansies', naturally, in a totally male society, made up of virile young men, whose sexual desires could not be diminished tamely even on the starvation rations dished out to them by their captors. Some scorned them; others tolerated them; and often they were, at least, good for a laugh when they appeared in the camp concerts looking more attractive and seductive sexually than the average 'English rose' most of the men knew back home.

Then there were the 'darkies'. There was only a handful of them and although this was an age when 'men of colour' were looked down upon by the pukka British sahib, these weren't. They were doctors of the Indian Medical Service, an odd Gurkha officer and a couple of officers from one of the private armies maintained by rich Indian maharajahs; but all had served with distinction in the British forces and after their capture had proved their worth as inveterate escapers; that's why they were in Colditz. 'Darkies', they might be called by their white fellow officers. But there was nothing particularly racial about the designation; it was just a common term of the time and, if anything, it was thought of – at least by the white – as an expression of endearment.

Still, for the handful of 'darkies', life in this predominantly white POW camp was not all that easy. Their religions, dietary habits and forms of worship, including the five times a day of the Muslims, did present problems. It was for this reason that on that snowy afternoon Captain Tariq Ali, formerly of the Pathan Scouts, happened to be in that snowy yard the moment that Major Dalby was shot. It was the same old question of the five times daily ritual washing and praying.

It was becoming more and more difficult in the crowded conditions of his own mess, where his fellow officers were sleeping in bunks three high and every bit of floor space seemed to be taken up with washing and the various hobbies, home-made stoves, etc. etc. of his comrades – and Tariq Ali, despite being a 'darkie', thought of them as comrades.

Now, his shoulders wrapped in a blanket against the biting cold, eyes half closed against the flying snowflakes, he wandered a little unhappily around the deserted courtyard. Then he heard it. The soft hush of a silenced weapon, followed a moment later by a low moan of someone in mortal agony.

The Indian captain's mood vanished immediately. He had been brought up with sudden death and treachery in his remote mountain birthplace. He recognized at once that it had not been the standard '08 model German Mauser rifle which he had just heard; it had been something more sophisticated – and that soft moan was of someone who had been gravely hurt by that strange rifle. In a moment he had found the dead major slumped at the base of the wall and with his hands cupped around his mouth against the wind-driven snow, he was shouting in German urgently, '*Alarm ... Alarm ... Man hat jemand enchossen ... ALARM!*'

The first searchlight clicked on suddenly.

Its beam cut the white gloom to illuminate the dark figure shouting crazily below. Abruptly German soldiers, grabbing their rifles, tugging on their helmets, were running to their duty posts everywhere with, in the background, the first hand-cranked sirens beginning their initial nerve-jingling wail.

The killer cursed. He reacted correctly, as he always had done in such situations. He realized immediately that he wouldn't be able to get out now. The special rifle, if nothing else, would be a dead giveaway. Besides he didn't have the correct pass for entry into Colditz. 'Shit,' he cursed in English. Then he got to work. Even as the first middle-aged sentry was slipping, sliding his way cautiously along the snow-slick battlements, he was pulling back the loose planks covering the medieval mullioned window that led into the dusty, long-abandoned interior of the castle. A moment later he was inside and had vanished...

Five

Colonel Langley patted his empty sleeve thoughtfully, as if he were wondering how he came to lose his arm and concluded, 'Well, Mackenzie, that's the way we have reconstructed the events at Colditz.' He pulled a face as if he had tasted something bitter suddenly.

Both the listening Mackenzie and Campbell 175 knew why. Langley, the head of MI9, the top-secret Intelligence organization dealing with the evasion and escape of British POWs, had once been a prisoner at the chilling Saxon castle himself before escaping and making a celebrated 'home run'. But they said nothing. They were here at Wilton Park, the secret outfit's HQ, to learn. They kept their own problems to themselves for the time being, though both of them wondered how the devil they had got involved in this whole mysterious affair of the dead Major Dalby.

'We can safely assume then,' said Langley, a tall, spare officer, his face lined as a result of the pain and privations he had suffered before he had got back to Britain, 'that Major Dalby was murdered. And we can add to that that it is ninety per cent certain that the Boche weren't involved. For once, it is the considered opinion of myself and my officers that the Germans are telling the truth. After all why should they shoot Dalby? We feel that they wanted him alive, just as they're keeping those two fools Best and Payne alive after all these years for some sort of show trial after they win the war–' he gave them a mockery of grin – 'which is hardly likely now, what?'

Mackenzie pursed his lips thoughtfully at the mention of the two MI6 men who had walked so easily into the German trap at Venlo back in November 1939. At the back of his clever mind a thought was beginning to uncurl itself slowly like some sluggish snake waking up from its sleep. Still he didn't say anything though he knew at his side Campbell 175 was looking at him significantly, wondering if his boss was going to react and start asking questions. But then, the former told himself, after yesterday's business with the mysterious 'Brigadier Clive', who had done a bunk after that telephone call, it was obvious that Mackenzie was playing this game with his cards close to his chest.

'We can assume, too,' Langley continued in his customary slow, careful manner, 'that the killer didn't escape the way he came in. Our people in Colditz are certain of that. So if he didn't get out, where the bloody hell did he go?'

That question gave them all pause, even Campbell 175, whose restless clever brain always seemed to have an answer for everything. Puzzled, their faces stoney, the Intelligence men half-listened to one of the cooks outside doing his 'spud-bashing', singing in a bored, weary voice, *'Up came a spider ... whipped his old bazooka out and this is what he said ... get hold o' this, bash-bash ... get hold o' that ... I've got a luvverly bunch of coconuts...'*

A little angrily, perhaps because he was so puzzled, Mackenzie dismissed the cook and his 'luvverly bunch of coconuts' and said, 'Colonel, let's have a recap.'

Langley nodded a little warily.

'According to the information with which you have supplied us, someone, apparently an SS officer or a person dressed as an SS officer, entered Colditz illegally. He stalked poor Major Dalby, shot him and would have got away with it, if it had not been for this Indian officer . . .' He clicked his fingers impatiently.

'Captain Tariq Ali.' Campbell 175 supplied the name dutifully.

'Yes, him ... hadn't raised the alarm. Thereupon, as is the drill, according to you, Colonel, all exits to Colditz *Oflag* were sealed and apparently he was unable to escape, according to the camp authorities.'

Langley nodded again, but said nothing.

'So if that is *really* the case, he, the killer, must have remained in the body of the camp. Here I see two possibilities: one feasible; the other hardly believable.'

Outside, the bored cook, his hands red-raw as he threw another poorly peeled potato into the great washtub full of cold water, had now launched into yet another dirty ditty to while away the time: '*Where was the engine-driver when the boiler burst?*' He was now chortling. '*They found his bollocks – and the same to you … bollocks.*'

Campbell 175 allowed himself a careful grin. These Intelligence brains never liked the realization there was another world out there, filled with bored, coarse Army types.

'Our killer, being presumably German, took refuge inside the German camp. I mean there must be scores of personnel looking after our poor chaps, and the way things are in Germany this winter, there must be lots of personnel changes so people won't know each other like they must have done at the beginning of the war. He could even be a cook like that ugly sod spud-bashing outside.'

Langley said, 'That is a real possibility. We signalled the SBO at Colditz to see that his chaps checked it out. Their duty pilots–' the one-armed Colonel meant the POW watchers who followed their captors' every movement twenty-four hours a day – 'know virtually everyone on the Hun side. And your other possibility, Mackenzie – the one that's barely believable?'

Mackenzie took a deep breath and hesitated. To Campbell 175, he looked like a man about to plunge into an icy lake in the depths of winter and was wondering whether he would survive the experience.

Mackenzie took the plunge. 'That our killer found an even better hiding place – even inside the British part of the *Oflag!*'

As Mackenzie had expected, Langley looked shocked. Even Campbell 175 was taken aback at his boss's bold suggestion.

Langley stuttered, 'Well, I know that Colditz Castle is a real old rabbit warren. I mean when I was in there we found rooms in the upper storeys, thick with dust and bird droppings, that looked as if they hadn't been entered for centuries. I'm sure the Huns themselves didn't know they existed. Nobody was ever able to work out a reliable plan of the place. All the same, what would a fugitive of that kind, hiding out like that find to eat and drink? I mean Colditz is bitterly cold at the best of times. He could freeze to death hiding out in that manner.'

'Agreed, Colonel, agreed,' Mackenzie said hastily. 'But what says he was not hiding out in the way I've suggested?'

'You mean . . .?'

'Yes.'

Langley looked at Mackenzie, as if the latter had suddenly gone mad.

'But you can't believe that, Mackenzie?' he said sharply. 'This Hun murderer mixing with our chaps! How could he pull it off? He'd have to speak English fluently, for instance ... How would he be able to explain his sudden appearance in the compound? ... Why, he couldn't just walk into somebody's mess and say, large as life, "I'm here, chaps. Can I have that bunk over there near the stove and what's for tea this afternoon...?" Langley stuttered out the questions wildly, totally unlike his usual calm, collected self ... 'I mean, Mackenzie, it's simply not on – not on at all.'

Mackenzie opened his mouth to explain. But before he could do so, there was a polite soft knock on the door.

'Come!' Langley cried, his thin worn face still flushed from his outburst.

It was another of 'Langley's Old Lags', as they called themselves, soldiers like the Colonel, who had escaped from enemy captivity and made a successful 'home run' back to the UK. In this case it was Staff-Sergeant 'Eyetie' Higgins, who back in '43 had escaped from Italy and walked seven hundred miles down the spine of Italy till he reached Allied lines in the south 'screwing my way home, as yer might, say, gents,' as he was wont to explain to the sergeants' mess. Now he was part of Langley's inner circle in the position of orderly room sergeant and trusted bearer of secrets.

'Well?' Langley demanded, 'what is it, you rogue?'

'Eyetie' Higgins indicated Campbell 175. 'Message for the Staff Sergeant, sir,' he said with exaggerated deference. 'Old Sweat' that he was, he was always exceedingly polite to senior officers, though as he confessed often to his cronies in the mess, 'Officers – I've shat 'em, gents. All this escaping lark – like a lot of bloody overgrown schoolkids!'

'All right, get on with it,' Langley said and dismissed the matter as Campbell 175 followed his fellow NCO outside into the corridor. He waited till they had gone, then said, 'How could this Hun chap have done it, Mackenzie – I mean infiltrated himself into our compound like you suggest?'

But again Mackenzie wasn't fated to answer Langley's question, for now Campbell 175 himself burst into the room without knocking and said, addressing himself directly and ignoring an annoyed Langley, 'Sir, this Brigadier Clive chap–' his dark face was flushed with suppressed excitement, dark eyes flashing – 'he isn't what he seemed to be.'

'How do you mean, Campbell?'

'Well, sir, he doesn't exist – at least on the Army List. The orderly room sergeant has just had it through from Army Records. No trace of any such person. Nor is there any trace in Signals of the message sent summoning us to the War Office.' He faltered, paused and stopped altogether, as if he had suddenly become aware of the enormity of what he had just disclosed to his boss.

Mackenzie stared back at him, equally shocked, while Langley glanced from one man to the other, obviously completely at a loss to understand what was going on.

Outside the weary cook, still 'spud bashing', despite the first flurries of snow beginning to fall from the grey winter sky, had now launched into the old favourite of that other age, the 'Phoney War' of 1939–40: *'Kiss me good-night, Sergeant-Major ... Be a little mother to me ... We all love you, Sergeant-Major...'*

Major Mackenzie couldn't help himself. Never in his long career in Intelligence had he been as puzzled and totally confused as he was now. Angrily he snorted, *'Kiss me bloody good-night, Sarnt-Major – indeed.'*

An hour later they were on their way back to London to the War Office to report, though in truth Major Mackenzie didn't know exactly what he should report. As he hunched in the hard leather seat next to Sergeant Campbell 175 at the wheel of the little van, he said a little helplessly, 'It all seems to me, Sergeant, to be a real dog's dinner. We're summoned to see a fake brigadier, informed of the murder of my old boss by this same fake brigadier, who promptly disappears, and then find out at Wilton Park that the murderer was – is – trapped somewhere in Colditz Castle and that he, the murderer, is not a German, at least not one of the Colditz Camp personnel ... We receive this information on what kind of basis?' He answered his own question. 'Not because we are *officially* concerned with a murder which had taken place way out of our patch and has nothing to do with us, *again officially*, but because persons unknown on this side of the Channel want to involve us in the affair.'

Campbell 175 took his eyes off the road for a moment and looked pointedly at his boss. He said, 'Not *us*, sir, but *you*.'

'Me – Christ, what do you mean?'

'You remember you told me about that business in Dieppe with Major Dalby?'

'Yes.'

'Well, in a way it was a false alarm, wasn't it? In retrospect, one could almost say that you were lured there to get rid of you.' He paused for a moment and let his boss consider his words. 'I mean there was a good chance that you could be killed attacking that Gestapo HQ, protected only by a handful of commandos.'

Thoughtfully Mackenzie nodded his agreement. As usual Campbell 175 was not wasting any time in getting to the heart of the matter. 'All right, I'll buy it. But why would anyone be interested in getting rid of yours truly – a lowly major of Intelligence?'

The smart little NCO at the wheel answered with a question of his own. 'Why should anyone be interested in killing poor Major Dalby two years later, sir?' He lowered his voice. 'It must be, sir, that you and he know something of great importance, something that may have happened a long time ago – at least before Dieppe in 1942 – which presents a threat now in late 1944, something quite frankly worth murdering for.'

There was silence for a while after that dramatic statement. Steadily the little van continued its journey back to London, with the two men in the unheated cab sunk in a cocoon of their own thoughts. Mackenzie realized that his sergeant was right. Even that car which nearly ran them down after their meeting with the mysterious 'Brigadier Clive' fitted into the picture. But what was the purpose of bringing the murder of Major Dalby to his, Mackenzie's, attention?

If there was a plot – and the strange

assassination of his old boss, Dalby, at Colditz indicated there had to be – what role did he play in it? Why had he been selected as a victim as well and why, more importantly, after two years since the Dieppe fiasco, had the matter been activated again?

After a while, as he pondered this strange mystery without really coming to any firm conclusion, save that he was involved in it somehow or other and there had been a deliberate attempt by this 'Brigadier Clive' to get him involved, Campbell 175 broke the heavy brooding silence with: 'I think we ought to be careful, sir.'

'*We?*'

'Yes, if you'll forgive me for being forward.' He grinned cheekily. He was always forward and he didn't care a tuppenny damn whether he was forgiven or not. Momentarily Mackenzie shared his grin, but said nothing. 'I know as much as you about what's going on. So–' he shrugged in that eloquent Continental fashion of his – 'I'm in the shit just as deeply as you are, Major. All for one and one for all sort of thing.'

As much as Mackenzie could be moved these days, he was touched. But he had long learned to conceal his feelings – five years of total war had taught him that. So he said in the same style that Campbell 175 had adopted: 'Cor fer a duck, don't go all ruddy wishy-wishy on me, mate ... and thanks.'

Thus they returned the rest of the way to London in silence, but animated now by a warm sense of comradeship, these two diverse individuals, the ruthless academic *manqué* and the little Jewish exile, who was determined to survive whatever might come...

BOOK TWO:

THINGS WHICH GO BUMP IN THE NIGHT

'They speak of murder ... I can't trust anyone any more. Assassination awaits me on the least suspicion.'

Felix Stidger, Union Spy, 1864

One

The Great Man rose from his bath in a flurry of soapy water. Immediately his valet handed him a glass of brandy and an already-lit fat Cuban cigar. He accepted them, as if he were totally unaware that he had been given them. Next to the valet, whose beaky nose was raised as if he could smell something particularly unpleasant underneath it, the second footman immediately began towelling the Great Man's plump, totally hairless body. Watching the little morning scene, the Prime Minister's Principal Private Secretary thought Churchill looked like some latterday Buddha, one who was without a single inhibition.

The towelling finished, the Great Man allowed himself to be draped with a warm silk vest which was far too short for him. But again he exhibited no shame at being seen standing there with his hairless genitals revealed to the servants, as he dipped the end of his cigar into the brandy and took a contented puff at it. He looked, at that moment, like a very happy man. But, of course, the Principal Private Secretary knew that the Great Man could never be happy, as long as he remained the 'King's First Minister', as he called the office of Premier in his old-fashioned manner. It seemed to him that, although the Allies were now winning the war, the Great Man's problems were mounting and mounting. There was trouble in Greece and Belgium; there was trouble with the 'Frogs' and with the 'Yanks'; there was even trouble back home. Not from the Labour people, as one might have expected – they still supported the combined effort loyally enough – but from within the ranks of the Premier's own party, the Conservatives. For some reason they were beginning to raise an old and secret issue: one that the Secretary thought should be best buried with the rest of the skeletons that all parties had to deal with.

The Secretary frowned and dismissed these myriad problems until the PM was dressed and ready to face up to yet another gruelling day. Let him enjoy this moment of peace with his brandy and cigar. Outside, an Army Humber had driven up and, after being checked by the Grenadiers who guarded the PM's private residence, was allowed to discharge its passengers. The Principal Private Secretary frowned. Yet more trouble for the Great Man, he told himself, and then watched as the second footman handed the Great Man's false teeth to the valet. The latter scrutinized them carefully to ensure that the third footman had done a good job of cleaning the dentures. Then in his turn he handed them to the PM. Churchill slipped them into his toothless mouth with a cherubic grin on his moonlike face and smiled at himself in the mirror. The Great Man's *toilette* was completed. He was ready for another day of attempting to save the British Empire from the dire fate awaiting it.

Mackenzie and Campbell 175 were understandably ill at ease. Both of them, for different reasons, held Winston Churchill in awe. Now, completely out of the blue they had been summoned from London by no less a person than the chief of MI6, the mysterious 'C', to come to meet him in his private residence at Chequers. As 'C' had explained over the phone in that soft upper-class voice of his, 'The fewer people at Whitehall who know you're meeting that – er – certain person the better.' But why they had been asked to meet Churchill away in the Home Counties, 'C' hadn't given them a slightest hint. As he had ended his conversation in that oblique fashion beloved by senior Intelligence figures: 'All will undoubtedly be revealed in due course ... goodbye.' And that had been that.

Now they were here at Chequers, sitting

nervously on the rather shabby chairs being served weak tea from what looked to Campbell 175 like real Meissen china, worth a small fortune. Every now and again, flunkeys and officials looked in at them perched on the edge of the spindly Queen Anne chairs, but whether they came to assist them or just to look, the two soldiers had no idea; for none of them uttered a single word. As Campbell 175 muttered out of the side of his mouth like some gangster in a Hollywood B movie: 'You'd think we were a couple of hairy-assed monkeys in a cage at Whipsnade.'

To which Mackenzie, equally ill at ease, replied also out of the side of his mouth, 'Shut it. One wrong word here, my friend, and we could both end up doing security work in the Outer Hebrides or somewhere equally exciting.'

The threat worked. Campbell 175 'shut it'.

Half an hour after they had arrived, with the weak tea untouched, getting cold in the fine eighteen-century Meissen cups, a young man popped his head round the door and said with a cheerful wave, 'My name's Colville. I'm the Prime Minister's Principal Private Secretary. The PM asks you to forgive him for keeping you waiting like this.' He lied glibly – he was accustomed to doing so. 'He has been detained, but he won't keep you much longer. Ring the bell for some more of that awful tea if you like.' He looked at his expensive wristwatch. 'Bit too early for a drink I'm afraid.' With that, he gave them an encouraging, if fake, smile and was gone again.

But if it was too early for them to have a drink, it wasn't for the Great Man. Shortly thereafter, he appeared, carrying a large glass of brandy in his hand, cigar stuck in the corner of his mobile, full-lipped mouth, to stand and stare at the two soldiers standing rigidly to attention, as if he were assessing them before he made any statement.

After what seemed a long time, he took the cigar out of his mouth, gave them a warm smile and said, 'Stand easy and please sit down.' He chuckled abruptly like the mischievous schoolboy he had once been so long before and added, 'I'm afraid you may need to.'

Uncertainly the two of them did so and stared up at Churchill, who remained standing. Outside, his bodyguard, the only one, Inspector Thompson of Special Branch, passed by, glanced in through the window and then continued his patrol. Apprehensive as he was, Mackenzie wondered again at the fact that one of the most important and endangered men in the world could get by with one single middle-aged policeman armed with a .38 revolver, as his sole protection. Then Churchill began to speak and he forgot the problem of Churchill's vulnerability.

'Mackenzie, it seems hardly fair,' he said, 'but unfortunately you have had a big secret thrust upon you – and a very dangerous one to boot.' He looked at an awed Campbell 175. 'And you, too, Sergeant.'

Campbell 175 swallowed hard.

'You didn't ask for this to be done to you, but there you are. You are both now stuck with it, two of only a handful of people in this country – and elsewhere,' he added, frowning darkly for some reason known only to himself. 'Indeed you both now know something that is enough to cause several people to be shot in the Tower for treachery and consorting with the King's enemies in time of war.' He paused to let the full impact of his words sink in, and took a careful sip of his brandy.

Mackenzie, his mind racing, told himself that Churchill probably needed the drink, but that it was also part of a pose, something that showed he had aristocratic blood flowing through his veins and that he disdained bourgeois values and pretence.

'Let me explain,' Churchill continued. He dug the thumb of his free hand in the corner of his waistcoat pocket in that characteristic manner of his when just about to address the House of Commons. 'It started back in November '39 when you, Mackenzie, accompanied your poor Major Dalby, your chief, on that Venlo foolishness.' Mackenzie had a pretty good idea where all this was leading. 'My dead predecessor–' he meant Premier Chamberlain – 'might have known something about what was going on. I hope he didn't. It will be an irrevocable stain on his memory if he did. But there were certainly important members of my own party who did know why those fools Best and Stevens were consorting with the Huns.' He frowned hard. 'They actively encouraged talks with the Germans – God damn their hide,' he snapped with sudden bitterness. 'They would have talked with that archfiend Hitler himself if it had meant achieving their treacherous aims.'

Mackenzie knew what the Great Man was getting at and he had a feeling that the clever little NCO at his side was tumbling to the truth as well.

'Since that time,' Churchill continued gravely, 'those people concerned have been actively involved with trying to remove all traces of their treachery. What about Best and Stevens? you may ask. They don't count. They have blotted their copybooks completely by blabbing to the Huns all they knew of our Secret Service. To all intents and purposes they are hopelessly compromised. No one will listen to them. Once they are returned to this country after the war, they will be cashiered and put out to pasture way out of the reach of the Press – and others.'

Immediately Mackenzie noted the change of inflection in Churchill's voice as he uttered the last phrase. Instinctively he knew there was more to this matter than what he had been told – and guessed – so far. He leaned forward, eager to hear more from the Great Man.

'You two and the unfortunate Major Dalby weren't compromised. So he and you, Mackenzie, were to be got rid of. In due course, Sergeant, you joined that select group.' Churchill allowed himself a cynical smile.

Campbell 175 couldn't help himself. He blurted out, 'Do you mean, sir, that our fellow Englishmen were – are – prepared to kill us because we know too much?'

Mackenzie wasn't even slightly amused at that use of 'our fellow Englishmen'; the situation was too grave. He looked at Churchill hard to see what the PM's response would be.

Churchill didn't bat an eyelid. He said, 'Yes, I suppose you're right, Sergeant. They are looking after themselves and their own future, now that it is clear we have won the war. But that in itself would be no problem under normal circumstances. I'm sure we could take care of such individuals without too much difficulty, once we know who they are.' He took a careful sip of his brandy, looking at them over the rim of the glass, as if he were trying to assess how far he dare go with these two soldiers.

'Right at the beginning when I took over as the King's First Minister in 1940,' he continued then, 'I sent some of the greatest plotters out of the country straightaway. To Washington ... Madrid ... and the like. I gave them high positions which would flatter their vanity, keep them busy and, naturally, *out of this country and its day-to-day affairs*. Thus they could do little harm. You understand?'

Hurriedly the two of them agreed they did. It was clear that Churchill had other more important things to say and would not like to be kept waiting to do so.

'Unfortunately there are others, who in the meantime have learned of their treachery back in '39 and how low this island sank in its attempts to appease Hitler. I have no power over these individuals and states. They can reveal our shame whenever it's going to suit their purpose politically.'

Mackenzie looked puzzled suddenly and Churchill, old as he was, noticed his expression immediately. He said to enlighten the Major, 'Devious individuals, Major, who call themselves our friends – allies. Now that this terrible business is almost over, they will not hesitate to ruin us, however loyal and friendly they may seem on the surface.' There was no hiding the bitterness in the old man's voice now and Mackenzie could sense the strain he had been under all these last years. Without Churchill, he told himself yet again, Britain would never have triumphed. He had guided her in those black years of the war through defeat after defeat. Now that the war was won, at least as far as the general British public was concerned, he was engaged in yet another secret battle to save the British Empire, seemingly against her current allies.

'Russia, sir?' he ventured.

Churchill shook his head and there were sudden tears in his eyes. 'I wish it were in a way, Mackenzie. Unfortunately it is not.' He dabbed away the sudden tears. 'It is the country of my own dear mother.'

Mackenzie looked aghast. The Great Man meant America. He stared at Churchill and wondered for a fleeting moment if Churchill had cracked under the great strain he had borne all these last years. The United States had been Britain's ally since 1941. Some said, perhaps rightly, that if President Roosevelt hadn't taken his country into the war against the fascist powers after Pearl Harbor, Britain would have lost the struggle against Germany. Now Britain's armies fighting in Europe were under the command of an American general, Eisenhower. Yet here was Churchill stating that the new danger came from that very same group and country with which most Britons thought we had a 'special relationship'.

Churchill interpreted the look on Mackenzie's face correctly. 'Yes, I know it is hard to believe, Major, but it's true all the same. As soon as the war is done, President Roosevelt and those of his kind in Washington will do their damnedest to ensure that the British Empire will go into a speedy decline.' He paused as if again he was considering how far he should go in his explanation to these two low-ranking soldiers. Finally, it appeared, he felt he had to tell them more and he said, 'President Roosevelt is, in truth, the meanest man I have ever met, Mackenzie, in my long political career. He owes no loyalty to anyone save himself. In all his years in public office he has stabbed colleagues and associates in the back or left them in the lurch – abandoned them – when he felt he no longer needed them.' He sighed and again tears were dangerously near. 'For a long time now Roosevelt has harboured a plan to get rid of the British Empire – and those of France and the Netherlands too. Now with America the world's supreme power, politically, militarily and economically, he intends to shape the world according to his own damnfool vision. That means the peoples of our own Empire will have to be set free, as he would put it, to control their own destiny,' Churchill's moonlike face contorted abruptly in bitter scorn, '–and what a damn fine mess they'd make of it, too, if that ever came about.' He shook his head and took a hasty sip at his brandy. 'So how can he start the ball rolling?' He answered his own question. 'He can do so by discrediting Britain and her rulers. He can show the world that at the beginning of the war, when we were actually supposed to be fighting Hitler's Germany, we were spineless cowards who were trying to save our skins and our precious Empire by talking secretly to the Huns. It would bring down the Conservative Party, in power at that time. It would be replaced by the Socialists at the first post-war general election and, as half-baked as that ilk are, most of them would be only too glad to give away the Empire so that they could finance their vaunted *"brave new world"*.' Churchill emphasized the last three words contemptuously. 'In short, I must tell you that President Roosevelt will not hesitate to use the most underhand methods to bring down my party and this country. And I must tell you this, too' – his voice had risen, as if he were addressing the House at the height of one of his great speeches – 'our erstwhile ally in Washington must be stopped before he can achieve this aim.' He looked directly at the two soldiers, his face red with effort, breathing harder than usual due to so much talking this early in the day.

Mackenzie and Campbell 175 waited apprehensively, knowing that they had been let into a great and highly lethal secret. There was no going back now, especially as Churchill believed that the fate of the British Empire was at stake.

Churchill nodded to his secretary. It was the signal. The two soldiers had had all the time allotted to them. The secretary stepped forward. 'I think,' he said, smiling encouragingly, 'Mr Churchill has finished with you. I shall take care of the paperwork. You will need power of authority at the very highest level...'

As he spoke the Great Man waddled to the window, glass untouched now in his hand. He stared out at the bleak winter garden to the low hills beyond, as if viewing some distant horizon, known only to himself. He did not look round when the two soldiers left.

Two

'Clive', as Mackenzie and Campbell 175 had known him, thought he knew his way around. Ever since he had 'gone on the trot' from the old 'Diehards' – the Middlesex Regiment – back in '40 after Dunkirk, he had dodged the 'redcaps' and all the other security organizations time and time again. How many times had he been in tight situations when any other deserter would have given up and tamely surrendered himself to that bunch of slab-faced military policemen with their fucking red caps? Not old 'Poxie' Pearson, or 'Clive' as he had been known for the last few weeks since the Yanks had hired him in the dirty little pub behind King's Cross Station, where he and other dubious characters – deserters, spivs, black-market operators and varied petty crooks – had hung out.

For over the years that he had been on the run, he had come to realize that the more important the pose or disguise the more successfully it worked. What was it his old dad had said to him more than once before they'd topped him at Pentonville back in the early '30s: 'Remember, son, the devil allus shits on the biggest heap.' Now that he was in really serious trouble – and he knew he was (for the rozzers and the redcaps were everywhere in London looking for a fake brigadier of his description) – he realized that he would have to aim high, if he were going get out of it with a whole skin.

Naturally, being the man he was, Poxie had already done some forward planning while he had still been playing the role of 'Brigadier Clive'. He had picked her just as he picked the whores he had lived with – and *off* – during his early years of being 'on the trot'. She had been dizzy, if not downright stupid, a junior subaltern in Army Records (Postings): one of those silly not very pretty girls from good families, whose rich parents had wangled her a job in army headquarters where, with a bit of luck, she might find a husband before the war ended and she found herself a spinster on the shelf for the rest of her dull Home Counties existence.

As a 'brigadier' he hadn't found it difficult at all to get himself 'into her knickers', as Poxie would have put it. A black-market dinner at the 'Dorch', a more expensive black-market bottle of bubbly at one of the drinking clubs that flourished illegally everywhere in Soho that winter and within ten minutes of locking the door of her *pied-à-terre* in a bombed Mayfair, he had her on her back, with her thick thighs raised high and spread wide, her khaki knickers thrown over the side of the divan, crazily like a bitch on heat, pumping away at her as if she were a deflated barrage balloon. As he might have boasted to his fellow criminals in that dingy pub behind King's Cross, 'As soon as I opened me flies, she was bloody well gasping for it ... I bet she'd never had a bloody good rogering like that in all her born days.' But naturally he didn't boast that to them; for he was keeping strictly away from that pub which he knew was the first place they (whoever they were in reality) would come looking for him now.

This winter afternoon with the barrage balloons like silver elephants straining to break their cables in the high wind, he had transformed himself yet again as he set out to re-acquaint himself with the Hon. Dolly of Army Records. Now he was Lieutenant Colonel Parker, MC and Bar of the Royal Tanks, lately of the British Liberation Army in Belgium until he had been badly wounded on the 'push' to save 'our gallant lads of the First Airborne' at Arnhem.

Naturally, thick as she was, the 'Hon. Dolly' would be surprised to find her brigadier lover suddenly transformed into a half-colonel of tanks. But as always he had his cover story ready. It was a bit poor. But he thought it would suffice to get her to do what he wanted before he took a powder. Besides he had nine inches of good solid meat inside his immaculately pressed khaki slacks to convince her, even if she did realize she risked being cashiered and perhaps sent to a military prison if she were found out. But then, Poxie Pearson alias 'Brigadier Clive' and now 'Lt Col. Parker, MC and Bar' reasoned, women like the 'Hon. Dolly' usually had their brains between their thighs. He'd convince her all right. Confidently he dropped out of the taxi which had brought him so far, put on his British warm to cover his tanker's uniform and then with a quick look to left and right and a glance at the reflection of the street behind him in the shop window behind, he set off to complete his way to her *pied-à-terre*. He wasn't being followed...

They'd met in the 'Mucky Ducky', as the Black Swan he frequented behind King's Cross was known to its habitués. They'd been in rough clothing and they thought at least that their speech was cockney. But they hadn't fooled Poxie for an instant. They were Yanks all right.

Still he had listened to their proposition attentively enough, knowing he could do it if they provided the brigadier's uniform and the right passes. They had said they could.

They'd take care of everything. Poxie felt under pressure to take the job since it was that stuttering slimeball who'd arranged the rendezvous. The fact that they were offering him a 'pony' down and another as soon as he left Whitehall had convinced him to take on the job – no questions asked.

But naturally Poxie being Poxie *had* asked questions of himself and then he'd realized he had got to know too much. For the two Yanks he presented a threat; and these days London under constant V-bomb attack was a dangerous place to be if you knew too much. People were dying all the time with not too many questions being asked.

A day after he had fled the War Office after the telephone warning during that interview with the two squaddies from Intelligence, a big camouflaged staff Humber had narrowly missed putting him in one of the mass graves which were being dug everywhere these days to take the scores of dead from the V-1 and V-2 attacks. Then he realized it was time to go on the trot again. But where? For, as he told himself, brooding over the matter in the backroom of the Mucky Duck, the 'Smoke' would be too hot to hold him now. They knew his haunts. They'd soon find him again even if he didn't take a dive – and this time he might not be so lucky as he had been with the Humber as it had come barrelling down the street right at him the day before. *Where?* The question had rolled round and round his brain all that dreary winter's afternoon until finally he had it. Who'd look for a bloke like him, who'd been on the trot for years now, at the fighting front – well not exactly in the line, but somewhere close to it? His face had lit up for the first time that gloomy afternoon when it finally dawned on him that it was the best idea he had had in months. Why, he had indulged himself in a double whisky at a price that had almost taken his breath away. He had downed it in one gulp, which was unfortunate. For while he had tilted his mean little face back to enjoy the full taste of the black-market whisky, he had missed the stranger watching him through the window from the lamppost opposite...

Poxie doubled up the stairs to her flat in a high good mood, confident now she'd do exactly what he wanted her to. 'Cor ferk a duck,' he said to himself in his native cockney, 'once I get the poor cow on her back, she'll do anything.'

He pressed the bell loudly. The speaker next to the door buzzed – 'Hello,' she said.

'It's me, old girl,' he sang out happily, 'my swagger stick under my arm and something equally stiff in my trousers, what?' He guffawed in his adopted horsey manner.

'Clive ... I'm almost naked ... I just got out of the bath.'

'All to the good, old girl. Saves us wasting a jolly lot of time, eh?' Again he gave her the full benefit of that horsey laugh that he had adopted years ago when he had first started playing toff roles.

'One moment, Clive.'

She removed the bolt and fumbled with the doorknob, while trying to towel her mousy hair, her bath robe barely concealing her ample form with one heavy drooping breast attempting to escape from the robe, which, even now when he needed her, didn't excite Poxie Pearson one little bit. Still he had his act to keep up and he said in the heartiest manner he could muster, 'I say, Dolly, that's a magnificent udder peering at me from your robe. In a brace of shakes, I'll just have to give it a good suck, eh.' He made a sound like a hungry baby at its mother's nipple.

'Oh, you are a naughty boy, Clive. I swear you've nothing else on your mind but you know what.'

'It's not on my mind though, babykins,' he assured her, 'but much lower down.' He gave her big dun-coloured nipple a light nip and she giggled too. Next moment the giggle died on her lips, as she raised her head from the towel and for the first time saw the change in his rank and uniform. 'Why, Clive,' she hushed as he pushed by into the apartment, which though she had sprayed with an expensive perfume still smelled of her perspiration for she sweated excessively, especially, as he put it, when she was 'randy', 'have you been demoted...? And why are you wearing the uniform of the RAC?'

He sat down, hastily pulled out his engraved silver cigarette case (naturally stolen), lit one of his Bond Street hand-made specials and lied glibly, 'I'm sick of staff jobs, old girl. This is the only way I'm ever going to get back to the front.' He let his hand drop on her plump knee and squeezed it firmly so that she'd know he was not going to waste too many words. Soon it was going to be 'Up Guards and at 'em', the phrase with which he usually prefaced their sexual coupling.

But for once she wasn't taken in so easily. 'But I don't understand,' she stuttered, ignoring the hand on her knee. 'You can't just change your rank like that—'

'Of course, you can,' he interrupted her, a huge smile on his face. 'When the old country needs one, who cares about King's Regs and all that paper rot! A soldier's first duty is with his regiment at the fighting front, even if he's only a common-or-garden subaltern, still wet behind the ears.' He pressed her knee even more firmly and she shivered, as if suddenly chilled. At the back of his mind a cynical hard little voice rasped, 'You've nearly got her, mate. Keep it up. She'll be spreading 'em soon and yer'll be inside them pearly gates before yer can say Jack Robinson. Then the daft bitch'll do any sodding thing yer want her to.'

She tried, however. She said, 'But you can't go to the front without proper papers and a posting, darling. I mean, it's simply not on.'

'I've got my officers' Record of Service, Dolly,' he answered without hesitation. 'You know, the jolly old 439.' He touched his battledress breast pocket beneath the ribbon of the Military Cross he had awarded himself at the Mucky Duck. 'All I need is a stamp and a signature. I'll take care of the travel documents myself. You could do the rest, old bean.'

She looked at him quite shocked. 'But I couldn't sign a posting like that, Clive. You know that. There'd be an awful stink if it came out. I—' She gasped, as he took his hand from her knee and slid it up the length of her thigh right between her parted legs. At once his middle finger slipped into the red wetness of the surrounding bushy hair. '*Clive!*' she exclaimed, melting into his other arm.

'Don't fight it, Dolly, old thing,' he whispered and thrust his wet tongue into her ugly ear. 'You know we're made for each other. When all this is over and I'm satisfied that I have done my duty as an officer and a gentleman, I am certain we can make a go of it–' he lowered his voice, almost as if he dare not trust himself to say the words aloud – 'as man and wife.'

'Oh Clive!' she simpered and leaning back, spreading her great ugly thighs willingly, let it happen, King's Regs and the problem of his Army Book 439 totally forgotten...

Outside, the tail strained, his head turned into the wind. Faintly from the direction of Putney or thereabouts he could hear the wail of the sirens. The V-1s were on their way from Holland again. He flashed a glance at his watch. It wouldn't be long now before the local sirens would start to sound. He'd do it then. Back in 1940–41 Londoners hadn't made much of the German blitz. Now two and a half years later they were running scared; the war had been going on too long. Once the sirens started to sound the alarm, they'd be running for the shelters, as if the Devil himself were after them, all stiff British upper lip vanished. Now they knew that only speed could save them from these mechanical monsters that fell from the sky. It was get to the shelter or snuff it. In an instant the street would be clear and there would be no witness of what he was soon to do.

Casually, as if he had just stopped to find his bearings and then thought he might pause for a cigarette, he took out one of the dreadful Woodbines he smoked as part of his cover, lit it, coughed furiously and with his gaze lowered stared at the window of the ATS officer's flat where the cocky bloody deserter was presumably dicking the ugly woman.

In fact, 'Clive' or 'Poxie Pearson' had just finished 'dicking the ugly woman'. Now she sprawled on the divan, legs still wide apart, revealing her wet inner thighs, panting hard as if she had just run a great race, while as casually as he could, 'Poxie' did up his flies and feeling very pleased with himself approached her handbag.

He was preparing for his contingency plan. If she acted up about certifying his posting to the British Army of Liberation, he ought to have her office keys. Once he was inside her section of Army Records, he'd soon make a pretty good attempt at authenticating his transfer. Then it would be frigging 'goodbye Leicester Square, hallo Brussels'. There it would not be too hard for him with his talent and experience to find some Belgie bint on the game and set himself up in business. He had heard from mates that there was a thriving black market in US goods, everything from trucks to blankets, in the Belgian capital. His eyes sparkled at the thought. He'd always fancied an extended trip to the Continent, especially if someone else was paying for it. Furtively, while she continued to pant on the sofa as if she might snuff it any frigging moment, he felt inside her bag for the keys and, with a bit of luck, her money, too. Outside, the sirens commenced their dreary, mournful wail yet again. He hardly noticed. The sirens these days sounded all the ruddy time.

The tail waited. Down the street he could hear the clatter of heels, followed by the cries of children, as a couple of mothers urged them to the shelters. A red-faced middle-aged special constable in a steel helmet shrilled on his whistle. Further on, another swung his rattle round and round yelling at the top of his voice, 'Now everybody ... off the street ... Come on now – *move it*!' From the west came the first faint ominous putt-putt of the flying bombs.

Instinctively the tail straightened up. He felt into the pocket of his dirty trench coat and into the hole in its pocket. Through it he gripped the hard, comforting butt of the pistol. In a minute the street would be cleared. There'd be no witnesses, and whatever noise the pistol made would be drowned by the roar of the doodle-bug and the thunder of the ack-ack. He smiled to himself and it wasn't a very pleasant sight. Everything was going exactly according to plan.

Three

'Christ Almighty!' Mackenzie swore. 'There are just too many bloody imponderables.' In a fit of exasperation he flung his pen down angrily on the desk in front of him.

Campbell 175 grinned to himself. It was sometimes good to see his boss lose his temper. Mostly he was so damned cool and collected: far too much a stiff-upper-lipped Englishman for his Continental taste. Still he could understand Major Mackenzie's frustration. It was a difficult case and it was taking them a devil of a lot of time to make any progress and Mackenzie was used to getting things done – *fast*.

It was now forty-eight hours since that strange interview with Winston Churchill at Chequers. The Prime Minister's influence had opened many doors, some of them very rarified, and the information had poured in from all sides. Still it was the interpretation of that information, turning it into some rational picture, that was proving difficult and had just caused Mackenzie's sudden rage. Still the clever little Continental with his sparkling black eyes knew that they were making progress. The problem was – in what direction?

Ignoring the guns blasting away outside as the V-1s fell out of the winter sky with frightening regularity, devastating Central London as if they would never stop until they had turned it into a stoney wasteland as Hitler in Berlin had promised, Campbell 175 said soothingly, 'Now, let's look at what we've got, sir.'

Mackenzie didn't respond. He continued to sit there at his desk, head in his hands, as if he could go on no more.

Campbell 175 pretended not to notice. He said, 'It's clear from what you've said, sir, and what Mr Churchill revealed that there was an important section of the Conservative Party and sundry other Conservative bigshots back in '30 who wanted *actively* to do a deal with Herr Hitler, as Chamberlain, the Conservative Premier of that time always called him. When it was clear years later that we were going to win the war, they wanted all witnesses to that deal, particularly those involved in the Venlo business, eradicated. Agreed, sir?'

'Agreed,' Mackenzie answered wearily, not raising his head from his hands.

'Now again, sir, from what Mr Churchill told us *durch die Blume** – he was forced to

**Literally – 'through the flower', i.e. indirectly.*

use the German phrase because he didn't know the English one – 'the Yanks are interested in that nasty business back then in '39 because they – Mr Roosevelt in particular – want to use those treacherous and cowardly negotiations to defame the British and help to bring about the end of our Empire.'

'Yes, yes, get on with it,' Mackenzie exclaimed impatiently. He didn't even comment on the little German Jew's reference to 'our Empire.' 'Sir!' Campbell 175 snapped dutifully. 'So we must ask, who paid the assassin of Major Dalby at Colditz and who did the same to this "Brigadier Clive" at the War Office, who brought us into the picture, obviously with the intention of –?' He didn't complete the sentence. Instead he cocked his forefinger as if he were pulling the trigger of a pistol.

'Yes – to eliminate us because we knew too much.' Mackenzie raised his head and for the first time seemed to be listening to what his sergeant was saying. '*Or conversely* to get the matter into the open again, perhaps to create the scandal that the Yanks would need if Churchill is correct in his estimate of Roosevelt's intentions.'

'The latter, sir, in my opinion.'

'So,' Mackenzie said thoughtfully his exasperation vanishing as quickly as it had come now that they seemed to be getting somewhere, 'we might fairly safely assume that there is a connection between the Major Dalby assassination at Colditz and this business with the mysterious – and now missing – Brigadier Clive?'

'That's my thinking exactly, sir.' Outside, another V-1 exploded, making the window panes, covered in strips of brown paper to prevent them from breaking, tremble violently. About a quarter of a mile away, a mushroom of dense black smoke rose to join the others which seemed to be everywhere at this moment. Campbell 175 told himself that Churchill wouldn't tolerate this kind of treatment much longer. Hitler was going to have to pay a bloody price for these attacks on England's capital, Churchill's beloved London.

'Well, if that *is* the case, Mackenzie continued, not appearing to notice the destruction and sudden death taking place just outside, 'from where are the Yanks directing their operations? I don't think it can be from Grosvenor Square. I don't think that the US State Department would run the risk of its official representatives in the UK being involved.'

Campbell 175 nodded his agreement and said, gaze following the course of a V-1 over the rooftops opposite, waiting for the moment that its engine cut out, praying at the same time that it wouldn't happen just yet – the bloody thing was too close to their office

– 'There are plenty of US Army undercover organizations operating in Europe now, sir, remember.'

'I hadn't thought of that. Yes, there's the CIC ... the OSS ... and half a dozen similar outfits, filled with all sorts of rum characters.' He laughed, but there was no happiness in it. 'We know ... we've come across some of them since D-Day.'

'Yes sir,' Campbell 175 agreed, giving a little sigh of relief: the V-1 had disappeared from sight, transporting its one ton of high explosive to some other unfortunate part of London. 'That kind of organization would be ideal for the job. Its men are trained in the use of weapons. They can travel anywhere, no questions asked by the civvie police when they're in US uniform and their seniors can arrange swift transfers from one military theatre to another if they're rumbled.' Mackenzie sat back, face very thoughtful. 'Yes the more I think about it, the more I'm convinced that it could be one of those undercover US military organizations that—'

He never finished the sentence. For at that very moment the phone on the desk in front of him started to ring urgently. He picked it up at once. For it was the red emergency telephone which connected him with the War Office, Scotland Yard and various other Intelligence agencies.

Campbell 175 tensed. It had to be something very important or somebody of very senior rank, or the switchboard operator wouldn't have put the call through; the ATS girls who manned the board knew Mackenzie's temper if he were interrupted during one of what he called one of his 'mind-bashing' sessions. He waited impatiently till the person on the other end had finished speaking and Mackenzie put down the phone with a curt 'Thank-you.'

'Important, sir?'

'You betcha,' Mackenzie snapped, rising and buckling on his belt. 'Get your car. That was Special Branch. Our missing Brigadier Clive has just been spotted – and there's been a murder. Come on, get your skates on, man.'

Campbell 175 needed no urging. This was the breakthrough they had been waiting for all along. He 'got his skates on'...

Poxie had reacted correctly and at once. In the past years since he had 'gone on the trot', he'd had plenty of experience of 'doing a bunk' when there'd been an emergency. As he had always boasted to his cronies, 'The frigging redcaps'll have to get up a lot earlier to catch old Poxie lads, and that's the frigging truth!'

She had leapt up from the couch when she'd spotted him fiddling with her purse.

Not bothering to close her gown, she had strode towards him, face suddenly flushed and angry, her pudding-like breasts wobbling crazily, crying, 'Clive, what in heaven's name are you looking for in my purse ... you've no right—'

That sudden attack on Dolly's part had saved his life. For while she had lain on the couch, her heavy body had covered the mirror positioned next to it (he always liked to watch himself 'perform'). Now in the abruptly revealed mirror, he saw the man in the shabby trench coat, gun protruding through the coat's open skirt, pointed directly at the spot where he was standing.

He had known immediately it was connected with 'them'. That instant recognition made him duck almost before he knew he was doing so. Next moment there was the sound of glass shattering. Dolly gave a piercing scream, one of absolute agony. In the same instant that the man darted forward, Dolly was propelled backwards, as if she had been punched by some gigantic fist. He caught a glimpse of her left breast. At that close range the bullet aimed at him had shattered it like an overripe orange. She was unconscious or dead before she hit the carpet. He didn't stop to find out. Still clutching her purse, he smashed through the door to the tiny kitchen. Below he could hear the killer clambering up the stairs looking for the door to Dolly's flat.

Scared stiff now, but retaining his wits, Poxie fumbled madly with the stiff catch of the kitchen window. He knew his number was up if he didn't get out immediately. The man who had shot Dolly instead of him wouldn't make another mistake. He was for the chop!

The catch wouldn't budge. The sweat pouring down his contorted face, he cried, 'For fuck's sake – *open!*' Still it wouldn't. Outside, the man had stopped. He was probably peering at the name on the door, trying to make out that it was Dolly's. Poxie would wait no longer. He slammed his elbow against the window. He yelped with pain. The glass broke and a sliver penetrated his arm. It didn't matter. He pulled on the outside. The cracked pane slid down. He didn't hesitate. There was a drop of perhaps twelve or so feet to the tiny yard, littered with paper and rubbish from an overturned rusty rubbish bin. Out he went. He slammed against the ground. His legs felt as if they were being driven deep into his stomach. Suddenly he felt very sick. He retched. From up above there came a shout of anger. It was followed immediately by a shot. A slug howled off the rusty bin. With the last of his strength, Poxie reached up and pulled himself up and over the yard wall. Next moment he was staggering blindly down the road that led to Victoria Station. But even as he ran, fear lending new strength to his legs, the deserter knew he had done it again. They'd never catch old Poxie...

Four

Victoria was like all the wartime stations that Poxie had ever seen. Naturally it was packed with troops in a bewildering variety of regiments and divisions and headgear, from the funny 'frontiersman' hats of the of the New Zealanders to the tricorns of the Poles, who were everywhere, clicking their heels, giving their strange two-fingered salute and crying '*tak*' at the top of their voices seemingly all the time.

There were women too: women of all kinds. Sobbing women; smoking women, careless now of what people thought of them smoking like this in public; silent women holding babies, who were equally silent. There were the other kinds, too. Women in the shadows, shivering in their flimsy frocks and high heels, whispering from the gloom at the passing men, '*Like a nice time, soldier? … Quickie for ten bob … Like me to show you it – half a dollar to you, duckie, with a free feel…*'

But it wasn't the leave men or the drafts heading for the Channel boats and the front or the women, which attracted Poxie's special attention. It was the hated redcaps: the hard-faced bastards in old-fashioned service dress, with leather-holstered pistols at their sides and eyes like steel gimlets under the peaks of the red caps which gave the military police their nickname. They were everywhere: pairs of them strolling up and down the platforms, stopping anyone they didn't like the look of; dodging in and out of the gloomy side corridors trying to find men who were absent without leave and were looking for one of the tarts who might put them up for the night – for a consideration.

The patrolling MPs didn't worry Poxie particularly. Normally, unless they were accompanied by the redcap officer, they wouldn't stop an officer, especially when he appeared to be a major as Poxie now did. It was those at the barriers, standing imperturbable next to the Railway Transport officers with their checkboards and worried looks, inspecting each individual's leave pass or paybook when the soldier tried to pass the barrier. No one seemed to escape their hawk-like gaze, even when the barriers were flung wide-open to let yet another draft of cannon fodder for the front march through to the waiting trains which would carry them to their particular dates with destiny.

Pausing under one of the blue-shaded

gaslamps so that he could be seen not to be trying to hide by anyone observing him – but not too clearly – Poxie made a great fuss of taking out his silver cigarette case and lighting one of his 'specials' with his silver lighter. But he hardly noticed he was doing so. His gaze was concentrated solely on the nearest barrier closing off the two platforms from which the troops trains departed for Folkestone and the Channel steamers for Ostend in Belgium. It was there that he would have to take a train, any train, that would allow him to escape. And he knew he didn't have too much time to waste. They'd be after him by now.

He frowned and coughed as the smoke caught him unawares. All the redcaps manning the departure barrier were sergeants, all old hands and bastards to a man, he could see that even in the gloom of the semi-blacked-out station. Besides, there was a sergeant-major in charge of the MPs, a warrant officer, second class, a real old sweat, who had probably sent more poor bastards to the glasshouse in Aldershot than he had had hot dinners. It would be ruddy hard to bluff his way through them without a travel order (and he had failed in that on account of the bastard who had tried to shoot him at Dolly's flat); they'd take no nonsense even from a supposed major, complete with Military Cross and Bar.

He bit his bottom lip. Time was running out fast. A draft from some Scottish regiment was passing through the opened barrier now. They were the usual undersized, bowlegged cocky Jock infantry, mostly teenagers, but full of the typical piss and vinegar of working-class lads brought up in the depressed Gorbals and the like. The redcaps were keeping a sharp eye on them, especially as a few of them had been drinking and all of them were 'bolshy' as the cannon fodder usually were once they got this far. After all, they knew the redcaps wouldn't attempt to put them 'inside'; riflemen were needed too urgently at the front.

Poxie eyed them. Their troop train was already getting up steam for departure. He could see the glare of the firebox, as the fireman shovelled coal into it and the guard was already fiddling with his flags, as if he would be only too happy when he had got rid of the troublesome Jocks. The train, Poxie reasoned, would be ideal for him. The escorting officer who would accompany the draft to the port would have his hands full of the young soldiers, trying to indulge in their usual larks, especially that of pulling the communication cord in an attempt to stop the troop train.

But how was he to get through that bloody barrier? he asked himself, face contorted in frustration. Once through, he'd be home and sailing. The escorting officer was a subaltern, who looked as if he had not begun to shave yet; he certainly wouldn't dare ask why a major in the Royal Armoured Corps had suddenly appeared in a draft of young infantrymen bound for the 51st Highland Division or the 15th Scottish.

Carefully, forcing himself to be calm, he searched for an opening, while the Scots now started to sing drunkenly, 'Why are we waiting *oh, why are we waiting*?' accompanied by a series of *baas* to indicate they were a bunch of lambs being led to the slaughter, which, in reality they were. Next to them, the redcap warrant officer was getting visibly angrier, his permanently brown old sweat's face turning a shade of puce with frustration. For he knew, there was not much he could do to stop the bolshy Jocks. The best thing he could do (and Poxie watching came to the same conclusion) was to get them on the train and on their way as soon as possible. His mind obviously made up, he strode across the platform to the waiting RTO officer consulting his all-important checkboard yet again and clicked his heels together in a perfunctory manner. It was clear to Poxie that the redcap NCO didn't think much of the young officer. The latter was bespectacled, weak-chinned and skinny and a member of the Royal Army Service Corp.

The redcap sergeant-major would obviously classify him as one of those who 'needs to get his frigging knees brown, lads, before he starts giving orders to the likes of me and thee'. The feeling would be mutual too. The RASC officer would be quite sure that the redcap looked down at him, made fun of him behind his back. Therefore, he'd be likely not to take any insubordination from the old sweat. Could he then, the officer, be his way through that damned barrier?

Poxie hesitated no longer. The draft of the rowdy young Jocks was now being crammed into the third-class carriage under the eagle eyes of the redcaps, stowing their kitbags, rifles and packs on the racks, fighting for the corner seats, though as soon as the train left Victoria Station it would be blacked out, baa-baaing furiously. Some of them were already singing drunkenly, 'We're no awa te gan awa', shouting, 'Scotland the brave' and making the usual noises Jocks did, Poxie told himself, as if Scots were the only troops ever to go and fight.

For a moment or two, the attention of the military police was distracted. Only the RASC officer seemed to concern himself with what was going on at the barrier itself. Poxie hesitated no longer. He had no other choice. Somewhere behind him he heard an American-accented voice say sharply, 'Major, say, Major could I have a word—'

He heard no more. He knew who that was. The Yanks had caught up with him. He pushed his way through the throng to the barrier and faced the pale-faced young RTO. 'I say,' he said in his best ladi-da voice, 'I wonder if I could have a look at these chaps' accommodations. The War Office has sent me down ... there have been complaints you know. The *Daily Mirror*'s got on to it. That cad Michael Foot, you know...' He rapped out the sentences, hardly knowing what he was saying. Behind him, he knew the killer would be preparing for his death – they never gave up. They were ruthless ... 'Just let me through for half a mo ... Be a good chap.'

The RTO was irresolute. He saw the rank and the ribbon of the MC. All the same, he knew he had strict orders not to allow anyone on the platform who didn't have a pass. 'I'm afraid, sir,' he began when the single shot rang out. Perhaps under normal circumstances that shot would have occasioned shouts, surprise, fear. But not here. These men had heard shots enough in their time. Besides hundreds of those crowded on the platforms of Victoria Station were armed; someone might have fired his weapon by mistake.

But Poxie Pearson *was* alarmed. He knew that shot had been fired at *him*. There was no time to reason with the RTO officer.

Already prepared for the worst, he lashed out using the old barroom brawler's underhand trick. The right hook with the gloved hand curled around a bunch of shillings from Poxie's inside pocket slammed the surprised RTO backwards and sent him sprawling the length of the dirty wet platform. In that same instant the guard shrilled his whistle and waved his green flag. The troop train, filled with the shouting, cheering, drunken Jocks, started to pull away slowly. Poxie knew it was his last chance. He vaulted over the barrier. 'Hey, you,' the MP sergeant-major yelled angrily. In his desperation, Poxie hit him, too. The redcap reeled back, his ugly yellow false teeth suddenly bulging from his lips and then the fugitive was running all out, as if his very life depended upon it, which perhaps it did. The guard leaned out of the open door and shouted something. Poxie ignored him. He grabbed hold of the door handle, gasping frantically, eyes wild with fear and excitement. With the last of his strength, he hauled himself on board and collapsed on the floor at the shocked guard's feet, completely out...

The Home Office pathologist, Bernard Spilsbury, felt in between the dead woman's spread legs, touched the right inner thigh and held his finger to his nose for a moment and then nodded to himself significantly. Mackenzie and Campbell 175 watched with silent curiosity, while on the chair in the corner, the young RTO officer held his badly bruised right cheek and moaned softly. Under other circumstances Mackenzie would have found the situation macabre, something out of a black comedy. Not now. He was too eager to hear Spilsbury's finding before he had the body of the dead woman taken away, though it was obvious what had killed her. Her large breast had been shattered by the bullet that had been fired through the window and the slug had killed her. He took his gaze off the breast splattered on to her pale body like a blood-red pomegranate. Next to him, Campbell 175 shivered.

Spilsbury wiped his finger off on a snow-white handkerchief, made a quick note in his black notebook and then, his well-known face as arrogant and austere as ever, turning to the two soldiers said, 'I need to do the PM of course, to be certain. But this is what I can tell you now, Major.' His words came in quick harsh bites, as if Mackenzie was one of his trial juries who naturally would accept his findings without the slightest doubt. After all, wasn't he the great Bernard Spilsbury, the twentieth-century medical Sherlock Holmes? 'The woman had sexual intercourse shortly before she was killed. Traces of sperm on the inner thigh. It wasn't forced. No bruising on the outer labia of the vagina for example. He had however made love to her quite vigorously. If you'll come over here, I'll show you.'

Hesitantly they did so and Spilsbury pointed a long skinny forefinger at the dead woman's left shoulder. 'You see there that he must have rested the collar of his tunic against her body during intercourse and pressed so hard that he left an impression of his regimental badge on her naked. flesh.'

Campbell 175 gave a little gasp and in his best imitation cockney, said, 'Cor blimey yer right, guv'nor. *That*'s the tank collar dog of the Royal Armoured Corps.'

Spilsbury froze him with a look and the words died on Campbell's lips. Hastily Mackenzie asked, 'Did this chap – the Tank Corps wallah – shoot her, sir?'

Spilsbury shook his head. 'No, Major,' he answered with that overbearing supreme confidence of his that he could never be wrong, 'I've had a look at the glass of the window.' He indicated the shattered pane. 'The bullet was fired from outside and besides if he – our tank corps wallah, as you call him – had killed her, there would have been a powder burn on her flesh. There wasn't. Someone else did it – from outside.' He nodded to his assistant waiting dutifully at the door. The latter turned and called down the stairs, 'All right, lads, you can take her away now.'

Moments later, a red blanket thrown over the dead woman, she was borne away by Spilsbury's mortuary attendants to be taken to St Pancras, where Spilsbury would carry out one of his celebrated post-mortems. Tipping his old fashioned Homburg to the solemn-looking soldiers, the great man followed like some grim minister of death bringing up a final procession to the grave.

Mackenzie waited till they had gone then he turned to the injured RTO officer, who was still moaning softly, cloth held to his swollen, injured face. Right at the beginning they had obtained a rough-and-ready description of his assailant from him, which had been telegraphed immediately to Folkestone and stations in between, then they had let him nurse his wounds. Now the time had come to find out more from the RTO.

It wasn't much. He described what had happened and how the redcap warrant officer had been put out of action, too, so he couldn't supply much else either.

'So why wasn't he stopped – our man that is – at Folkestone, Lieutenant?' Mackenzie demanded sternly.

'Well, sir, we were too late,' the young officer answered thickly, as if he had suddenly acquired a lisp, for that cruel punch had split his lips badly and knocked out a couple of his front teeth.

'This new flap in the Ardennes with the Jerries attacking all along the line and our people over there screaming for reinforcements from the UK, there's mass confusion at Folkestone and the troop embarkation point. The lads are hardly off the trains from Victoria and they're on the troop ships bound for Ostend and the front. We're shipping hundreds out every night—'

'But did he go to the Continent or didn't he?' Mackenzie interrupted the flow of words harshly.

The young officer spat blood from his damaged gums into his handkerchief and looked glumly at the red stains, as if they were the harbinger of some dread disease. 'Well, we're certain that he didn't stay in Folkestone. The place is swarming with civvie police and our own redcaps on the lookout for blokes trying to jump ship – lots of 'em try it on and risk the glasshouse–' he meant the military prison at Aldershot – 'rather than risk having their head blown off at the front.' He sucked more blood from his damaged gums. 'Yessir, we're sure he got on a boat to Ostend. How?' He shrugged and left that particular question unanswered.

Mackenzie nodded his understanding. On the previous Saturday, the Germans had launched a massive surprise attack in the Belgian Ardennes. Now with the Yanks falling back everywhere in confusion, the Hun spearheads were heading for the River Meuse, their final objective apparently the great Allied supply port of Antwerp. Naturally there'd be mass confusion on the Continent. It would be an ideal situation for a man like this supposed brigadier, now apparently masquerading as a major in the RAC. 'So,' he summed up the report from the injured officer, 'our suspect should have reached Ostend with one of the Channel ferries and with the situation being the way it is, he could easily vanish once he got off the boat?'

'Exactly, sir,' the RTO said miserably. 'As soon as the boats arrive, the troops are marched to the railway station on the pier only five minutes from the docks and marched off. The reasoning is that one day *soon*, the Luftwaffe will launch a massive raid on Ostend and the docks to stop the influence of new troops for the front.'

'Yes, that could well be—' Mackenzie stopped short. He could see the young officer was suffering. 'All right, Lieutenant, thank you for your help. We won't need you any more. Off you go and get yourself patched up.'

The RTO rose, put on his cap and gave Mackenzie a shaky salute. Mackenzie was in no way a kindly man – the years of war had quashed most of his altruism. Still he took pity on the poor young sod. The way he had messed up the situation at Victoria, it was more than likely that his CO would get rid of him tootsweet and he might well be one of that mass of cannon fodder himself heading for the front and an untimely death. 'Oh, and tell your commanding officer,' he added, as the RTO buckled on his belt, 'that you have been a great help to us. I can recommend you to him as a good officer.'

The other man's injured face brightened considerably. 'Thank you, sir,' he said with new hope as he went through the door, leaving the two Intelligence men alone and Campbell 175 remarking wrily, 'If you'll forgive me saying so, you're getting soft in your old age.'

'Forgiven.'

'Now what, sir?'

'This. How would you like to join the infantry?'

Campbell 175 looked aghast. 'But sir, what are you thinking of? You know it's against my religion. Besides I'm a devout coward.'

Mackenzie chuckled, 'And you are quite right, old chap. You're far too valuable – or cunning – to have your head shot off in the poor bloody infantry. Still you must realize two things. One, whoever's behind all this must know we're on to them by now, so we've got to assume another identity, if we're going to carry on.'

'And two, sir?'

'The only lead we've got is this fellow – let's call him Clive, shall we? That elusive bugger will lead us to them, with a bit of luck, and perhaps, whoever they are, they know that too. So, they'll chase him and us as well. Perhaps the equation will work out, and we'll be able to put all the bits and pieces together in the end.' For a moment the shadow of a doubt crossed Mackenzie's lean, almost hawk-like features.

'Yessir, I guess that's the only course we can take. But where do we find Clive on the Continent? It's an awfully big place and there must be at least five million or so Allied squaddies under Eisenhower's command over there.'

Mackenzie answered with a question of his own. 'Where do swine like Clive go when they want to take a dive?'

'Big cities, where they can find ladies of the night who are stupid enough to take them in and where there are easy pickings on the black market and such like.'

'Going to be dangerous over there just now, sir,' Campbell 175 reminded his boss, 'what with old Jerry bashing away westwards.' He assumed that cockney whine of which he was so proud. 'A geezer could get hurt over there just now, guv.'

Mackenzie ignored the comment. 'All right, digit out of the orifice, we're off to the Continent ... and let's start where all good Americans are supposed to go when they die.'

'And where's that, sir?'

'Paris!'

Five

Paris was no longer gay this December. Indeed it appeared to the two newly created infantry officers, both majors, to be on the verge of a nervous collapse. The slushy streets of the French capital were still packed with troops of half a dozen Allied armies, GIs, both black and white, drunken Canadians, British HQ staff immaculately turned out down to the obligatory swagger stick as if they were still back in Whitehall – there were even green-faced, shivering Indian soldiers, looking very out of place in their turbans. But there was something subdued about the lot of them, the newly created Major Campbell of the Somerset Light Infantry told himself. They hadn't the normal exuberance of young men let loose in a great city filled with beautiful girls who could be had for the price of twenty Woodbines on the black market which flourished on every street corner.

Campbell 175 could guess why. There were police, military and civilian everywhere. Each main intersection seemed to be guarded by the sour-faced *flics* in their *képis* and cloaks and most of them were carrying not only their normal service automatics but also submachine guns slung over their shoulders. To support them there were the 'white mice', as the French called the white-helmeted MPs, protected by sandbagged emplacements, with here and there a heavy half-inch machine gun pointing down the street, as if they were expecting the Germans to come marching down it at any moment. Everywhere, it seemed, to the two observers shivering in the MI6 jeep sent to fetch them from Orly Field, there was an air of impending gloom about Paris. It was if its citizens and the authorities had already half succumbed to the conviction that the *Boche* were on their way here as they had been in 1940 and nothing was going to stop them achieving that objective – not even General Eisenhower's vaunted Americans.

Major Mackenzie tugged at the end of his red frozen nose and wished they were already at their destination in avenue Gabrielle; he felt his feet had become blocks of solid ice. Only 'C' in London would have dared to show his contempt of Military Intelligence, to which they nominally belonged, by sending an open jeep to take them to MI6's Parisian HQ, even though they had priority from no less a person than Prime Minister Churchill himself.

For a while Mackenzie forgot the cold, as he listened to a burst of rapid machine-gun fire somewhere to their left, followed by the tinny-sounding siren of a French ambulance. Moments later an American command car, filled with grim-faced heavily armed MPs, the driver blasting its horn at the jeep, swept by, driving at a crazy speed. Mackenzie looked at Campbell 175. The latter shrugged, as if there was nothing more to say. This was simply Paris, December 1944, with the Germans on their way. It wouldn't be long before the refugee columns started heading south again like they had done in 1914, 1918 and 1940.

'*Frogs*.' Mackenzie cursed, as if that said it all.

But if the French and their American bosses were tense, the entrance to MI6's HQ in the French capital was a haven of peace, or so it seemed. A fat grey cat dozed underneath the entrance hall radiator, with a saucer of milk next to it while its master, presumably, a fat bespectacled sergeant with the green flash of the Intelligence Corps on his shoulder, did the same at his desk. His booted feet were on top of it and next to him lay his sten gun, its magazine not attached. Not far away there was a half-empty bottle of Haig, possibly the reason for the fat sergeant's slumber.

'The eye of the nation – always on the

alert,' Mackenzie said cynically.

The sergeant continued to snore softly.

'Typical English calm in the midst of chaos,' Campbell 175 agreed with equal cynicism. 'When everyone around you loses his head etc. etc....' He grinned wickedly as, hooking his boot under the chair leg, he pulled sharply.

The fat sergeant slammed to the floor with the upturned chair – hard. 'What the hellus—' he spluttered, eyes flashing open. Then he saw the two officers facing him and said quickly, rising to his feet, 'Must have dropped off, sir.' Hurriedly he tugged at his ill-fitting battledress blouse.

'Helped by a little sleeping draught no doubt,' Mackenzie said, pointedly glancing at the bottle of Haig.

The fat sergeant had the decency to blush, but before he could respond, a voice from inside the next room said in a mild manner with a trace of a stutter, 'Anything ... ha-ha-happening out there, Sergeant Green?'

Mackenzie turned to face an untidy-looking civilian, dressed in a sloppy well-worn tweed jacket and baggy unpressed pre-war flannels. He was smiling in an apologetic way, but there was no mistaking the mocking look in his eyes. *Don't trust him*, a little voice at the back of Mackenzie's brain snapped harshly. *Don't trust him as far as you could throw him*. Aloud the Major said,

'Mr Philby ... Mr *Kim* Philby?'

'The s-s-same, Major. Please come in. I expect you, gentlemen, would like a stiff peg.' He looked at Campbell 175, but the latter kept his gaze lowered. Like Mackenzie, he had taken an instant dislike to the civilian, though for the life of him he couldn't understand why. So the two of them allowed themselves to be ushered into the inner duty room while the sergeant waddled off to find a fresh bottle of Scotch.

Grateful for the instant warmth engendered by strong spirits, cradling their glasses in their stiff frozen hands, the two of them listened in silence while Philby stuttered his way through the situation as he saw it in Paris.

According to Philby, the balloon had gone up immediately that the news of the great German breakthrough in the Ardennes had reached Eisenhower's headquarters at Versailles, some ten miles or so away. 'The Supreme Commander sl-slapped a news blackout on at once – and that d-d-didn't help matters much either. It only confused the situation. N-now, the Yanks see the Germans and their agents everywhere. It's not wise to go out after dark, gentlemen,' Philby ended, 'without a pass. The Yanks are so nervous. They tend to shoot first and ask questions afterwards.'

Mackenzie took another thoughtful sip of

his Scotch. 'So where does that leave us ... with, er, our problem?' He hesitated, because somehow – he didn't know why – he didn't feel like telling Philby everything. The man was obviously astute and wise to the ways of the world; yet at the same time he gave the appearance to Mackenzie, who was skilled in such matters, of a man who couldn't quite be trusted.

'In some d-difficulty,' Philby answered and shoved the whisky bottle over to them to help themselves to another drink. 'We've put the word out to look for this chap of yours – er – Clive – to our Provost Branch, here and in Brussels, and with the Prime Minister h-himself behind us, they are naturally backing us to the hilt. Besides, the redcaps are busy rounding up deserters everywhere. Either they volunteer to go up the line and fight as riflemen or they go inside for a very long time.'

'Good,' Mackenzie said and accepted another drink. Outside there was another burst of muted machine-gun fire followed by the shriek of a police siren. 'And the civilian police?'

'Bolshy – very bolshy. I'm afraid we can't get much co-operation from them. The Belgies are going communist. As for the Frogs, they'll play it any way they see best for themselves. If the Jerries come back, I'd g-give you odds on that they'd be co-operating with them again like they did with them when the Germans were the occupying power here in France. No, gentlemen, we're in this strictly alone.'

'And the Yanks?' Campbell 175 asked quickly, telling himself that this Kim Philby of the Secret Service was not only somehow shifty, he was also a cynic.

'Yanks?'

'Yes, are they helping us – you?'

Kim Philby seemed to ponder the question for a while, keeping his head slightly bent. Mackenzie, watching him, wondered if this was because like so many people who suffered from a stutter he tried to avoid eye contact, which would make his stutter worse, or whether he didn't want them to see the look in his eye. But if it was the latter, why didn't he? After all they were on the same side and he knew Philby was supposed to be a favourite of 'C', a coming man in the Secret Service.

Finally Philby spoke. He said slowly, 'What do you think, Major, should we tell the Yanks?' Now his stutter didn't seem so pronounced at all and Mackenzie remembered the old trick of someone being interrogated. To give yourself time to think over your answer to a tricky question posed by the Interrogator, you feigned a speech defect, a coughing or sneezing fit, something like that. Was Philby's supposed pronounced stutter simply a device to allow him to deal with difficult or awkward situations? If so, who was he afraid of on his own side? Abruptly and without real reason, he decided there and then that Mister Kim Philby should know only as much as he thought the civilian needed to know. He finished his second whisky with a gulp and rose to his feet.

Philby looked surprised. But Mackenzie didn't give him time to comment. Instead he said with a fake smile on his face, 'Well, that really warmed us up, Philby. Now what about having your sergeant show us to our quarters? It's been a long cold journey. We'd both like to get our heads down. Tomorrow is another day.' He feigned a yawn.

Philby seemed about to hesitate, then he said, his stutter returned, 'W-well, yes, of course, Major.'

Five minutes later they were back in the freezing open jeep, with Mackenzie whispering urgently to Campbell 175, 'A word in your shell-like—'

But Campbell beat him to it with a quick, 'I know, sir, I know...'

'Keep your mouth shut, Campbell, I don't trust the stuttering bugger.'

'Exactly.'

Inside, a waiting Philby waited till he heard the jeep depart, then finally he picked up the phone with fingers that had been itching to do so ever since Mackenzie and Campbell had been announced by the fat duty sergeant. 'Give me Schaef Main Exchange,' he demanded of the switchboard operator, 'and please make it quick ... It's urgent.'

Six

Kerrigan was born to hate. Since he could remember he had been filled by that particular virulent Irish-American hatred of the 'English oppressors'. Not that he had ever been in Ireland, the source of that hatred, save for a day or two when he had been first sent overseas back in 1943 – and then it had been to the equally hated 'Protestant bastards' of Northern Ireland.

No, Kerrigan's hatred was based on half-baked legends, boastful tales, nearly forgotten memories of an 'old country', passed on to him by his parents, who had fled Ireland back at the times of the 'Troubles', and their Irish neighbours in that little part of New York which would always be 'more Ireland than Ireland'.

That hatred, so clearly expressed in his runtish, bitter twisted face that could never exhibit the careless, open-hearted generosity of the race to which he was so proud to belong, had been why he had been selected for the task he was now to carry out. As he crouched in the shadows of the smelly old stairs, replete with the odour of garlic, cat's piss and ancient lecheries, he remembered the chief's words: 'Kerrigan – Charley – there have been too many slips of late. That bastard Poxie escaped in London and sooner or later will spill his guts if we don't stop Mackenzie and Campbell getting to him. We don't want any slip-ups on this one.' The chief had risen from his big desk, decorated with the one star of a brigadier-general and standing next to the furled Stars and Stripes banner, had extended his big hand and shaken his warmly, saying, 'I'm depending upon you, Charley. Remember you're doing this, not only for the good ole US of A, but also for Ireland. 'He had bowed his great handsome head to indicate that this was a very solemn moment and he had been so moved, the tears had sprung spontaneously to his eyes. 'Don't worry, sir,' he had said thickly, very moved, 'Charley Kerrigan won't let you down, sir. The English bastards won't live to see another day ... I swear that on my mother's head.'

'Thank you, Charley,' the boss had replied softly. Unknown to the man now preparing to carry out that promise, he had waited till he had left his office before reaching for the bottle of bourbon and hastily pouring himself a large drink, saying in mock wonder and with a shake of his handsome head, 'Oh, where in Jesus Christ do we find 'em!'

Kerrigan cast a quick glance at the green-glowing dial of his wristwatch. It was nearly midnight, well past the time of curfew. Outside, Paris had finally grown almost silent. He could hear the measured beat of a couple of *flics* patrolling the opposite side of the street and from far off the noise of the troop-and-supply trains being shunted at the Gare d'Austerlitz. But the indiscriminate firing had ceased and the only MP jeep in the street was his own – the MP jeep was the best cover he had been able to think of at short notice – parked discreetly at the back of the old hotel which had once served as a brothel until it had been requisitioned by the US Army.

Kerrigan took a careful breath and, feeling inside his pocket, gripped the handle of the razor-sharp knife with a hand that had grown damp with sweat abruptly. It was time to get on with it. It would be six hours or so before the maids came fussing about their jobs. By then, the boss had informed him, he had to be well out of Paris. Carefully, keeping his foot on the inside edge of the stairs so that his weight didn't make them creak, he took his first pace upwards. On the first-floor landing above him, where their bedrooms were, there was no sound, save the soft rumble of someone snoring gently. All was going according to plan. There was not even a single whore in the place, who might rouse her bed-mate at this unearthly hour. The night duty man, fast asleep in his cubby hole behind the reception desk had been strictly warned against allowing any of the officers in transit to bring a woman in. Everything was as the boss had planned it ever since he had had that telephone call from that snivelling, stuttering little two-timing bastard of an Englishman – *God rot his black English soul!*

Slowly, taking the ancient stairs one by one, stepping in and out of the patches of icy spectral moonlight cast through the unblacked-out windows, he controlled his breathing, which had begun to become more rapid. He had to be in perfect control. There would be no slip-ups when he was on the job.

He reached the landing. He halted. He turned his ear to left and right and listened hard. Nothing. Just the steady soft snoring of a happy man, far away in a warm world of his own, remote from the bloody conflict raging fifty miles or so away. He tightened his grip on the knife. It was the weapon he preferred to work with. It left no traces – empty shell-cases, powder burns and the like – like a pistol did. Hell, you didn't need any special knife – just one from the kitchen of the nearest house. He moved on.

Carefully, very carefully, he crept down the corridor. Through the dirty window at the end of the landing he could see the spectral sickle of the moon, casting its icy unfeeling light on this scene of impending death. The sight pleased him for some reason. Perhaps it reminded him of the tales of the 'Troubles' that his old dad had told him and how the 'boyos' had murdered the proud English in their big houses before they set fire to them. The boyos had always attacked silently at night when the 'Black and Tans' were in their barracks, getting drunk and fucking the poxed-up whores, the only Irish women who'd sleep with the murdering pigs.

He stopped. There it was. Number Nineteen. That was the room they'd given to the older of the two English swine. Twenty was that of his companion. Not that the fact there were two of them worried Kerrigan. The first one would be dead, his throat slit from ear to ear before the other one could turn over in his bed and by then he'd be in Number Twenty, ready to perform the same quiet little operation on the other Englishman. He smiled softly at the thought and repeated the words 'the same quiet little operation' to himself in the fashion of lonely, secretive men. He liked the sound of them.

Unfortunately Kerrigan had been misinformed. On the surface it might have seemed a minor thing. In effect it wasn't.

For the room he had picked for his first 'quiet little operation' was not that of Major Mackenzie, but that of Campbell 175 – and Campbell 175 had come from a different world than that of the young academic Mackenzie. His had been the world of the hated Jew, living constantly in fear in those years before he had made his escape to England, that remote island where his favourite poet Heine had always maintained he would like to die because in England 'everything happens a hundred years later than anywhere else'. Campbell 175 had lived in dread of that knock on the door in the middle of the night and that gruff official voice demanding, *'Polizei ... aufmach ... hier deutsche Polizei!'* It had become second nature for him in his youth to be prepared for any and every emergency. Thus it was he had prepared this night too in this strange French hotel – to the trained killer Kerrigan's cost.

Slowly, the key already well oiled, Kerrigan turned the reception's pass key into the lock of Room Nineteen. There was no obstruction for they had already made sure the two Englishmen had no room keys to lock their bedrooms from within. It had been the old excuse: 'The Boche, gentlemen, they took the keys with them when they left in August.' In France it was the convenient excuse for their own looting of the buildings evacuated by the fleeing Germans: that the latter had stolen everything before they had departed at top speed.

The door opened halfway. A slight breeze wafted on Kerrigan's hard killer's face. The Englishman had his window open, it appeared. He grinned cynically. The swine wouldn't be needing fresh air much longer; his health was about to go into an abrupt decline. He clutched his knife more tightly. He took another pace. Next moment he cursed. The newspaper Campbell 175 had spread out all around his bed as a customary precaution when he believed that he might well be in danger rustled.

An eternity. Kerrigan stopped short, felt his heart beating away like a trip hammer. Had the man sleeping in the bed – a vague shape under the thick cover – heard?

Kerrigan swallowed hard and tried to control himself. Nothing moved. Should he risk it? His mind raced as he considered what he should do next. Something squeaked softly. He jumped. Was it the man in the bed? Sweat dripped down his forehead suddenly in thick opaque pearls. Again he waited, body tense, electric with suspense. Again nothing. If the man in the bed had heard him, surely he would have sat up and shouted out something. Outside a church clock chimed two o'clock.

Kerrigan pulled himself together. 'Bad

cess on ye,' he said in the old tough Irish manner. Whether he was speaking to the clock, the man in the bed or to himself only, no one ever would find out for Erin Kerrigan would never see another dawn and his interrogators wouldn't have the time to find out what had gone through the dying Irishman's mind in those last hours of his angry, violent young life. For as the hollow boom and echo of the last stroke of two faded away, a cool, but foreign voice snapped, 'Stand where you are, you bastard, and don't move.'

Kerrigan started as if struck by an electric shock. The next moment the light behind him went on and lit the room a pale ugly yellow, illuminating the peeling ceiling, the semi-pornographic picture on the wall next to the crucifix, of two cropped-haired women engaged in a suggestive kiss, the scuffed pages of *La Liberation* spread around the bed and the small, Jewish-looking young man in shirt and underpants, holding what looked to Kerrigan like a fountain pen in his hand.

Momentarily Kerrigan's mouth dropped open at the sight. What was the crazy limey about, trying to hold him up, if that's what he was attempting to do, with a fountain pen? He tightened his grip on the knife and prepared to lunge forward.

But Campbell 175 beat him to it. *'Don't!'*

he snapped and raised the fountain pen threateningly.

'Fuck you,' Kerrigan snapped. He bared his teeth in what might have been a grin of triumph or contempt at this damned silly Englishman and his frigging fountain pen. 'Try this on for fuckin' size—'

His threat ended in a gasp of pain, as if someone had suddenly slammed a hard fist into his lean guts. He stopped in mid-stride and stared down at his stomach in utter disbelief. Where the pain was, a sudden small hole had appeared. From it squirted dark-red blood. Abruptly the knife tumbled from suddenly nerveless fingers. 'But ... but...' he stuttered and went down on one knee. He stayed there swaying wildly like a tough old boxing pro, refusing to go down for the final count.

Campbell 175 watched, the fountain pen at the ready. He showed no pity, only cagey alertness. The dying man had tried to murder him ruthlessly and without mercy in his sleep; why should he feel anything for him now? He raised his voice just loud enough perhaps to waken Mackenzie in the other room, but no one else on that floor. 'Sir, in here ... it's urgent ... Sir.' He stopped. Already he could hear the squeaking springs of the bed, broken by years of greedy 'mattress polkas'. Mackenzie was awake immediately.

A moment later he had opened the adjoining door. He, too, was clad in his underpants, but he had slipped a khaki pullover over his shirt against the freezing night cold. He took in the situation at once. The fountain pen, which housed a .22 pistol, supplied by C's Quartermaster; the newspapers, now stained with the stranger's blood; the dropped knife and the still conscious Kerrigan writhing with pain, his lips bitten bloody with the agony, obviously dying. 'Yes?' he asked.

Campbell 175 nodded, not taking his eyes off the dying man for a moment. At this time he felt no mercy, not the slightest compassion for the killer on the floor, writhing in a pool of his own blood. He had been brought up in the hard school of Jewish persecution in Germany of the mid-thirties. It had been a world of dog eat dog. There was no time for mercy in those days.

Mackenzie looked down at Kerrigan. He made his own quick assessment of the Irish-American. He'd last a few hours at least if he got some rudimentary treatment: long enough to answer some of those questions which had plagued him ever since he had been informed of the murder of poor old Dalby at Colditz. 'All right, I'll do my best,' he snapped, very businesslike now. 'Ring up that stuttering twerp Philby at his office. We want a doctor – a discreet one – tootsweet.

They'll have someone like that at hand. Don't tell Philby why. We want to keep him–' he indicated Kerrigan, whose face had turned a deathly white, the tip of his nose abruptly very pinched, a sure indication that he was going to die soon – 'in the world of the living long enough ... well you know. Off you ... Let's get some action on this one.'

Campbell 175 hesitated, as if he was worried that his boss might not be able to cope and Mackenzie said in mock irritation, 'Well, don't just stand there like a spare penis at a wedding. I can manage ... don't fuss, man.'

Campbell 175 grinned despite the tension of this scene of sudden death and answered in that pseudo-cockney accent of his, 'Yessir. The King said crap and a thousand assholes bent and took the strain, for in them days, the word of the King was law.' With that, he fled the room.

Mackenzie bent down. The Irish-American started back up at him, his eyes filled with pain and hate. 'Ye'll not get anything outa me, Englishman,' he said thickly, a trickle of dark-red blood running down the side of his bitter mouth.

Mackenzie wasn't impressed. 'That's what you think. Now then shut your mouth and save your strength. You're going to need it ... But first I'm going to help you.' Unfeelingly he ripped open the dying man's shirt and began to work on him. In the new silence, broken only by the sound of the wind outside and the harsh hectic breathing of the man on the floor, he started to plug pieces of the sheet into the gaping wound, the blood spurting upwards and staining his hands until finally it ceased to flow and he knew that Kerrigan would live for another couple of hours, enough time for what he wanted. 'All right,' he said, breathing a little hard with the effort, 'I'll make a deal with you. I'll see you live, if you answer a few questions.' He shrugged. 'I'll let you die otherwise.'

Kerrigan looked up at the Englishman's impassive, hawk-like face. 'You limey bastard.' His burst of anger vanished as soon as it had come. 'All right,' he said weakly, 'you fuckin' win ... What do you want to know?'

Mackenzie grinned.

BOOK THREE:

TO DESTROY AN EMPIRE

And many more Destructions played
In this ghastly masquerade,
All disguised, even to the eyes,
Like Bishops, lawyers, peers, and spies.

Shelley

One

Joe Kennedy grimaced, as if he were in pain. In fact, the girl under the big desk in the White House's outer office was doing wonders with his flagging libido and the grimace was, in reality, one of utter pleasure.

On the desk in front of him he had been trying to note the points he would make to the President in a few minutes. But now the ornate pen he had been using lay sprawled across the White House notepaper, a series of blots obscuring the little he had been able to write before his 'research assistant' had agreed to 'do a number on him'. And what a number it was!

All maidenly blushes and downcast baby-blue eyes, she had whispered huskily that she had never 'done that kind of thing, Mr Kennedy, sir' ... even with her steady. But when he had mentioned Hollywood and the next movie he was funding and that if 'you play your cards right, honey, I might just be able to find a bit part for you,' that had changed the matter completely. She'd had his flies open, his dick standing to attention and her mouth open, ready to give head, as if she had been doing it professionally for years.

Suddenly his spine arched and his ugly tortoise-shell glasses slipped from the bridge of his big nose with the delightful body-churning shock of his ejaculation. 'Hold it!' he hissed through gritted teeth, his long face contorted with unbelievable pleasure. 'Don't let go, honey ... for Chrissake!'

She didn't and a few moments later she was cleaning him up while he patted her blonde head absently, saying without belief, 'Just you contact my secretary, dear, and she'll fix you up with the producer. He'll see you're all right.'

Privately he told himself that the producer would – on the casting couch. A girl who gave that kind of head would go far in Hollywood. But not in the movies. Then as he heard the squeak and hiss of rubber wheels which indicated that the President was on his way to the Oval Room, he knew it was time to dismiss the pretty blonde with the fabulous tongue back to her 'research'. Some men would have tried to get her telephone number. Not Joe Kennedy, ex-Ambassador to the Court of St James. He knew there were plenty more dumb blondes willing to perform and do almost anything for him, old and as ugly as he was, as long as he could offer them the glamour of a film role in Tinseltown.

At the door, she curtseyed in a fashion which she probably thought was cute and blew him a silent kiss. He smiled, showing his big square ugly teeth and told himself, 'Stupid cunt,' wondering yet again on how gullible people were, but telling himself he was glad they were. The knowledge of that fact and how to use that knowledge had made him a rich and powerful man. Why would he be here otherwise, a former boot-legger and the son of a Mick ward boss, one of those black Catholic Micks, who had never been invited across the doorstep of those fancy Bostonian WASPs who had ruled Boston when he had been a kid. Roosevelt had no real affection for him. All that the President wanted from him was – frankly – money, the votes money could buy and, now and again, as was the case now, a certain cynical expertise: the knowledge of where the bodies were buried. And brother, did he know that?

The squeak of the 'Boss's' wheelchair was getting closer. He'd better be on his way. He gave his flies a quick check, brushed his jacket to remove any blonde hairs she might have left, but even as he did so, he told himself with a laugh, the blonde hairs, if there were any, would be at the other end of his anatomy. Then he went out, happy with himself, whistling under his breath, like some Mick street urchin of his youth, 'Phil the Fluter's Ball'.

Henry Wallace, the Vice-President, and Morgenthau, the Secretary of the Treasury, were waiting in the Oval Room as he entered. He liked neither of them. Morgenthau was a Jew and he hated Jews. Wallace was a fool and a 'pinko' and he hated 'Reds' even more than he did Jews. Still he smiled warmly at both of them, knowing he didn't want to make enemies of two of the most powerful men in the Boss's cabinet; he might need them. Besides, Morgenthau, in particular, was a personal friend of the President. He didn't want the former bad-mouthing him when the two got together for one of their informal little chats, which, in reality, were gossip sessions about the lives and loves of their fellow bigshots on Capitol Hill.

Outside, the squeak of the wheelchair had ceased. Kennedy knew why. Roosevelt was going to put on his act, thinking he'd impress them. Now he was rising from the small armless presidential wheelchair with the aid of Irvon McDuffie, his valet. Together they'd be clicking the catches on the braces which kept his wasted, pitiful, useless legs still so that he could walk the handful of yards to his chair at the big table. It was a customary performance he sometimes put on for people like the other two and himself. For his part, it didn't impress him one little bit. Roosevelt, who hadn't a kind bone in his whole body and would stick a knife in your back at a moment's notice, if it suited him, was, in reality, a goddam pathetic cripple!

Next moment the great man himself appeared. He walked very stiffly with an awkward legs and arms movement like an automaton. But there was that usual great smile on his lips, his white teeth dazzling, his cigarette-holder thrust upwards cockily. Behind him came the valet pushing the wheelchair – just in case. For already the effort of these few paces had brought him out in a muck sweat and a watching Kennedy knew that usually after such a performance, McDuffie would have to strip him of his shirt and underpants and towel his body dry. Somehow Roosevelt reached the chair. Hastily McDuffie clicked the catches off the callipers which kept his crippled legs upright and the President collapsed gratefully into the chair. The meeting could commence.

Roosevelt wasted no time. He never did. He knew the others only too well. Indeed he knew more about them than they knew he did – their strengths and, more importantly for him, their weaknesses. 'You all know,' he commenced, 'why we're here. The war has changed in America's favour. We are certain now to beat the German in due course after the defeats of Stalingrad and El Alamein and although the little yellow men are tougher than the Germans, we'll beat the Nips too.' He favoured them with that brilliant smile once more – not that it impressed his listeners; they knew *his* weakness too. 'Thus we and the Russians will emerge from this war the top dogs ... Though I firmly believe there will only be one post-war superpower, as they call it now – the United States of America!' He beamed at them again.

All but Wallace, the 'Red', smiled back. But his reaction didn't matter. The Vice-President was on the way out. For the 1944 presidential election, Roosevelt would pick another, less controversial Vice-President hopeful.

'So, gentlemen, if we are going to decide the fate of the world, we'd better start giving some thought to it – *now*.' There was a sudden unexpected sharpness in Roosevelt's voice. It made them sit up, even Kennedy, the arch-cynic. Roosevelt wasn't ribbing them. He meant to be taken seriously, very seriously.

'Our allies,' the President continued, 'are really bankrupt, financially, militarily and morally. France, the Netherlands and Britain all really depend upon us to keep them in the war, which of course is our aim.

But what of after the war? Why should we support empires, such as the French, Dutch and naturally British, which are morally corrupt? Is that what we are fighting this war for, gentlemen?'

Wallace beamed in his usual childish manner and exclaimed, 'Exactly, Mr President.' Morgenthau looked thoughtful, probably wondering what any decision might cost his jealously guarded Treasury funds. For his part, Kennedy told himself cynically: Yeah, get rid of the Frogs, the Cheeseheads and the Limeys with their protective tariffs against US goods, and American manufacturers could make a killing by selling to empire markets which had been closed to them so far. Boy, wouldn't that just be great! His weathered lecher's face cracked into a wintry smile at the thought of how much dough he personally could make then.

Roosevelt let them absorb the information and then raised a finger of a hand heavy with brown liver spots, as if in warning. 'I doubt if we shall have much trouble with the French and Dutch,' he continued. 'But we will with Churchill. He is fanatical about the British Empire, as you well know. The trappings of Imperial power have been part and parcel of his life ever since he was a blue-blooded infant.' He paused, and a look almost of sadness passed momentarily across his heavy, bejowled face; it was as if he felt sorry for his long-time comrade-in-arms. 'Churchill will fight to his last breath to defend his Empire.'

'Economically,' Morgenthau interjected in his usual dry-as-dust manner, 'Churchill hasn't a leg to stand on. The British are bankrupt.'

'Deservedly so,' Wallace chimed in. 'They have exploited their natives cruelly for far too long.'

No one took any notice of Wallace, but the Vice-President didn't seem to notice. As always he listened only to his own crazy inner voices.

'So,' Roosevelt said, 'we must work towards compromising or discrediting Churchill. Not a single man in his cabinet, Conservative or Socialist, could replace him in a crisis. Churchill stands out alone – he is a great man of his kind—'

'A big fish in a little pond,' Kennedy interjected bitterly.

'I guess you're right,' Roosevelt said mildly, though he hated to be interrupted. But he needed Joe Kennedy. If anyone was prepared to do the dirty work for him, it was the one-time bootlegger. He was the hatchet man he'd need in the future *par excellence*. Why, hadn't Kennedy once said openly, 'The future capitalist class is safer under a Hitler than under a Churchill'? Terrible, but typical of Joe, who was obsessed with gaining wealth and keeping it.

'What can be done, therefore, to undermine Churchill?' Roosevelt asked. He answered his own question. 'We destroy his power base, which is his own Conservative Party. Show that party as being corrupt, self-serving and above all *treacherous* and we destroy Churchill's credibility. Why, he might not even be re-elected in the first post-war general election over there in England – and then our problem is solved. The Socialists who would then rule would hand over the British Empire on a silver platter to the natives.'

Only Wallace noticed the use of the word 'natives', but before he could open his mouth to protest, the President had continued with, 'If, however, Churchill did get re-elected as the man who led England to victory, then we must set about speedily discrediting him.' He took a deep breath, his sick face flushed an ugly pink with the effort of talking. Behind him his valet tensed anxiously. Of late the President tended to collapse frequently; he hoped he wouldn't now in front of these tough, self-seeking men who really ran America whether they were in the government or not.

But Roosevelt didn't collapse. Instead he mopped his sweat-dripping brow with a large flowered handkerchief, which he kept tucked up his sleeve in the effete English fashion and said a little weakly, 'Joe here knows what went on in London back in 1939 just after England declared war. As you gentlemen know he was our ambassador. He can give chapter and verse how leading politicians in Churchill's own party engaged in treacherous talks with the Germans *after* war was declared. Bring that out into the open when the time comes and Churchill and his Conservative Party are dead ducks. The party that represents the Empire will be destroyed. Joe,' he ended weakly, 'you've got the floor...'

Two

One year to the day after they had tried to settle the fate of the British Empire in Washington, they stabbed 'Poxie' Pearson, alias 'Brigadier Clive', to death in Central Brussels. It was the way that Poxie was fated to die, but even in his wildest dreams, the long-time deserter had never expected death would come so soon.

At first he had thought of going to Paris, but the great German counter-attack, now over, had changed his mind for him. He had headed instead for Brussels, the Belgian capital, firmly in British hands. Here he'd reasoned he'd be safer. He knew his English too, in particular the ways of the redcaps, and he believed he could dodge them better than the Yank MPs in Paris.

It had turned out to be a wise decision. He'd soon got his feet under the table. He'd picked up Simone flogging her wares in the rue Neuve, tried her out at a price which made him skint and decided she was a valuable – as well as expensive – commodity that would keep him throughout the winter at least. As long as she could spread her long legs that seemed to go on for ever till they reached that naked hairless vulva of hers, he'd been rolling in it.

In the meantime he continued his own modest business centred on the 'Bon Marché' and the 'Boule Max' flogging black-market fags, marge, and anything that he could stick in his pocket and do a runner with whenever the rozzers appeared, which was often in the Wild West atmosphere of Brussels, packed with troops from the front with money to burn. But in the week leading up to that Thursday where the Grim Reaper finally caught up with him, Poxie had ventured into the big league, as he called it. It had been a fatal move. For trading in black-market penicillin, stolen from military hospitals in Louvain, Verviers and the surrounding towns was a dangerous business. Unwary dealers were stabbed in the back, strangled, shot and thrown in the nearest canal just for the sake of a couple of vials of the precious, life-saving drug. Poxie should have known that. But he had grown greedy and, believing that his luck would never run out, had taken the chance of sudden violent death.

Thus it had been that he had not taken his usual precautions when he had been approached in the Café Texas, just off the Gare du Nord that Thursday night, the last he'd spend alive on this earth. The place was packed with Allied soldiers in various stages of drunkenness from tipsy to the falling-down stage, dressed in a bewildering variety of winter uniforms. Most of them were from the front and had plenty of money to spend, or they'd brought with them rations and other items they could sell on the Brussels black market, which again provided them with huge bundles of greasy Belgian francs. They had reckoned with a short, brutal life at the front – sooner or later their 'number would come up', and they were intent on enjoying themselves before it did; and enjoyment meant 'booze and bint', as the English among them put it.

The noise was terrific. Everywhere they were crammed together like sardines, shouting at each other, shouting at the waiters, shouting at the musicians and, most of all, the whores, who obviously wouldn't be spending the night in their own beds. Indeed, some of the tarts looked as if they hadn't spent a night in their own beds for a very long time, though all of them obviously had passed a lot of it on their backs with their legs spread.

Poxie wasn't particularly interested in the women – after all he did have his Simone, though, as he told himself, he wouldn't object if one of them put her hand in his flies and suggested they should become engaged for an hour or two – for free, naturally. Poxie Pearson never paid for 'it'. It was a matter of honour and pride with him.

He smiled faintly at his own humour, as he fought his way through the noisy throng, coughing and blinking in the thick fug, heading for a chair at the back of the packed place where he could observe the types. For since he had gone into the 'medical supplies business', as he called it, he had learned that some of the blokes from the front had discovered penicillin too. Nicked from some unwary medical officer or field dressing station, it bought more tarts on the black market than did a tin of Players or other contraband that the redcaps might seize upon easily in one of their routine searches of leave men heading for a thirty-six-hour pass in the Belgian capital.

He slipped the sweating waiter a hundred franc note and nodded to a table near the sign marked '*cour*' at the far end of the room. It was always handy to be next to the 'yard' where the lavs were, just in case there was a police raid.

He ordered a cognac – 'none of yer bath-tub-brewed muck, mind you – the real stuff' – and sat down to watch the action. It was the usual stuff he had become accustomed to in his time in Brussels: suddenly enraged soldiers drawing their pistols and threatening to shoot some other poor sod who had looked at their girls; whores, as drunk as the soldiers, pulling off their drawers and dancing stupidly on the table exhibiting their hairy bushes, as if they were displaying some unique sexual toy; surly soldiers arguing with the waiters about the bill; furtive, baggy-eyed civvies trying to flog obscene photographs that must have been taken a hundred years before to soldiers who couldn't even see straight.

Once, a fat whore with triple chins, took off her drawers and, squatting over the band's big drum, offered to suck up anything the audience threw on it with her vulva as long as she could keep it. It was a parody of a popular radio show 'Penny on the Drum' back home. But after the first few 20 franc coins, a bored soldier tossed a tin of black-market corned beef, stolen from somebody's compo ration on to the drum and the 'exhibition', if that was what it was, came to an end. The whore pulled on her voluminous 'art silk' black drawers and withdrew with a sulk. The drummer reclaimed his drum and after a careful examination of it began to thump it again with the rest of the Belgie 'orchestra' playing the jerky *bal musette* music.

Poxie was bored. There seemed none of the action he was looking for about in the Café Texas. Not even one of the free whores, lounging moodily at the zinc-covered bar, sipping cheap beer, had approached him yet. And so far he hadn't spotted anyone who might be interested in business. Thus it was that he was about to drain the rest of his cognac and go when the tall, willowy sergeant in the lighter grey battledress of the Canadian Army nodded at the empty chair at his table and said politely enough, 'That chair taken, chum?'

Poxie looked up at him. There seemed something soft about the Canuck. Was he a pansy, perhaps? But at the same time, the deserter's quick gaze noted the sergeant's three stripes and the red patch of the Canadian Medical Corps on his shoulder. He smiled warily. Perhaps the Canuck was in the business? Extending his hand like a waiter to a guest who was known to tip well, he said, 'Take a pew, old lad. Costs nothing.'

'Gee, thanks,' the other man said and now Poxie noted with increased interest that the Canuck was carrying a haversack and it was full of something; that was a good sign. It meant he might have something to flog. 'Thought I might look over the talent,' the Canuck said with a smile, revealing a mouthful of excellent teeth.

Poxie with his built-in antennae for dubious characters like himself knew there was something fishy about the other man; his look was too intense. He wasn't there to watch the ‘talent’ at all. Perhaps he was a Mary Ann. It didn’t matter. It was what he had in that haversack that counted. After all, homosexuals had to buy their bit of the other just like ordinary decent blokes had to do with their tarts. The Canuck was up to something, of that he was sure.

Ten minutes later, now on their second cognac each bought by ‘Curt’, as the Canuck introduced himself, they were deep in conversation, trying their best to understand each other in a room now bulging at the walls with screaming, shouting whores and their clients and the *bal musette* going full blast.

Poxie had been right. The Canuck was fishy. He had something to flog, but seemingly he didn’t want to show the illegal wares inside the Café Texas. Drunk as everyone seemed to be, still he was scared that they might be observed and, as he put it, ‘be shopped by some goddam pimp or other low-life ... Perhaps,’ he suggested, looking to left and right as he did so, as if he were afraid he was being observed, ‘we could go to a little place I know off the rue Neuve – very quiet and discreet. We could talk business there?’ He looked pointedly at Poxie.

The deserter hesitated.

The Canuck still seemed dodgy somehow, though he couldn’t quite put his finger on how. Perhaps it was because he was a pansy, of that Poxie was sure. Was he using 'business' as some sort of excuse to get him, Poxie, outside? But Poxie didn't see himself as being exactly a pansy's typical dreamboat; they fancied sweet young lads with plump arses. He frowned. But in the end greed got the better of him. He said, 'Buy me another glass of that rotgut and we'll go.'

Poxie should have been warned by the haste with which the Canuck NCO complied with his request. It was a fatal oversight. Five minutes later they were descending the stairs to the Canadian-run 'Pro-Station' in the traffic island in the middle of the Boule Max. Here, worn and weary but happy soldiers of all nationalities lined up at zinc troughs, their khaki trousers around their ankles, busily engaged in squirting purple liquid from rubber tubes attached to the walls up their penises before powdering their organs and tying little muslin bags around them. It was the standard operating procedure that the Army insisted upon after sexual intercourse. Failure to comply would result in thirty days in the glasshouse if a soldier who had failed to carry it out caught VD.

The sight caused Poxie some degree of relief. It explained why he had thought the Canuck was a pansy; all, the medical personnel who dealt with soldiers' pox diseases seemed to be homos. Besides it might mean, too, that the Canuck had the wonder drug, penicillin, to flog.

'This way,' the sergeant said. 'My office is at the back of this place. Disgusting isn't it!' He indicated a corporal in some Highland regiment or other who had lifted his kilt to expose his naked loins, but who was too drunk to direct the rubber tube up his penis. Instead he was spraying potassium permanganate solution all over his boots.

Poxie nodded without interest. But that use of 'disgusting' confirmed his belief that the Canuck was 'the other way'. No ordinary squaddie would have used a word like 'disgusting'; that was left to yer officers and gents.

But the Canuck was not an officer and definitely no 'gent'. What happened next proved that, but by then, it was too late for Poxie to do anything about it. With his key the Canuck seemed to open the door in the dark, smelly corridor behind the troughs, or at least appeared to fumble with the lock, while Poxie waited, unaware of the impending danger, too concerned with wondering what the Canadian might sell to him and hoping it was penicillin.

Suddenly, startlingly, it happened. Out of the gloom at the end of the corridors, two shadows detached themselves. The Canuck hissed something in French. Poxie half-turned, abruptly alarmed and knowing instinctively that something was going badly wrong. Too late! The knife blade slid between his third and fourth ribs like a red-hot knife into butter. In that same instant his cry of mortal agony was stifled by the hard calloused hand that wrapped itself around his gaping mouth.

Desperately and already dying Poxie tried to break that hold. In vain. Once more that killing blade sliced into his side and pierced his lungs. His spine arched in excruciating pain like a taut bow. But he couldn't break that hold. He felt his life fluid drain out of him, as if someone had opened a tap. In the smelly gloom, he saw the Canuck staring at him, gazing without the slightest mercy, assessing how much longer it would take the trapped man to die.

With the last of his ebbing strength, Poxie tried to break away. He bit the calloused palm holding that vice-like grip on his mouth. '*Sale con anglais!*' his assailant snarled angrily. But he didn't let go. Bright red and silver stars started to explode in front of the dying man's eyes. He knew he hadn't much time left. He kicked backwards with his heel. But he was too slow, dying as he was. The man avoided the kick easily. He increased the pressure. 'Die, you bastard ... *die*,' he gasped in heavily accented English.

Poxie gasped incoherently. A red mist had

replaced the stars. It was threatening to engulf him. He fought a moment more and then it descended for good. Suddenly he went limp in his killer's arms. The other man sensed that it was all over. But he didn't relax that murderous pressure for a while. He wanted to make quite sure.

The Canadian sergeant wanted to as well. He peered at Poxie's brick-red face, his tongue hanging out from purple lips like a piece of coloured leather, and said then finally in French, 'Comrades, get rid of him now.'

The one who had stood by in the shadows, just in case, raised his clenched fist in the Communist Party salute before the two of them set about dragging the body outside into the blacked-out streets. The 'Canadian', if that was what he really was, waited till he heard the outer door close behind them, then he raised the telephone from its cradle. Comrade Philby would need to know immediately that his orders had been carried out.

'Comrade' Philby gave a little sigh of anticipation. He always felt like this when he could report directly to his case officer in Moscow. A Moscow signal filled him with a sense of achievement, even pride, that he was helping the cause of the 'Great Patriotic War' that the Soviet Fatherland was waging with the Fascist beast. He liked to feel sometimes that occasionally his top-secret signals from Paris were read by no less a person than Comrade Stalin himself. Now he read through the signal before he encoded it and used the clandestine radio of the Parisian Communist Party, which was the securest transmitter in the whole of Western Europe, to dispatch it to the Soviet Fatherland. It was fairly long, but he couldn't help that. Besides the French 'pianist', as the Résistance called their radio operators, was a genius at dodging the *flics*' detector vans.

'Situation here clarified,' he read after speeding through the various technical instructions to the 'pianist'. 'The link'–' he meant the dead Poxie – 'has been liquidated. However, situation is now in the open. It is clear to Brit. authorities that US actively working against Brit. interests. London reacting. Very optimistic that a break between London/Washington take place soonest.'

He smiled, obviously pleased with his efforts. The sooner the British and the American imperialists started fighting each other, even if it was just in the council chambers of the Western World, the better. The Soviet Fatherland needed all the help it could get to survive and triumph over the next post-war months. He dropped the 'flimsy'* and reached for his big glass of whisky. He raised it as if in a toast, staring at his reflection in the mirror on the wall opposite, just next to the traditional consular portrait, to be found in British establishments all over the world, and stuttered, 'F-f-fuck you, King Emp-peror!'

On the wall, his fellow stutterer, King George VI, the last King Emperor of the dying British Empire, stared back at him stonily. The arch-traitor laughed again and then got on with his encoding.

**Wireless message.*

Three

Seven abreast, the band of the Brigade of Guards packed the shabby London street, as they swung towards the saluting dais. At their head the massive drum major, resplendent in pre-war red and silver, twirled and swung his mace with majestic ease. His eyes were fixed on some distant horizon, blind to the miserable world of the grey-faced, undernourished civvies packed on both sides, watching the rare spectacle.

But the stirring music seemed to have little effect even on the schoolkids whom someone had supplied with cheap paper Union Jacks. A few waved in a desultory fashion, but for the most part the civilians watched without much interest. It was snowing again and the soft flakes falling on their heads seemed to deaden their mood even more.

Standing behind the dais where the Great Man would take the salute together with the rest of the well-nourished Anglo-American brass, Major Mackenzie told himself the spirit had gone out of the British people.

The war had simply lasted too long. There had been too many deaths and years of defeat. Now that the great conflict was finally turning in the favour of Britain, the people no longer cared. All they wanted was for the war to end.

But if Major Mackenzie's mood was sombre, that of his companion, Campbell 175, was exactly the opposite. Every time the drum major threw up his silver mace high into the sky and caught it effortlessly when it seemed it had to crash to the ground, he gave a little gasp of admiration, entranced by the spectacle, almost like a pre-war British schoolkid, Mackenzie couldn't help thinking. It irritated Mackenzie for some reason he couldn't quite make out and he grunted, digging his sergeant in the ribs, 'Don't have a bloody orgasm, Campbell.'

The little Jewish MCO with the dark sparkling clever eyes wasn't offended. He said, 'But you must admit that they are really putting on some show. There's no other country that could do it like this – even the Adolf Hitler bodyguard strutting and stamping down the *Ost-West Axis* before the war couldn't beat a spectacle like this, sir.'

'I'm glad you think so,' Mackenzie said, adding a little cynically, 'Yes, I know the Yanks think we turn out some good military bands – for all the use they are.'

Campbell 175 could see the 'old man' was tired. There were dark circles under his eyes and when he took off the steel-rimmed spectacles he was now forced to wear, Major Mackenzie looked very old and worn. The little sergeant felt it had been the strain of this Colditz affair and all its ramifications. At least they had mastered most of the 'imponderables', as Mackenzie had called them originally. They knew from the dying OSS killer what Roosevelt and his fellow bigshots planned for post-war Britain and its Empire; they knew that 'Brigadier Clive' had been sorted out, though who exactly had killed him so brutally in that underground VD station was uncertain – Belgian communists were suspected. Yet how *they* had got into the act was still a mystery. And they knew, too, that the Great Man was planning to go over to the offensive. That was why, Campbell 175 thought, they had been brought here.

As he had remarked to a sombre Mackenzie a little earlier on when they had been summoned hastily to attend the Prime Minister's celebratory parade, 'The Old Boy's not going to give up without a fight, sir. He'll do the Yanks yet.'

Mackenzie had not shared his enthusiasm. He had remarked in that subdued manner which seemed to have afflicted him ever since they had come back from the Continent two weeks before, their task there seemingly completed, 'You know in the early fifth century when the Roman Empire was on its last legs and about to go into its fatal decline, the Roman patricians hired barbarians to protect Rome from their fellow barbarians from the north.' He looked pointedly down at Campbell and the latter had begun, 'By that, sir, you think I'm one of the barbarians defending a declining British Empire when real Britons are no longer prepared—'

The stamp of the massed band coming to a halt, followed by the harsh commands of the drum major echoing and re-echoing in the stone chasm of the street had cut into his words. Now the two Intelligence men watched as the band and the crowd waited for the Great Man and his entourage to emerge. Steadily, sadly, the snow continued to fall and the crowd huddled closer together like a flock of sheep, cowed by wind and weather, waiting numbly for God knew what.

Suddenly an American officer came hurrying out of the building. He was beautifully dressed in immaculate olive drab and 'pinks', his plump face glowing with radiant health. Mackenzie told himself he was a worthy representative of the 'new order' – keen, alert, fresh. He said something to the bandmaster. The drum major raised his mace. Next moment the band broke into a Sousa march, again fast, racey, vibrant with pulsating life. A moment later General Eisenhower, the Allied Supreme Commander, appeared together with Churchill, wearing his strange square nineteenth-century bowler hat and supporting himself on his stick. Eisenhower paused. He grinned. His smile seemed to spread from ear to ear. It appealed to even that war-weary crowd of Londoners. They cheered. Churchill smiled, but Mackenzie felt he didn't look too pleased. The contract between the old and the new was only too obvious. Mackenzie sank back into his mood of despondency, hardly aware of what the two men said, the snow gathering unnoticed on his bowed shoulders.

It was only half an hour later while they waited for the crowd to disperse and for their audience with the Great Man, thawed out a little by hurried sips from Mackenzie's silver flask (of late a worried Campbell had notice the boss was beginning to drink a lot during the day), that Major Mackenzie started to become aware again that they still had a job to do.

He watched Eisenhower finish his little address to the crowd, which actually cheered afterwards, and remarked, 'I don't think Ike has got anything to do with this bad business, Campbell. It's clear he's too honest—'

'Or too simple,' Campbell 175 interjected.

'Who's the cynic now?' Mackenzie retorted without rancour.

Then the two of them waited for Churchill to finish and for the signal to approach them, for the authorities had insisted that the two Intelligence officers could be seen in a fleeting conversation with the Great Man, but not closeted privately with him. The Yanks of the OSS working under Roosevelt could be watching them, especially here in London where they had one of their headquarters in Europe.

Finally it was over. Eisenhower departed to the strains of 'God Bless America' played badly, perhaps deliberately so, by the band of the Guards and surrounded in his armoured, bullet-proof Cadillac by a V of white-helmeted MPs on motorcycles. It was time for them to receive their instructions from Churchill.

The Prime Minister looked worn and not too well. His face was sickly-looking and the usual mischievous sparkle was absent from his eyes. At last, Mackenzie told himself, the strain was beginning to tell on him, just as it had long done on the nation he was now finally leading to victory.

But if the Great Man was ill, his instructions were clear, precise and very much to the point. 'I have read your report,' he announced while all around him his staff hovered nervously, as if they were afraid that Churchill might keel over and die on them on the spot. But Churchill ignored the falling snow. He continued with: 'It is obvious that we have cleared up the – er – matter – in question somewhat. Your report makes that clear. We know more of the role of our cousins across the sea and that those devils of traitors from my own party are prepared to go to any length to cover up their tracks. Now we must take the matter a step further.' He hesitated, as if he wondered how he was going to phrase his next few words. Finally, as his Secretary attempted to hold an umbrella over his head but was waved off immediately with a growled, 'Let the people see for God's sake. I'm not made of sugar, you know!' he said, 'Now we – *you* – must make it clear to the Americans that we know what they're about.'

Mackenzie and Campbell 175 looked puzzled.

Churchill didn't seem to notice; perhaps he didn't want to. He continued with: 'What I am asking of you two is highly dangerous and under normal circumstances, I wouldnot ask you to volunteer for it. But the future of the Empire is at stake. There can be no quibbling.'

The two looked even more puzzled.

'It has to be you, Major Mackenzie. The

Yanks know your involvement in this delicate matter now. So you have to be seen doing what I plan so they know we're on to them. Perhaps they will desist.' Abruptly Churchill's bottom lip trembled as if he might break down and cry there and then, but he contained himself just in time and went on with: '...desist at least for a little while. So, Major, you and your sergeant will report to Air Marshal Harris at his headquarters – everything has already been arranged – he will brief you on your mission.'

Churchill was now very businesslike and for the first time he seemed to notice the snow which was beginning to settle on his bowed shoulders. He nodded and the umbrella was placed over his head to protect him. 'I shall not shake your hands in the manner that one should part from brave men such as you. I shall also say this: I will never see you again and you, in your turn, must never mention what you have done and what you know to anyone outside of this circle. This matter must remain part and parcel of the secret history of this titanic struggle between good and evil...'

Even though he was greatly puzzled by what the Great Man had in store and the role 'Bomber' Harris of the Royal Air Force had to play now, Mackenzie could see he and Campbell had already been almost forgotten. The Prime Minister was no longer addressing them, but perhaps the whole British nation. Holding the umbrella, the Secretary nodded as if he knew that too. He indicated that they should go. Together they saluted. Churchill did not appear to notice. He was still talking.

Silently in the snow they moved away and into the crowd which was beginning to drift away in a kind of listless silence, not even excited by the spectacle on this grey winter's day. They passed the band and the drum major, who somehow seemed to have shrunk in size until he looked just like any other soldier, despite his scarlet and silver uniform. They were packing away their instruments and clapping their red hands together to restore the warmth. Just as they reached the edge of the crowd, Mackenzie looked back. Churchill had vanished inside the building again. Instinctively he knew they really never would see him in the flesh again...

BOOK FOUR:

RETURN TO COLDITZ

April is the cruellest month, breeding
Lilacs out of the dead land...

T.S. Eliot

One

It was now over a month since 'Bomber' Harris, head of Bomber Command, had received them at his underground HQ just outside Oxford. He had peered at the two of them, both now clad in the uniform of RAF pilot officers, with his suspicious little eyes. Probably he didn't like them, for without any kind of preamble he had barked, moustache bristling, 'This morning I was stopped by a fool of a young policeman for speeding. He told me to be careful or I would kill someone one day. *Me*!' Harris's face had turned almost puce with the memory. 'But I put him in his place very smartish. I said to him, "Young man, I *kill* thousands of people every night!" '

The anecdote had flabbergasted both of them. Neither Mackenzie nor Campbell had been able to react. Harris had. 'Why am I telling you this?' he snapped. 'I'll tell you – because I think this operation is a ruddy waste of time and more importantly a waste of aircraft. So the two of you better shape up or, Prime Minister or not behind you, I'll cancel the whole bloody op. All right get on with it.' And he had dismissed them there and then, leaving them not one wit wiser what this 'op' was.

Thereafter the days and weeks passed at an amazing speed. From morning to night they were on their toes, being given a bewildering variety of instructions by senior staff officers, mostly behind closed doors. Their first week was apparently to acquaint them with RAF procedure, drills, even slang, which they were ordered to use. By the end of that week they were talking about 'kites' 'prangs' and the like in the mess, as if they had been using such terms all their service life. They were also growing RAF-type moustaches and Mackenzie had been told to get rid of his glasses; aircrew didn't wear glasses.

That 'aircrew' had puzzled them for a while until on the following Monday at eight hundred hours precisely, they were told by their new instructor, his chest ablaze with the ribbons of the DSO, DFC, AFC and the like that 'it's no use trying to train you as navigators or pilots. Too long and you haven't got the ability. You'll have to be the lowest form of aircrew life – tailgun Charleys,' he had twirled his absurd moustache with a flourish, '–air gunners to you brown jobs.' So it was out to the ranges to fire twin Browning machine guns at the targets until they were both deafened, their heads ringing with the incessant chatter of the powerful turret machine guns.

But at night in their separate Nissen hut listening to the drunken singing of the pilots in the officers' mess and the shouts and cries of the usual rowdy mess games that followed, they both couldn't sleep. It was not that they were afraid of what was to come; it was the unsettling feeling of not knowing exactly what it was. By now the Allies had crossed the Rhine. Soon Eisenhower's great armies would be spreading out over the Reich, bringing an end to that murderous empire which Hitler had once boasted would last a thousand years. In a matter of weeks possibly the war in Europe would be over. So why were they still training and for what?

At the end of their third week at the bomber base in remotest North Yorkshire they received their first clue. The officer with the medals and the enormous moustache departed. In his place there was a much older officer, who limped and walked with the aid of a stick. His skinny chest bore the ribbons of the Old War and he had none of the brash ebullience of their first trainers.

'Just call me Wingco,' he introduced himself quietly, eyeing the two newly fledged pilot officers, now sporting the half-wing of an air-gunner with its 'AG' roundel. 'It's better if you don't know too much about me.' Immediately Mackenzie guessed he was one of them – Intelligence. But he contained himself, keeping his thoughts to himself. 'Right, as you know, you've come to the end of your training.' He gave them a tired smile. 'Thank God, you're not going on ops. You're not exactly the best of machine-gunners.'

Again neither Mackenzie nor Campbell 175 responded. They were back playing their old role of Intelligence. The less they said, the better. So they listened in silence. Outside they were revving up the Lancasters. Obviously there was going to be an op this night. There always was. Bomber Harris seemingly hadn't noticed the war was coming to an end. He was working his hard-pressed crews full out to the very last.

'Wingco' said, 'You've been trained as air gunners because if and when the Huns interrogate you, a knowledge of air gunnery is easier to fake than that of navigator or flight engineer. That's why you had to get rid of your spectacles, Major Mackenzie.' His eyes twinkled for a moment. For he could see the surprise on the faces of the two 'brown jobs'.

Campbell 175 opened his mouth to express his surprise, but 'Wingco' held up his hand for silence. 'Not now, Sergeant Campbell. Just listen, please, for the time being. All will be explained in due course.'

Mackenzie frowned but said nothing. The RAF officer seemed too clever by half, but he seemed to know what he was about and, besides, for the time being he was boss, so he didn't comment.

'Now then, let me brief you a little on the gear you'll be wearing when you go,' Wingco went on. He touched the highly polished brass button of his tunic, adorned with the proud wings of the RAF. 'Now, these buttons are ideal places for hiding things. Fortunately the Huns haven't cottoned on to that yet – they're a slow peasant race, in my lowly opinion. Well they did once, but we soon rectified that.'

'I don't understand,' Campbell 175 ventured.

'Of course you don't. Not your field exactly, is it?' Wingco said pleasantly enough. But Mackenzie felt the RAF veteran was treating them as if they were typical thickheaded Army types who didn't know their arses from their elbows. Outside someone was shouting above the mounting roar of the engines being tested, 'Watch that frigging hydraulic fluid, Chalky. It don't grow on the frigging trees, yer know...' The shout was followed immediately by an angry 'I saw that look, White! That could be classed as dumb insolence. I'll have yer on a frigging charge, if you pull a face like that agen.'

'You see,' the RAF officer continued, 'you unscrewed the button by turning it to the left – anticlockwise. After a few years of searching our chaps who were shot down and captured, the Huns cottoned on to the trick. They still do it. But we turned the tables on 'em.' He smiled at them, as if he had just pulled a rabbit out of a top hat for a bunch of tiny tots and was pleased at their childlike reaction. 'We reversed the thread so that when the Huns turned the button to the left, it only tightened the assembly. The button stayed in place, its secrets undetected.'

Campbell looked at Mackenzie. His look said, 'Does this RAF Brylcreem type think we're bloody idiots?' Mackenzie frowned as if to indicate that he should keep his mouth shut. The sooner the little lecture was over, the sooner they'd find out what all this was leading up to.

'Now here's another little gadget I'd like to recommend to you, gentlemen,' Wingco went on. He pulled out a khaki military handkerchief. 'A perfectly normal snotrag, you'd say.' He held it up for them to see, again like a conjuror lulling his audience, before he pulled off his trick to their total astonishment. He beamed at them paternally and said, 'However, if we do this.' His finger sought and found the key thread at the handkerchief's edge. 'Pull and our snotrag is transformed. *Voilà*!'

Wingco had a point, Mackenzie told himself. For now the perfectly ordinary handkerchief had abruptly changed colour. The khaki-brown had vanished. In its place it had become green: a green criss-crossed by a myriad of black lines. 'What is it?' Wingco proudly answered his own question. 'Why, a very detailed map of central Germany to the east of the River Elbe. Now what do you say to that, gentlemen?'

Mackenzie thought it was time for Wingco, whoever he was and despite his age, to be put in his place. 'I take it then we are being prepared for an op. somewhere between the Elbe and Berlin, the territory which will soon become a battleground between our people advancing from the west and the remainder of the *Wehrmacht*, trapped in that area by the Russians coming in from thc east.'

His words caught the older man by surprise. That was obvious by the look on his face. 'Yes,' he stuttered, 'you're right.' He recovered quickly, however, and added, 'But you're not supposed to know that – *yet*. It is my job to brief you on the tricks of the trade that you might need—'

Mackenzie didn't give him a chance to wiggle out and continue with his exposition of the various 'tricks of the trade' that downed aircrew might use to fool their

German captors and aid a possible escape later. He snapped, 'I'm really sorry to interrupt your fascinating disquisition. But time is running out.' He looked pointedly at his wristwatch. 'The war might be over by the time we get started and why do we need to know about escaping when we've not been captured and, as far as I'm concerned, don't intend to be–' he lowered his voice and looked directly at Wingco as if challenging him – 'unless you want to inform us of something to the contrary.'

Abruptly the RAF officer looked deflated and very old. Mackenzie saw him that moment for what he was: a retread from the Old War, feeling that he was doing an important job briefing the young men flying out to do battle, while he remained safely behind in a nice warm mess, smoking his pipe and nursing his pint. In reality he was just a minor bureaucrat, who would soon be put out to pasture again in some bloody awful suburb, clinging to his old rank and knowing all that awaited him was boredom and the release from old age by death. Mackenzie relented. He said, the anger gone from his voice now, 'Sorry for rabbiting on like that, Wingco. But you can understand our impatience. We've got a lot on our plate and we want to get on with it before this show is finally over.'

Campbell 175 looked at his boss out of the

corner of his eye. This business seemed to be mellowing him. A couple of months before, Mackenzie would not have been so kind to the old man and his bloody 'tricks of the trade'. Or was the boss simply bloody fed up to the back teeth of the whole business? It had been going on just too long.

The Wingco recovered. 'I take your point, Major.' He raised his voice, but the defeat still remained in his faded grey eyes. 'Right. This is the drill. You are going to be shot down over Central Germany – or so it will seem. We're going to fix a kite so that it appears to have been badly hit, forcing the crew – you two – to hit the silk. We've done it before.'

'And when are we going to be hit and bale out – more importantly, *why* are we going to do so, Wingco?'

'All right,' the sergeant-fitter was shouting outside. 'NAAFI tea-van's up. Fall out, you lot of pregnant penguins and get yer char. Ten minutes – no more. You heard me, Chalky White, ten minutes, just hark on.' The rear of the Lancaster's four engines died away and abruptly a heavy silence descended upon the field outside. It seemed to emphasize the sudden brooding quality of the mood inside the little freezing Nissen hut.

For what appeared a long while, the old RAF Intelligence officer didn't reply. Then he said, voice barely audible, 'You're scheduled for a daylight op on Jena tomorrow.'

'And then?' Mackenzie asked.

'The drop will be faked. You and Campbell here will be the two who will bale out.'

'And then?' Mackenzie persisted, iron in his voice now.

Campbell caught his breath, wanting to know why they were going to fake a drop and at the same time not wanting to do so.

Winco said, 'Off the record?'

'Off the record,' Mackenzie echoed, not taking his gaze off the old man.

'You'll get sealed orders tomorrow when you're on the Lanc. But this much I can tell you – again off the record.'

'Go on.'

'You are going to let yourselves be taken prisoner. But you have to look the genuine article to the Huns who capture you. Hence the buttons, handkerchieves and the like. But you *have* to be captured.'

'Why?'

Wingco shook his greying head slowly. ' 'Fraid I can't tell you that. That'll be in your sealed orders. But I know this. The PM gave the order for you to carry out this mission of yours, whatever it is, personally.'

Outside the sergeant-fitter blew his whistle. 'Get fell in now. ... Come on, Chalky, get that frigging rock bun down yer and move it.'

Presumably 'Chalky' moved it. There was the stamp of boots marching in unison down the gravelled walk next to the flight path. The sound faded into the distance, then there was silence, leaving the three of them staring at each other, frozen into their postures like cheap characters at the end of the third act of a fourth-rate melodrama...

Two

Somewhere a gramophone was playing the 'Boogie-Woogie Bugle Boy from Company B'. It was accompanied by the sizzle of frying bacon and sausages. For there'd be a big breakfast for the aircrews after the briefing, that is for those who could eat it.

Inside the briefing room, the crews stared at the red string, illuminated by spotlights in the ceiling, stretched from North Yorkshire, across the North Sea and then on to the heart of what was left of Germany. The senior Intelligence officer let them gaze at the route for a moment or two and then tapped the map with his long pointer. 'Jena ... your primary today.'

There were low whistles from the surprised aircrews and someone at the back said in an Aussie accent, 'Strewth! ... That's on the other side of the ruddy world.'

Campbell and Mackenzie said nothing. They felt totally out of place among these young fliers from all over the Empire. Besides if anyone knew they wouldn't be coming back this day, it was the two

Intelligence men. They had nothing to lose. So they sat on the hard wooden chairs and listened.

'Your aiming point is the centre of the optics factory – here,' the Intelligence officer went on, tapping the map again with his pointer. 'We have been informed it is a vital target. Knock it out and the Jerry war industry will be blinded. Their tanks, cannon, planes etc. will be without their essential optics.'

The information didn't impress the young men. Someone groaned in mock anguish, 'D'yer think I can get an immediate transfer to the Pay Corps.' Someone else warbled, *'My eyes are dim, I cannot see, I have not brought my specs with me.'*

The Intelligence officer ignored the comments. He said, 'We're going in in two boxes, Yankee-style. One will cross the Dutch coast south of Texel at zero plus ten. The other will follow at zero plus twenty. All planes will carry Tokio tanks due to the distance...'

Someone touched Mackenzie on the shoulder. He started. It was a senior flight sergeant. He said in a whisper as the briefing continued, 'There's a wingco outside from Air Marshal Harris's HQ to see you, sir. Urgent.'

Mackenzie nodded to Campbell. They rose and all around them the jeers rose immediately as a young voice cried out, 'You tailend Charleys got the wind up already? We'll have to get an extra Elsan for you.' He meant what the aircrews called among themselves very crudely 'the shit bucket'.

Mackenzie felt himself go red, but he controlled himself. They were young men perhaps going to their deaths this day. They could be forgiven almost anything. Together, he and Campbell 175 pushed their way past the raised knees and followed the flight sergeant outside to where an immaculate wing commander was waiting beside a camouflaged staff car. Surprisingly he was wearing a service revolver around his waist.

They snapped to attention and saluted.

The staff officer returned their salute stiffly, as if he were on the parade ground and demanded, 'ID, please.'

A little surprised, they produced their cards and the other officer examined them at some length. Finally he said, 'All right.' He snapped his fingers at the young pilot officer waiting in the staff car. He jumped out immediately and Mackenzie was surprised to see that not only was he armed, but he was also carrying a briefcase chained to his left wrist. Mackenzie told himself this was it. These were the all-important sealed orders they had been expecting.

They were. The wing commander said, 'In

a moment, you'll sign for these orders as Air Marshal Harris has commanded. He has instructed me to tell you that they must not be opened and read until your plane is airborne. Is that clearly understood?'

Mackenzie was too intrigued to attempt to reply in his usual caustic manner. Instead he contented himself with, 'Yes, understood, Wing Commander.'

'Good.' The staff officer nodded to his subordinate.

He undid the chain and handed the briefcase to his superior. The latter produced a key, also attached by a thin chain to his belt, opened the case and brought out an official brown enveloped, which had been sealed and then crossed twice with a thick blue pencil. With it he produced a form. 'Please sign,' he ordered.

Hastily Mackenzie did so and was handed the envelope. 'You understand, don't you,' the wing commander repeated severely, 'not to be opened till you are airborne. You will then destroy the order.' Then, surprisingly enough, he snapped to attention and saluted the two pseudo pilot officers before returning to the staff car, leaving Campbell 175 to gasp with astonishment, 'Holy cow, sir, he actually *saluted* us. Oh, my aching back, the condemned man ate a hearty breakfast.'

'That he did,' Mackenzie agreed. 'Well,

come on, let's tuck into those eggs and bacon. You never know, they might be the last we scoff for quite some while.' And for once Campbell 175 had no smart retort at the ready...

They crossed the Dutch coast an hour later. Breaking out of the low cloud over the North Sea they were dazzled momentarily by the blood-red ball of the sun lying on the horizon. It was a beautiful spectacle after the dull greyness of the cloud over the water. But neither Mackenzie nor Campbell at the back of the aircraft just behind the regular 'tailend Charley' in his revolving turret were struck by the beauty of the moment. They were still digesting the contents of that order which had been passed on to them via Bomber Harris.

It had been brief and very formal. It had read: 'You will proceed, using your own resources, to Colditz. There you will search out all traces of the Dalby affair. This is imperative. Any risk can be taken.' The message had been unsigned – indeed there was none of the usual officialese to identify its sources. But Mackenzie had reasoned that there was only one person who could have penned the order.

'The old man – Winnie – Winston Churchill,' he had exclaimed to Campbell 175 as the latter burned and shredded the charred embers ever the Elsan bucket, which reeked

– as yet – of Jeyes Fluid, only.

'But what does it really mean?' Campbell had asked, puzzled to the extreme. 'I mean – proceed to Colditz ... and search out all traces of Dalby?'

'I think it means we are supposed to be taken prisoner and then make such a nuisance of ourselves that we will be transferred there. After all, Colditz is supposed to be called the "bad boys' prison". So we've got to make bad boys of ourselves.'

'OK, I'll buy that. But what are the traces we're supposed to find? I mean, the man who killed your Major Dalby can't still be inside Colditz, can he? Is that what the PM means? And if he does, how can this, sir, stop the Yankee plot?'

But Mackenzie had no time to reflect on how he might answer this overwhelming question. For now the first flak was blossoming up all around them in bursts of even more brilliant scarlet light. Shrapnel pattered against the Lancaster's fuselage like pecks from some gigantic predatory bird. Immediately the pilot took violent evasive action, throwing the heavy four-engined bomber all over the sky, or so it seemed to the two fledgling air gunners. Behind them a Lancaster was hit. For a moment it seemed to stop in mid-air, as if it had run into an invisible wall. Then the port wing broke off and went whirling down to the ground like a huge metal leaf. Almost instantly it went into its dive of death. No one baled out and then their own pilot had shaken off the flak and they were closing up to the rest of the formation, flying on majestically, as if nothing at all had happened.

They crossed the Belgian–German frontier. Below the territory was in the hands of the victorious Allies by now and the crew knew they could relax. The flight engineer went to the bucket in a great hurry and Mackenzie could see he was shaken and frightened. The 'tailend Charley', a mere boy of nineteen, spun his turret round after asking the skipper's permission and they opened the thermos and poured him a cup of hot coffee. His own hands, despite the electrically heated gloves he wore, seemed too cold to open the flask. The boy gulped the coffee down, winked and hurried back to his turret. Campbell 175 shook his head and shouted above the roar of the engines, 'What a frigging life, sir!' He indicated the air gunner, already scanning the sky once more for the first sight of enemy fighters.

Mackenzie nodded, but said nothing. What was the use? he asked himself. The war was still raging. The god Mars still had need of his doomed youth. They flew on, heading north-east. Below, the earth was silent, but there was an uncanny brooding feel about it. There was trouble ahead,

Mackenzie could sense it – lots of bloody trouble.

The Rhine came up out of the ground mist. It glistened like a sluggish silver snake as it wound its way through the Rhenish plain. It was over a week now since Montgomery had forced it with his great crossing, but there was still activity down there. Through the drifting low cloud, Mackenzie and Campbell 175 could see the tiny figures of engineers working on new Bailey bridges over the river, with long lines of military vehicles of all types crowded on the western bank, waiting to be transported to the other side and the battle beyond. A couple of Spitfires guarding the bridgehead from possible German air attack came up and buzzed the fleet of bombers but in the end, as the Lancasters ploughed steadily towards the River Elbe, they waggled their wings in farewell and zoomed back to the Rhine. Now the two Intelligence men knew they were approaching their objective. They'd better prepare for what was to come, once the flight engineer had dropped the canister which could imitate the impact of a shell hitting the Lancaster and setting it alight. They set about struggling into their parachutes.

But everything turned out differently from how 'Bomber' Harris and his planners had anticipated at their underground headquarters in the Home Counties. Over the Elbe a slight mist had formed concealing the artillery duel taking place down there between advancing American troops and the hard-pressed last-ditch German defenders. Thus it was that, surrounded by swirling grey fog, the head RAF squadron was caught by surprise as the first Messerschmitt 262 jets came barrelling in at well over 600 m.p.h., cannon thumping away, tracer shells hurtling at ever-increasing speed towards the sluggish, slow-moving four-engined bombers.

'Bandits at—' the pilot called over the radio and broke off, as he ducked instinctively, as the first burst of cannon fire ripped the length of the Lancaster's fuselage. It was an unquestionable signal for the battle to commence. For now there seemed to be the latest German jets everywhere, attempting to break up the British formations and destroy their massed gun power.

In an instant all was crazy confusion. Radio messages crackled back and forth. 'Yellow noses twelve o'clock high ... Gunner ... gunner, for Chrissake, lead him in ... Here Tango One ... bailing out ... Tango—' From all sides red and white tracer zipped back and forth like flights of angry hornets. The first aircraft was hit. The crew bailed out. What looked like a ball came flying past Mackenzie's Lancaster. It was a severed head, complete with flying helmet and earphones. A jet was hit. It staggered on a few metres, black smoke pouring from its fuselage. Desperately the pilot tried to open the canopy. It wouldn't budge. Next moment the Messerschmitt exploded in a flash of blinding scarlet light. When it cleared there was nothing there save shards of silver metal.

Frantically their own skipper broke formation. It didn't matter really; the Germans had already penetrated it. The Lancasters' air gunners could no longer bring massed fire to bear on their attackers for fear they might hit their own comrades. He took the great bomber down in a steep, terrifying dive that had her shaking at every rivet. Campbell 175 turned a ghastly white. Mackenzie nudged him hard. 'Get that parachute on,' he yelled above the deafening roar.

'Sir,' Campbell answered thickly, as if he were trying to choke back hot vomit. With fingers that felt like clumsy sausages, he started to fix the straps of the chute. Mackenzie did the same.

The pilot's desperate evasive action was failing. One of the twin-engine jets now clung to the Lancaster's tail. Its pilot pumped shell after 20mm. shell at the fleeing bomber. Desperately the boy 'tailend Charley' attempted to fend the German pilot off.

In vain. He was eager for a kill. He hung on, firing burst after burst. The rear turret perspex shattered in a glittering spider's web. Blinded, the tail gunner reeled back, his face looking suddenly as if someone had thrown a handful of strawberry jam at it. Campbell made as if to go and haul the blinded boy, who was moaning piteously, out of his shattered turret. Mackenzie caught him just in time. 'No,' he yelled, face contorted and scarlet, the veins sticking out at his threat. 'No time for that ... leave him, and that's an order!'

The Lancaster lurched. The bomb aimer had released his bombs. Lightened immediately, the diving bomber's speed increased. Below, the bombs exploded over some stricken burning village. But the measure didn't help. The German fighter pilot clung to the Lancaster. Now the bomber was taking impossible punishment. Its outer port engine was shattered. To starboard both engines were pouring out thick black smoke. She was flying literally on one engine. The fuselage was now ripped apart, with the wind howling through shell holes everywhere and in the cockpit the red warning lights were flashing their urgent alarm. The Lancaster was not going to survive the impossible dive.

But the pilot's voice when it came over the intercom, though distorted, was very calm.

He said, as if he did this sort of thing every day, 'All right, chaps, this is it, I'm afraid ... Bale out now. God bless you ... Bale out *NOW!*'

Three

The big bomber gave a series of gigantic lurches. The two Intelligence men held on for dear life. At the controls, the pilot, his face lathered with sweat, fought to keep the Lancaster airborne. They had already pushed the blinded tailend Charley out. Now the flight engineer, dragging his shattered leg, the bone gleaming like polished ivory in its red-gore hole behind him, was following. With a howl of sheer agony, he flopped out of the plane, the wind cutting off his cry immediately. Now it was their turn. Mackenzie cupped his free hand around his mouth and yelled as the wind plucked at his words, 'You first ... me straight after ... stick together ... avoid the others ... Good luck.' With that, holding on to the fuselage for dear life, he gave Campbell 175 a mighty kick in the seat. The younger man flew out of the plane.

At the controls, the pilot gave up. He slumped over the controls and began to sob, his shoulders heaving as if he were heartbroken. For a moment Mackenzie was tempted to go and help him. The man had simply collapsed. He needed aid. Then he thought better of it. His mission was more important. He hesitated a mere fraction of a section longer, the fierce wind plucking at his overalls. Then he took a deep breath. Next instant he launched himself into space.

Instantly the breath was dragged forcibly from his lungs. He gasped and choked. He was falling at a tremendous rate. For a moment he panicked. Would his chute never open? Was he going to die as a 'Roman candle', as the aircrew called it. No! With a tremendous crack, the canopy blossomed open. It was as if his arms were being dragged from their sockets. He yelped with pain. Next moment that frightening descent ceased. Above him the canopy opened fully and he was drifting down silently, gently. He swung from side to side. He caught glimpses of dark fir forests marching up and down the hillsides like spike-helmeted Prussian grenadiers. Here and there there were patches of frozen snow still. He pulled at the shroud lines. The wild oscillation ceased. Above him he could see the rest of the Lancasters sailing on to Jena, with a couple of stragglers, trailing black smoke against the hard blue of the April sky, turning and heading back home.

Now the ground was looming up ever

closer. Mackenzie threw a look to left and right. The countryside seemed deserted. Not that he wanted to be found by the enemy, but he knew he must. Still he reasoned that someone would spot the downed Lancaster and there'd be German patrols out soon enough, looking for its crew. He craned his neck to see if he could see Campbell 175. But his chute had carried him beyond a patch of firs on the slight rise to his right and he was now out of sight. But Campbell would soon get his bearings and find him, he told himself. As they said in German, Campbell hadn't fallen in his mouth; he was a smart chap. So he concentrated on landing safely, as he had been taught to do.

He clapped his legs together. At the same time, he kept his knees slightly bent so that the impact wouldn't be too much of a shock for his lower limbs. It would be fatal if he broke a leg now. He was veering to the firs. Hastily he pulled at his shroud lines. But it was too late. He hit the firs. They tore and lashed at his body. He yelped as a prickly branch slashed his cheek. Then he was submerged in the penetrating smell of firs. Next moment he hit the ground at their base and hardly felt the impact. The firs had broken his fall.

All the same he was winded. Thus for a few moments he lay there, swamped in the deflated chute, fighting a little to recover his breath. There was hardly any sound now, except the soft rustle of the breeze in the tops of the firs and the dying drone of the Lancasters as they headed for Jena. He might have been the last man left alive on earth.

'But you aren't,' he told himself. 'Now get that digit out of the orifice and move it.' Obeying his own advice, he started to free himself from the parachute harness and prepared to conceal it. After all, he wanted the Germans to think he was a genuine escaper, ready, once he'd freed himself, to make a run for it back to the American lines on the Elbe.

But even as he scraped the chute together and had begun kicking foliage over the limp silk, he could already hear the baying of the dogs and the shouts of the searchers. The Germans were quick off the mark. They had their search parties out already. He shrugged. Soon he'd have to face up to them. He prayed they wouldn't be a lot of hot-headed Hitler Youth fanatics who'd shoot first and ask questions afterwards. These days the kids in their short black pants were the only real fanatics left in an almost beaten Third Reich.

'*Zu mir Leute!*' The command alerted Mackenzie to the fact that they were on the other side of the wood now. He touched the fountain pen, his only weapon, and prayed he wouldn't have to use it – yet.

They caught Campbell 175 first. He was still struggling with his chute, billowing in the breeze that swept across the open ground, when they appeared, almost as if from nowhere. One minute they weren't there; the next they were. In the lead was a fat policeman in his green uniform and leather helmet. He was shaking as if with rage and in his fat paw his pistol trembled dangerously. But it wasn't the fat cop that frightened Campbell, it was the man and couple of women behind him.

They were all heavily armed, bandoliers of machine-gun ammunition criss-crossing their chests, stick grenades thrust down the sides of their jackboots, carbines and machine pistols at the ready in their dirty paws. That in itself was frightening enough, but it was the tarnished silver numerals and death's head badge on the battered rakish caps which frightened the former German Jew the most. He had seen the insignia often enough in the days when he had been on the run, with, it had seemed, every man's hand against him. It was the badge of Himmler's ruthless and fanatical killers – the SS!

At the same moment, slowly and carefully, very carefully, Mackenzie started to raise his hands. *'Hande hoch,'* the fat cop shrieked. *'Hande hoch, du Luftterrorist oder isch schiesse!'* Then when he saw that Mackenzie was already raising his hands, he looked puzzled and, turning to the SS mob, raised his shoulders, as if querying what he should do next.

A scar-faced sergeant, minus his helmet, but with a bloody bandage wrapped around his forehead, shoved the fat cop out of the way. *'Weg da, Opa,'* he growled. 'Get out of my way, granddad. ... You,' he pointed his machine pistol at Mackenzie threateningly, '–hand over your cigarettes – *quick!'*

Mackenzie fumbled in his overall for a packet of Players in his inside pocket. There was no use fooling with the SS NCO. He looked the type who might well shoot an unarmed man for a single cigarette. He found the packet and handed it to the NCO. He smelled the cigarettes and said to the others, *'Echt Virginia Tabac, Kameraden! Prima...'* He tossed the packet to the nearest woman, a fat blonde, whose enormous breasts threatened, it seemed, to burst the buttons of her dirty, soiled tunic at any moment. She caught it neatly, took a cigarette and tossed the packet on to the rest, who were staring at their prisoner as if he were an alien creature who might just as well have fallen from outer space.

Not the NCO with the Schmeisser though. His red-rimmed eyes were full of hate and suddenly an alarmed Mackenzie realized that his very life was hanging by a thread. This roving band of SS were killers. They weren't the kind who took prisoners. Why should they? Once Germany lost the war, which it soon would, they were the quarry, hunted down by the Allies, probably with no quarter given.

Slowly the NCO raised his machine pistol. He clicked off the safety with a loud metallic sound. He grinned, displaying a set of gold teeth, enjoying the spectacle of the growing fear reflected in the prisoner's face. Mackenzie knew he had to do something – and something quick. He flashed a glance around the mob. Not one of them seemed to be startled by the sound of the catch being raised. It appeared they'd already guessed their NCO was going to shoot the prisoner.

The SS man raised the pistol. He tapped the magazine to check if it was firmly in place. Mackenzie felt a cold bead of sweat begin to trickle down the small of his back unpleasantly. He realized he had only moments to live. He had to act. He looked at the red-faced cop. He was his only chance. 'There's another one of us – over there,' he croaked, hardly recognizing his own voice, 'beyond the trees!'

It worked.

The fat cop tried to reassert his authority. He said, 'Did you hear the prisoner? ...

There's another air gangster over there.' Probably the policeman was too stupid to realize that Mackenzie had just spoken to him in fluent German. 'We must take him, too.'

'*Jawohl*,' the fat woman with the enormous breasts, who was scratching her loins, as if she might be lousy, agreed, 'we must take him. He might have more of these splendid cancer sticks.' She indicated the cigarette stuck behind her right ear.

A look of indecision passed over the NCO's villainous face. Mackenzie held his breath. Would his little trick work? It did. The NCO lowered his machine pistol slightly, and half turning, said: 'All right then, let's find the other Tommy bastard. Then I can shoot both of 'em together.' He laughed coarsely and the others joined in. Without looking at Mackenzie, he commanded '*Mitkommen!*'

It was the last thing he ever did. In a flash Mackenzie had the little fountain-pen pistol out of his pocket and had fired. At that range he could not miss. There was the soft hiss of compressed air and the softer *thwack* of a tiny .22 bullet striking flesh. The next instant the NCO was stumbling forward, dead before he struck the damp ground...

Four

The rickety wood-burning German truck bumped and chugged its way up the rutted hillside track to Oflag VIII. Handcuffed in the open back, watched by two guards armed with captured Russian tommy guns, Mackenzie and Campbell 175, both bruised and bloody about the face from their recent beating, stared at the hilltop camp.

It seemed typical of the POW camps which dotted Germany in 1945: several acres of mud shaped in the form of a hexagon by triple electric-wire fences. These four-metre-high fences were presided over by stork-legged wooden towers guarded by elderly or formerly severely wounded *Wehrmacht* soldiers, who manned the searchlights and machine guns. In between the two outer fences, fierce Alsatian dogs prowled on a moveable chain ready to go for any would-be escaper's throat – or testicles.

Inside the hexagon there were lines of neat wooden huts on low stilts so that the guards or 'goons', as the POWs called them, could probe under them with their long metal-detector rods, looking for contraband or escape tunnels. Now everywhere in the compound, skinny men in a variety of army and air-force uniforms wandered about slowly – for they were too starved and weak to move fast – enjoying the first rays of the weak April sunshine. As Campbell 175 remarked through bruised and thickly swollen lips, 'A real home from home, sir.'

To which Mackenzie, who was still hurting too from the beating he had received before the SS mob had handed them over to the Luftwaffe officers, contented himself with a nod. For he was not only sore, but worried too. In the confusion before they had been handed over by their rescuers, the *Luftwaffe*, to be sent to the *Oflag*, there had been no mention of the SS NCO whom he had shot. But soon, he knew, it would reach the camp and what would happen then? He felt he knew. In the state the last remaining part of Germany in Nazi hands was in, they might just shoot him and Campbell out of hand. Now, it appeared to him, the sooner they got out of the *Oflag* and on their way to Colditz, with its high-ranking prisoners being held as hostages by the Nazis, the safer it would be for the two of them. Now Colditz might well be their only hope to stay alive till the war ended with an Allied victory.

The gates swung open slowly and the

handful of scruffy guards held back the POWs crowding forward to look at the 'new boys' and presumably pump them for the latest news of the war. Gasping as if on its last legs, the truck, moved on and deposited them and their guards in front of the '*Lagerbüro*', the camp office.

Here they were surrounded by a motley crowd of British officer POWs in clothing ranging from RAF uniforms, complete with medal ribbons, to ragged civvies, and clogs made of wood. But in spite of their clothing and starved, pinched faces, which gave their eyes a wild bulging look, the POWs were, Mackenzie could see, in great heart; they hadn't lost their fighting spirit and that pleased him no end. He felt a renewal of hope. These men would help him and Campbell to do a bunk as soon as possible; he knew that implicitly.

'*Meine Herren ... bitte meine Herren*,' said a tall sergeant, with his right arm missing and the black wound medal prominent on his chest, forcing his way through the throng, adding 'Please, English gentlemen ... you are officers.' The remark was met by a series of jeers and wet raspberries, but still the POWs moved back to let the two 'new boys' through.

Five minutes later they found themselves in a wooden shower room, where the one-armed NCO informed them in his accented

English, 'Off with ze clothes. You will wash.' He indicated the showers. 'Then you vill be searched, yes?'

'Yes,' they agreed as one, while Mackenzie flashed Campbell 175 a warning book. The latter nodded. He still possessed their only weapon: something they might well need soon.

The search of their upper bodies, hair and ears was routine and swift. Then came their lower halves, something which seemed to embarrass the German *Feldwebel*. 'I am now searching your private pieces,' he declared, while behind him a dim-looking private began examining their discarded uniforms. 'I do not like. But *Befehl ist Befehl*.' 'Orders are orders.' He cleared his throat, holding his hand in front of his mouth very politely. 'You vill now bend please.'

They bent and the NCO groped their bottoms in embarrassment. It was then that Campbell 175 pulled his trick, which Mackenzie couldn't have done in a thousand years. In the same instant that the NCO began to fumble with his anus and the dim-looking private picked up the lethal fountain pen and unscrewed the cap, Campbell farted. It was loud and wet. The NCO jumped as if he'd suddenly been shot. His face flushed an angry red. '*Du Schwein!*' he exploded, '*Du Dreckschwein!*' He shook his hand, as if it might well be dangerously contaminated. 'What for an English gentleman are you?'

Campbell 175 gave him a careful smile, while his eyes followed the private's every movement. 'Sorry, old chap ... Call of nature ... Just couldn't hold it in any more. One of those things, what,' he added airily.

The NCO wasn't impressed. Perhaps he didn't understand the words. Instead he bellowed at the private, still holding that killer pen in his pudgy hand stupidly. '*Abfuhren!* Take the swine out of my sight at once.'

Minutes later they were back in their uniforms, pen returned, and being released into the compound. For the time being they were safe, but even as they were summoned to meet the Senior British Officer for an initial briefing, they both knew they were living on borrowed time. That murder of the SS thug would catch up with them sooner or later; they were both sure of that...

Colonel Ryder, grey-haired, clipped old-fashioned moustache, collar and faded khaki uniform well pressed (by means of a can of hot water used as an iron), looked exactly how an old-style regular army man was supposed to. Instantly Mackenzie knew he could tell Ryder only so much; he'd flap if he knew the two of them were killers. Still he needed the old man's help if he were going to get out of the camp and into

Colditz as soon as possible. For a while, he knew, he'd have to bide his time while he tried to ascertain just how far the old boy might be prepared to go.

Ryder offered them a cup of tea politely enough – 'Sorry, no sugar, chaps. Precious as gold these days.' Then he made a fuss of lighting his pipe, filled with a mixture of cigarette ends and dried tea-leaves and puffed away happily, while he watched them sip the scaldingly hot, bitter tea. After a while he took the old pipe out of his mouth, fussed again with it, tapping the bowl, puffing through the mouthpiece before saying. 'Naturally, chaps, it's your duty as officers to make an escape. But things have become damned different since the early days when the Boche were damned sporting about escaping.'

Mackenzie could have groaned at the expression. Ryder made it sound like bloody public schoolboys' high jinks. But aloud he contented himself with saying, 'I understand, sir ... and we will try to do our duty.'

'Good show. But, as I said, the Boche have become bloody-minded since they know they're losing the war. Half the chaps in this camp have marched to and fro all over Germany since January when the Russkis invaded – and the Boche didn't treat the poor chaps with kid gloves, I can assure you. If they fell out of the column, the guards finished them off with bayonets or if they were lucky with a bullet at the back of the head. Definitely bad show. But there you are. Fact of life.' He took up the pipe and gave it a trial puff. Satisfied that it was drawing properly, he lit it again and paused.

Next to Campbell 175, Mackenzie stepped in, knowing that if the old regular went on much longer like this, Campbell would put his foot in it by making some sort of snide remark or other. He said, 'We'll take the risk, sir. But we're fit and would like to have a go. Perhaps you could give us some help.'

Ryder's weathered face cracked into a wintry smile. 'Of course, old chap. My job to do so. But as SBO, I can't be seen getting too close to you escaping types. The Kommandant wouldn't like it, you know. Better give you over to the Escape Officer, Ramsbotham.'

As if he might well have been listening outside the door of the SBO's quarters, there was a quick knock and even as Ryder snapped, 'Enter,' Captain Ramsbotham, Royal Army Service Corps, appeared and clicked to attention with a curt 'Sir'.

He looked at the two Intelligence men and said, 'Hello, chaps.' He didn't offer to shake hands. Mackenzie for his part took an immediate dislike to him. It wasn't because he was an old-school regular like Colonel

Ryder, it was because Ramsbotham had a smug, self-satisfied air about him – and in view of what the SBO had just told them, Ramsbotham looked surprisingly well fed. Indeed he was almost plump, his cheeks red and healthy-looking with none of the prisoner greyness of most of his fellow POWs. Ramsbotham, Mackenzie concluded, had some means of getting close to a well-filled trough. He frowned.

Ramsbotham turned back to Ryder. 'Searched their gear, sir. Nothing untoward.'

Ryder explained. 'We've always got to be on the lookout for Boche stooges, planted on us. The Boche will go to any lengths to find out what's going on. We have to take our precautions. All of us have been through it. Standard Operating Procedure, you know.'

'Yessir,' Mackenzie and Campbell 175 replied as one, but both of them didn't like the fact that the fat, well-nourished RASC officer had searched their bits and pieces without their knowledge. Mackenzie, for his part, made a snap decision there and then. Ryder was harmless, but he wasn't so sure about Ramsbotham. Whatever plans for escape they now developed, Mackenzie told himself, he wouldn't entrust them to Ryder and Ramsbotham...

'Sheep's Arse,' the tall, half-starved Com-

mando officer said contemptuously. 'Sheep's Arse.' He spat in the mud of the compound. 'That sleek bugger couldn't escape out of a wet brown-paper bag even if you gave him a pair of scissors!'

The three of them squatted in the evil-smelling latrine with the spring rain beating down like a drum roll on the tin roof of the place. Outside, the compound was a sea of mud. It was empty too, save for some miserable middle-aged guards trudging around, their rifles slung over their bent shoulders. To Mackenzie, it looked like a minor version of Dante's Hell, from which there was no escape, though he knew there had to be for them. They didn't have much time left.

It was for that reason he had sought out the lanky Commando officer, captured in the Normandy landings and now a veteran of nearly ten months in the camps. Commandos, Mackenzie knew, had been specially trained in escaping. But although the tough soldier, with a nasty bullet-wound scar running the length of his right cheek, had been eager to help, his information had not been very encouraging.

'I'm a bit of a new boy like you two,' he had told them when Mackenzie had approached them in the 'senior officers' crapper', reserved on Ryder's orders for officers above the rank of major. 'I've cased the place. There are opportunities, but not many here have the mentality for escaping – and Sheep's Arse–' he meant Ramsbotham – 'isn't exactly enthusiastic.'

'I'd gathered that myself,' Mackenzie had agreed. 'But go on.'

'The wire's negative. There are no tools available, or so Sheep's Arse says. Besides–' the Commando had shuddered dramatically – 'there are those bloody hounds. They could make a right mess of a bloke's family jewels.'

Campbell 175 had laughed in a shaky sort of a way and he closed his naked upper legs hastily.

'Tunnel?' Mackenzie had queried.

'Again tools and it would take too long,' the Commando had replied. 'Besides, this Elbe soil is mostly sand. You'd need plenty of timber to shore it up – and as it is, most of the bunks' wooden slats have gone into the stoves for heat and cooking.'

For a moment or two, the three had lapsed into a gloomy silence while the rain beat miserably on the tin roof above them, dropping on to the mud floor through the joints.

'Any ideas then?' Mackenzie asked.

'Damned well fly,' the Commando had suggested, a wry grin on his lean face. 'I heard of a bloke at the another camp who—' He didn't finish his story. For at that moment no less a person than 'Sheep's Arse' himself appeared at the open door of the latrine, clad in a waterproof, munching a sandwich and carrying a roll of real lavatory paper in his other hand. He stopped short at the sight of the three officers crouched there miserably, slacks around their ankles, his plump face worried for a moment. Obviously he hadn't anticipated anyone being here in the pouring rain. Then he recovered quickly and smiled. 'Having a little chat?' he asked and swallowed the rest of his big sandwich, which dripped with hot fat and smelled deliciously of roast pork.

'No.' Campbell 175 could not stop himself. 'We were just having a sly wank together.'

It was in that instant, as Sheep's Arse's face flushed an angry red, that Mackenzie had his idea. 'I say,' the Escape Officer snapped, 'there's no need for that kind of filth, even in here.' With that, he sniffed, clutched his precious German toilet paper more firmly in his fat hand and stalked off to the rearline of thunderboxes, as if he couldn't stand being close to them. As he went, the Commando gave a fat raspberry and quipped in what he thought was a feminine falsetto, 'Oh, do excuse my breaking wind like that. It'll be the rich food the kind Germans feed us on.'

The two Intelligence men laughed, though both of them, in reality, had never felt less like laughing...

Five

For the next twenty-four hours or so, the hasty plan started to evolve and mature in Mackenzie's mind. Outside it rained and rained and rained, as though some god on high had decided he'd had enough of the crazy, war-torn world below and intended to obliterate it in one great flood. But despite the persistent heavy rain, now and again Mackenzie could hear the muted rumble of the permanent barrage in the distance and told himself, with a sudden sense of urgency, that the coming battle was getting ever closer.

By now he had concluded that Sheep's Arse was working with the Germans. Twice he had watched him with the one-armed *Feldwebel* who dealt with the POWs and both times he had been eating greedily, jaws working overtime. Mackenzie surmised that in return for those special rations which kept the RASC officer nice and plump (in contrast to his wretchedly skinny fellow POWs living on a diet of potato soup and two thin slices of black bread smeared with artificial honey a day), the Englishman passed on information about his fellows. After all as Escape Officer, Ramsbotham was in the best position to know about any impending trouble in the *Oflag*.

Naturally he would not consider himself a traitor. He wasn't actually *betraying* anyone. He was just warning the Germans to nip any POW trouble in the bud. For Ramsbotham believed in a better future for his fellow Englishman. He openly proclaimed that he considered 'when victory is achieved, it'll be our turn to run the old country. Churchill'll be out. Then our people – Bevin, Bevan, Mr Attlee will be running things. We'll have a National Education Act, better schooling for all. A Welfare State, National Health. Why,' Ramsbotham had breathed in awe to his bored audience of younger officers, 'only the other day, Mr Beveridge said, according to the *Daily Herald* that for four shillings and tenpence a week paid in, each working man will never have to worry about the future again. What d'you think of that?'

No, Captain Ramsbotham wanted to see a British victory and the Brave New World to come all right. What he didn't want was to risk his own health and perhaps life achieving it. As Mackenzie told Campbell 175 grimly, 'There's a lot of the treacherous buggers around, you know. The more of 'em we get rid of now, the more likely we might even see a little bit of that bloody Brave New World of theirs...' Campbell forced a grin. 'Unfortunately,' Mackenzie went on, 'that bloody so-called security officer, Sheep's Arse, is out to prevent us escaping. With him in charge of security we'll never get out of Oflag VIII. We won't be able to make enough attempts to be transferred to Colditz. So, we'll just have to break out for real – and then break in.'

'Break in where?' Campbell asked puzzled.

'Where everybody else was trying to break out. ... Colditz, old friend. We'll be the only two Kriegies in World War Two who actually broke *into* Colditz.' And he began to laugh. But it wasn't a pleasant sound. For half a moment, Campbell thought his old chief had gone crackers – absolutely *meschugge*...

On the morning of 2 April, 1945, Mackenzie and Campbell 175 set their plan into motion. It was still raining hard and they were happy it was. It would keep the guards under cover and the POWs confined to their crowded huts, thick with cigarette smoke and the stink of unwashed, sick bodies. Boldly, they approached Sheep's Arse as he was leaving Ryder's quarters and whispered without any preamble, 'We're going under the wire tonight. We want your help.'

Sheep's Arse's mouth fell open like that of

some dumb village yokel. 'What ... what did you say?' he choked.

They repeated their request.

He looked at them as if they had suddenly gone mad. 'But didn't you hear the guns last night? It can't be much longer till the Yanks are here, man.'

'We can't wait,' Mackenzie replied. 'The place here is driving us crackers. We're going tonight.'

The traitor could see it was no use reasoning with them. So he said, 'And how am I supposed to help you, eh? I have no tools, no German currency, no extra concentrated food. You know the situation here. We're down to rock bottom.'

'I know. But we could use your help all the same. The Jerries trust you, we know.'

Sheep's Arse shot them a quick glance, but their faces revealed nothing. He decided Mackenzie had simply made a statement of fact. 'Go on,' he said.

'We want you to get us as far as the gate, the back one near the latrines. With you there, they won't suspect anything.'

'And then?'

Mackenzie shook his head. 'Better you don't know, old chap,' he answered with fake friendliness. 'We don't want to land you in the shit afterwards. So what you don't know, can't be held against you.'

At that moment the two Intelligence men

could almost see Sheep's Arse's brain working, the wheels and gears clicking and churning, as he figured out how he could profit from the attempt of these crazy fools to escape, when the war was almost over bar the shouting. 'All right, it's my job as Escape Officer to help you–'

'To betray you,' a harsh, cynical little voice at the back of Campbell's brain snarled.

'–what do you want me to do?'

'This. As I said, we want you to get us as far as the back gate near the latrines. The prisoners don't use it. Kriegies are only allowed in and out where they can be checked at the main gate.'

'Yes, I know. Get on with it,' Sheep's Arse said impatiently. 'So why are you – *we* – approaching the main gate?'

'Because you suspect something fishy is going on – we'll leave it vague about what. You're marching us to the guard there to report us. Why are you reporting us to the Jerries?' He answered the question swiftly before a puzzled Escape Officer could stop him. 'Because you know the war's about over. You don't want any trouble that could cause any loss of life or any reprisals on the part of Jerries. That sounds logical, doesn't it?'

'Yes, I suppose ... so,' the other man said hesitantly. 'But what are you going to do then? – you said, you're going under the wire. And how do I fit into your plans?' He added quickly, 'I mean if you *do* manage to make a break, it'll be me who has to take the can back. And at this stage of the game, I don't fancy doing that. After all, the Jerries are not above putting me against the wall without trial and shooting me out of hand, especially if one of their people gets hurt.'

'Calm down ... calm down.' Mackenzie attempted to allay his fears. 'The only person who'll get hurt is you.'

'What!'

'Yes, once you engage the guard in conversation, telling him that we are planning to be naughty boys, we sock you – not too hard, but hard enough – so you're out of the game. Later you can say, you knew nothing more.'

Sheep's Arse looked fearful. At the same time, however, his mind seemed to be working, as if he were seriously considering Mackenzie's bold plan. 'All right, let's say that I went ahead with this damnfool scheme of yours, what would you do?'

Campbell 175 answered. He smiled, but his dark eyes didn't light up. Indeed they were full of menace. 'Make a run for it to the Yanks westwards,' he said easily. 'They'll probably be so glad to see a couple of limey heroes like us that they'll feed us steaks and ice cream for a week or two.'

'I see,' Sheep's Arse said thoughtfully,

obviously warming to the idea and Mackenzie felt he knew why. The traitor was going to profit personally from the cock-up which would result from the botched escape attempt that he would ensure it would be. He'd be led to the trough once more and if the Germans decided at the last moment to evacuate the *Oflag* as they had done with other Allied POW camps once the enemy had got too close, if anyone received favourable treatment from the Germans it would be Captain Ramsbotham, Royal Army Service Corps. He'd survive to see the post-war Brave New World, that would be for damned certain.

'All right,' he said finally. 'What do you want me to do?'

Mackenzie wasted no time. It was getting dark earlier than expected. More rain was on its way and the dark threatening clouds were rolling in rapidly from the west and it would be a shame to waste the cover heavy rain would provide. 'This,' he commenced...

It was pouring down. With elemental fury in a solid grey wall, the spring rain slanted into the mud of the compound. On the tin roof of the latrines it rattled and splattered, drowning out any other sound. The huts to which the POWs were now confined by the downpour were only yards away yet the usual noises of mouth organs, shouts, cries of anger were completely cut off. Even the usual murderous growling of the savage, half-wild Alsatians between the lines of barbed wire were drowned out. And with the rain had come a sudden unseasonal coldness. Not that the two men waiting in the stinking shadows of the lines of thunderboxes noticed; they were hot with excitement. Any minute Sheep's Arse was scheduled to make his appearance and then the tense hectic business would commence.

Mackenzie and Campbell 175, their pathetic bits and pieces stowed about their person, knew that they were supposed to be walking into a trap. After their meeting with Sheep's Arse, they had watched him discreetly until an hour or so later he had made contact, with the one-armed *Feldwebel* with his fractured English. They had sheltered in the porch of the *Lagerbüro*, deep in conversation, smoking fitfully, passing a flat bottle of schnapps to one another at regular intervals, planning what they were going to do. And as far as they were concerned, they guessed the one-armed NCO would ensure it was something unpleasant – very unpleasant. What else could the German do? In these last days of the already lost war, any German soldier who failed in his duty could expect to be shot summarily and without trial himself. As they said themselves cynically, it was 'march or croak'. They had no alternative but to carry out their duty to the very end, or else...

Campbell 175 nudged Mackenzie suddenly. 'He's coming,' he hissed and the two of them shrank back further into those evil-smelling shadows. There was indeed the sound of boots slogging through the mud and it could only be their contact. In the huts the POWs could use their own overflowing 'piss buckets' until the rain ceased.

The footsteps stopped. From their hiding place, they could see the Escape Officer outlined in the open door, the sacking which covered it normally pushed back. 'Are you there?' he queried, the rain slashing down with vicious fury behind him. 'Christ, hurry up, I'm getting frigging soaked out here.'

'You'll get frigging worse soon, if you don't watch it,' Campbell 175 mouthed until Mackenzie's warning look shut him up.

'In the rear – over here,' Mackenzie called softly. 'Come on in ... We're just getting our things together.'

Sheep's Arse frowned and hesitated. 'I haven't all day—'

'Come in quick, for God's sake, we don't want anyone to see you there,' Mackenzie cut him off harshly.

'Oh, all right.'

He pushed the sacking curtain further to one side and came in hesitantly, boots squelching in the mud of the gangway.

Campbell 175 tensed with the stave of wood. Behind him Mackenzie slipped off the last slat covering the thunderbox. The nauseating stench of faeces was suddenly overpowering. Campbell 175 gagged and felt very sick. But he didn't relinquish his grip on the wood.

Sheep's Arse turned the little corner. Abruptly he stopped short. He saw them crouched in front of the open pit of stinking yellow ordure white with thousands of wriggling fat maggots. His normally red face blanched. 'What in heaven's name are you about?' he demanded thickly, vomit rising in his throat and threatening to choke him.

'Can't you see?' Mackenzie said threateningly and nodded to Campbell 175 poised there with his slat of wood.

Mackenzie didn't wait for an answer. He said brutally. 'You're a fucking traitor—'

'I'm not—'

Mackenzie wasn't listening. 'We've checked. Your German friend with one arm has had a machine gun set up just beyond the back gate. As soon as we're in sight, you know what he's going to do.' His eyes glittered angrily.

Sheep's Arse threw up his hands in front of his face, as if to ward off a blow. 'I didn't know ... Honest ... I didn't know,' he quavered. 'I thought I was going to do you a favour ... save you from being bloody fools, getting yourselves killed...' The words died away on his bloodless lips, as Campbell 175, his eyes blazing with unrestrained rage and hatred, prodded him abruptly so that he staggered towards that evil stinking yellow pit...

Six

Campbell 175 hit the Escape Officer again. He staggered and nearly fell into that stinking pit. Eyes wild and crazy with fear, the tears now rolling down his pudgy face, he choked, 'Oh, please ... please don't do it ... Don't put me in...' He could not finish the words. The plea died on his lips. The thought was too horrific to be expressed.

Coldly Mackenzie watched his assistant torture the sobbing traitor. He felt no mercy for him. Sheep's Arse had his excuses, but in the end, he would have sent them to their deaths to save his own precious hide.

Once more, Campbell 175 slammed the slat into the other man's back. Now he was bent gasping and vomiting and sobbing all at once, his terrified face only inches from the pit. One of his hands had slipped momentarily and had penetrated the yellow mess, before he had pulled it back as if the slime were red hot. Now he stared at the dripping hand aghast, unable even to wipe it clean, great tears coursing down his cheeks.

Finally Mackenzie held up his hand. 'He's

had enough,' he commanded.

Campbell 175, panting heavily with the effort of beating the traitor, nodded his agreement. Yet his dark eyes still blazed with rage and though he lowered the slat, he held on to it just in case.

Still sobbing, Sheep's Arse wiped the mess from his hand, muttering, 'I'm all shit ... Oh, my God, look at me, I'm covered in shit—'

'Shut up,' Mackenzie cut in harshly. 'Get a grip of yourself. Now you know what'll happen to you if you betray us. You know, too, what to do?'

'Yes ... yes...'

'Good. Then let's get on with it. They'll be locking up the prisoners in thirty minutes.'

Campbell jammed the wooden slat once more into their prisoner's back, but more gently this time. He wanted him to be able to walk to where the trap had been set for them. 'Move it,' he ordered.

Sheep's Arse moved it with surprising speed, considering his condition. Perhaps he had summoned up the last of his strength so that he could get away from that awful pit.

Outside it was almost dark now. In the barracks, there was the flickering yellow light of the home-made candles. Here and there the first searchlights had been switched on and were beginning to sweep the compound with their icy light. But the rain was still coming down in solid sheets and the searchlights weren't having much success. Mackenzie, bringing up the rear behind Campbell 175 and his prisoner, was grateful for that. The situation was now very nip-and-tuck. One wrong move and they'd be dead men. They needed all the luck on their side they could achieve. Darkness was what they wanted.

Slowly, Sheep's Arse, reeling from side to side as if he were drunk, in the lead, with Campbell next at five yards and at another five yards, Mackenzie, armed with the pen-pistol, casting swift glances to left and right, they advanced on the stark-black silhouette of the rear gate. Mackenzie strained his eyes. A lantern glowed dully in the window of the guard hut, but he couldn't make out any other sign of life. But then, he told himself bitterly, the swine wouldn't want to be seen, would they? They'd let him and Campbell 175 get within range, which would be very close in the pouring rain, and then they'd rip the two apart with their machine gun.

Slowly, very slowly, they got closer and closer to the back gate. Still the rain kept pouring down. All three of them were soaked. Their feet, squelching through the mud, must have made a hell of a noise, Mackenzie couldn't help thinking, but he knew the patter of the rain drowned any sound they made. He peered through the gloom. But each time he did so, his gaze was blurred by the raindrops lashing his face. Time and time again he wiped his face purposelessly. They plodded on.

Up front Sheep's Arse attempted once to look back. He didn't complete the move. Campbell 175 growled something and whacked him with the dirty slat. Their prisoner yelped, stumbled, nearly fell, caught himself in time and went on. Mackenzie whistled. It was the signal. They were getting very close to the trap. It was time for the two of them to fall back, ready to move immediately, once the balloon went up, which would be very soon. Mackenzie felt a vein in his right temple begin to throb. He controlled himself. He didn't want his nerves running away with him now. He *had* to keep calm.

Now, he estimated, they were about twenty metres away from the trap. Soon, he knew, their captive would shout – a warning, a greeting, an attempted exclamation. Before that they had to be running like hell for the place of escape, while the heat was off.

He whistled again. Despite the savage hiss of the rain, Campbell 175 had been expecting it. He dropped the slat. Mackenzie took a deep breath. Next instant he hurled the rock with all his strength. It slammed on to the tin roof of the guardhouse. Even with the noise of the rainstorm, it could be heard. One moment more and the two of them had dashed to the right and were running, as if the Devil himself were after them, sloshing through the puddles, heads tucked into their shoulders, arms jerking back and forth like pistons.

An angry cry. *'Halt!'* someone challenged ... *'Oder ich schiesse.'*

'Don't fire,' Sheep's Arse cried in despair. 'It's me—'

The burst of vicious white tracer ripped into his guts. He screamed, high and hysterical like a woman. He stopped in his tracks. His hands flew to his savaged stomach. Too late. His entrails started to slide out of the bloody raw, gory hole like a steaming grey reptile. He gasped in horror. Slowly he began to sink to the mud, dying as he fell.

Now wild firing commenced at the back gate. Even in the pelting rain they could hear the angry shouts, orders and counter-orders. Somewhere a siren began to wail. Behind them the prisoners in their huts went crazy. They began beating their tin mugs and canteens against the rough wooden tables in unison. Someone began to sing in a jeering voice, *'Right in the Führer's face,'* accompanying his rendition of the dirty song with simulated wet farts.

As Mackenzie ran after Campbell, he hoped the noise from the barracks would fool the guards. If they thought there was a mass breakout being attempted, they'd concentrate on bringing up reinforcements before they dared enter the compound. Already he could hear the rattle of chains as they started to loosen the Alsatians. They'd need the dogs for the compound. In front of him, Campbell 175 gasped, 'Come on, sir – bash on ... we're nearly there.'

They were. Now the stork-legged tower, their objective to the right of the main gate, was looming up. Up there the elderly guards would already be fumbling with their machine gun. Mackenzie prayed they'd be directing their fire at the huts if and when they opened up.

Moments later they dropped into the dead ground in the shadow of the tower above them, wheezing like ancient asthmatics. But there was no time for resting. Already they could hear the sound of guards wading through the mud from the main guardroom, ready to enter the compound. The Germans were reacting.

Now they squirmed forward on their bellies. They were almost exhausted, soaked to the bone. But in their urgency, carried forward by an almost overwhelming fear, they had no time to notice the cold. They worked their way between the tower's legs.

Now they could hear the guards above quite clearly. But they were certain *they* had not been heard. They headed for the spot they had already selected: an area in the first fence where the wire had rusted over the years and finally snapped open. Mackenzie had guessed the gap might be just big enough for them to squirm through. He was right. In the lead, Campbell turned and whispered, bending the wire even more as he did so, 'We'll manage, sir. I'm off.'

'Bash on,' Mackenzie hissed back.

Campbell 175 pushed on to the next line, crawling silently, any sound he might have made drowned by the drumbeat of the rain and the noise from the rear gate. He came to the wire. Behind him Mackenzie now followed, panting a little. Campbell 175 grabbed the lower strand of the second wire fence. It was, as he had hoped, rusted almost through, too. He tugged. Nothing. The wire didn't give. He cursed. He tried again, exerting all his strength. The wire gave with a slight sound. Campbell 175 could have cheered. They were doing it; they were getting away. But he knew there was no time for congratulations now. Every second was precious. It only took the guard above them to crane his neck over the side of his watchtower and he'd spot them, even through the pelting rain.

Hastily he started to turn the broken

strand upwards and at the same time fumble with the next strand with his other hand. More than once the cruel barbs ripped his flesh painfully. But he ignored it. He had to widen the gap. Another strand snapped. He could have shouted with joy. Mackenzie had reached him now. He joined in widening the gap while Campbell 175 worked on the third piece of rusty wire, telling himself that if he could break it the gap would be big enough even for Mackenzie who was broader in the shoulders than he was.

Suddenly he stiffened. His hands froze on the wire. A dark shape had moved out of the patch of shadow to his left. For a moment he thought it might be his over-excited imagination playing a trick on him. But it wasn't. The shape, low and close to the ground, moved again. Next to him, Mackenzie froze; he'd seen it too.

The shape raised its head and now Campbell, with a sudden sensation of absolute fear, recognized it for what it was. One of the savage, half-wild Alsatian dogs. They hadn't been taken into the compound, as he thought. At least this one hadn't. For a moment he lost control of himself, as a cold finger of absolute fear traced its icy way down the small of his back. What was he going to do?

Next to him, Mackenzie fumbled cautiously – very cautiously – inside his tunic, not taking his gaze off the Alsatian for an instant.

Across from them, so close that they could smell the beast's disgusting, fetid odour, the Alsatian sniffed the air, as if it were not sure whether there was someone there or not. They waited, hardly daring to breathe. But now Mackenzie knew what to do if the worst happened.

It did the very next moment. The Alsatian emitted a long, low growl. It inched back on its hind legs. It bared its fangs. Its ears fell close to its evil sloping skull. It was about to spring.

Campbell 175 was quicker off the mark. His right hand shot out. In the same instant that the beast was about to launch itself forward, he grabbed it by its ugly snout. The dog's bark was stifled and it didn't spring. Wildly it wriggled and tried to throw off Campbell's grip. It threshed its trapped head back and forth. It lashed out with one of its front paws. The cruel claws ripped the length of Campbell's face splattering blood everywhere.

Grimly he held on, panting wildly with the effort.

The Alsatian thrust its hind legs into the mud till it had a firm grip. It dug in its clawed feet and started to attempt to pull Campbell backwards, while trying at the same time to throw off that killing grip on its jaw. Campbell gasped, 'I can't ... can't hold on ... much longer.'

Mackenzie didn't reply. He hadn't the time. He lunged forward instead. With all his strength he found the beast's genitals and pressed hard. The Alsatian's whole body quivered crazily. But now the two escapers were in control and the dog seemed to sense it. Suddenly, startlingly, it went limp, as if resigned to its fate.

Mackenzie didn't give it a chance to recover. Still holding on to the beast's sexual organs, nostrils filled with the animal's revolting stink, he pressed the little pen pistol into the Alsatian's pelt just below its right ear. He pressed the catch. A soft plop. The Alsatian arched its back. In its death agony it twisted and tore itself free from Campbell's grasp. A moment later it lay stretched out on its side in the mud and pouring rain – dead.

Five minutes later they had broken through the last fence and were hurrying wordlessly into the rainsoaked darkness...

BOOK FIVE:

END RUN

'Ye have scarce the soul of a louse,' he said,
'but the roots of sin are there...'

Rudyard Kipling

One

'Holy Strawsack!' Campbell 175 whispered in German. 'The place looks like the castle out of one of these American horror movies. Frankenstein and all that.'

Mackenzie had never seen an American horror movie, nor had he ever heard of Frankenstein. But he could understand his companion crushed next to him on the wooden seat of the crowded country bus. Towering above the plain, the great medieval castle, with its series of slate-roofed turrets, did look eerie and somehow threatening, even now bathed as it was in the spring sunshine. 'It looks a hard nut to crack,' he replied sotto voce in German, too. 'But somehow we've got to do it.'

Campbell 175 opened his mouth to say something, but decided not to. His German was, naturally, perfect, but his accent was that of the Rhineland and it stuck out badly against that of the Saxon peasants of the area. For up front, the armed SS private who was probably returning to his unit had turned and was staring at them with that hard arrogant look typical of the SS.

Not that, Campbell 175 told himself, they were anything much to look at. Their ragged *Joppen** had been stolen from a barn and a scarecrow respectively and their black peaked caps worn by the local peasants and workers had been picked up from the bus station waiting room. The only thing, he felt, that might give them away was their RAF boots, muddy now, but definitely of best-quality leather unlike the shoddy, ersatz ones of the others passengers on the wood-burning country bus.

The young SS man turned to his front again and the two fugitives relaxed. Not that they expected much trouble out here in the country. Germany was on its last legs. Allied fighter-bombers were everywhere shooting up everything that moved during the daylight and the sound of the approaching Americans was getting louder every day. Now soldiers and civilians alike were concerned with saving their own lives. Naturally there were a few patrols about, mainly consisting of heavily armed officers who were trying to stem the rot, picking out soldiers without documents or men of military age in civilian clothes, who might well be deserters, too. The patrols made

**A thigh-length coat worn mostly by country folk.* Transl.

short work of anyone they felt had run away. They were prosecution, defence and execution. They had usually dealt with their unfortunate victim within five minutes, leaving him lying in a bloody pool at the readside or hanging stiffly from a tree with the usual sign attached to his corpse – *'I am a Defeatist and Traitor'* – as a warning to others of their ilk. The bus had passed two such victims already in the half-hour since they had chugged out of the bullet-scarred bus station, trailing wood gas behind them.

Soon both of them knew they'd either have to evacuate the bus on account of yet another low-level strafing attack by Allied planes or because a patrol stopped them. But before that happened, they hoped the bus with the mattresses tied to its roof as a pathetic form of protection from air attack, would get closer to the great 'bad boys' prison'. Though at the moment, neither Mackenzie nor Campbell 175 had much idea of what exactly they were going to do when they got there.

From the front seat behind the driver, the SS private had begun looking at them again, this time with the aid of the bus's rear-view mirror. Instinctively Campbell 175 touched his left cheek where the hound had mauled him. The wound had long ceased bleeding, but when he had washed in the lavatory of the little bus station, Campbell had attempted to pull off some of the scab so that the wound wouldn't be so noticeable. Now it was leaking a little blood again. Hastily he attempted to wipe it away. It was a gesture the SS private noted. Suddenly, frighteningly, he gripped his rifle more firmly. Out of the side of his mouth, Campbell 175 whispered, this time in English, 'I think that bugger's on to us, sir.'

Mackenzie didn't appear to hear. Instead he nudged Campbell's leg with his knee and indicated the '*Notausgang*', the emergency door, to their right. A twist of the handle labelled, as seemingly everything was in Germany, '*Verboten*' and they would be tumbling out into the road. Campbell 175 nudged him back to indicate that he had understood. It was risky, even though the old bus was just crawling; an unlucky fall and they'd be in real trouble.

But Fate took a hand and the jump from the bus proved unnecessary, though jump they had to in one way or another.

It was just when the SS private started to stir nervously in his seat, as if he were about to make a move, and the bus driver throttled back and engaged second gear prior to entering the little hamlet of Colditz that with startling suddenness the two Lightnings fell out of the spring sky. One minute it was a blue calm stretch of nothingness; the next the twin-boomed American fighter-bombers were zooming in at tree-top height, machine guns and cannons already spitting death.

'*Jabos!*' the SS man yelled frantically, the two civilians forgotten immediately.

The bus driver hit the brakes. The old bus shuddered to a halt. Next moment all was panic, as the passengers scrambled and fought before the dreaded *Jabo* fighter-bombers came in for another run, which would probably spell doom for the bus now slewed across the road. It was every man – and woman, too – for themselves. Mackenzie and Campbell 175 fought with the rest, pulling aside those who got in their way, English standards of politeness forgotten.

They tumbled out and, hopping over the passengers' pathetic bits and pieces, now abandoned in their panic, they pelted for the leftside drainage ditch. Just in time. The first Lightning came barrelling straight down the road, its prop wash whipping and lashing the trees to left and right. They could see the pilot quite clearly behind his shining perspex screen. His face radiated such all-American confidence that the two of them hated him at that moment just as much as the terrified Germans. Hastily they ducked as a burst of shells ripped the length of the ditch just above their heads. Some of the screaming hysterical civilians were just not quick enough. Women fell, their heads blown away. A baby tumbled into the ditch, dead and shattered like a broken doll. An old man lay back almost gently and with his eyes wide open, pipe still burning between lips that were growing ever slacker, died. The pipe continued to burn.

It was horror upon horror and then in a flash the second plane had gone too, leaving the two shocked Intelligence agents to stare wide-eyed at this terrible scene of death – even the suspicious SS man had been killed, his face looking as if someone had thrown molten red wax at it, as his features dripped on to his chest.

'Oh my God,' Campbell 175 breathed in German, breaking the loud echoing silence that followed the departure of the second Lightning, already streaking upwards, twisting and turning in a joyous triumphant victory roll as it did so. 'My God!'

'Don't blame God!' a female voice said hotly. 'It's not God who did this.'

The two of them turned, startled. A young woman had risen from the ditch. Her face was streaked with dirt and her clothes were shabby and dirty, too – she looked as if she had been on the road and sleeping in her clothes for a long time – but there was no denying her prettiness. She was dark with equally dark flashing eyes – now full of anger – so that she looked more Slavic with those broad cheeks than German, with a slight but provocative figure, especially now as her breasts beneath the tight sweater heaved with emotion.

'Yes,' she cried, that bold unconventional face suffused with rage, 'you heard me, don't blame God ... blame man. It was man – men – who did that!' Dramatically she flung out her hand to indicate the shattered bodies further up the ditch and Mackenzie saw she had been wounded. There was bright red blood running down the side of her hand.

'You've been hit,' Mackenzie said.

For some reason, Mackenzie never found out why, even afterwards, but her anger vanished abruptly. Her face crumpled and suddenly she had bent her head and she was weeping uncontrollably...

Thus they met Irma Novak for the last week of her young life. She was from Colditz, but at eighteen she had been sent to work as a telephonist in Berlin's Air Ministry. But that April, as the Russians started to draw their circle around besieged Berlin ever tighter, she and the other young female employees of Göring's Ministry had been ordered to break out and go home. As 'Fat Hermann', the enormously fat head of the *Luftwaffe*, had decreed, 'I will not be the cause of our young German maidens losing their honour to a bunch of rapacious subhumans.' 'Maidens', they might not have been, but Göring had been right. Once the Russians captured the German capital, there would be mass rape of German women from sixteen to sixty.

So she had fled to her home village, suffering God only knew what kind of outrages and indignities, ones that she only barely hinted about to Mackenzie in the short time that they were together – 'the last and happiest time of my life', as he would tell Campbell 175 when he was drunk, which became increasingly often *afterwards*. Now within sight of Colditz village she had been subjected to what she thought was the final horror and for a little while she had cracked, unable to take any more.

It was while the two men attended to her wounded wrist, using part of her dirty petticoat to bind it and stop the bleeding, while other transport from the village – carts, hand-towed wagons, even a baby's pram – took away the other wounded, that she pulled herself together and told them they could shelter in her father's house for the night. Her father would probably have some potatoes at least down in the cellar, perhaps even a slab of smoked bacon too, with which he '–we – can feed you'. At first they hesitated. But when she told them, wincing a little with pain, as they tightened the makeshift bandage, that her father – Fritz – worked up in the castle, they agreed.

Besides they knew they needed a base for the night. They were without documents. After curfew anyone in authority could arrest them on the spot without identification – and more than likely, under the conditions prevailing in a dying Germany, that would result in a speedy death with the backs of their heads blown off by some SS thug.

It was Campbell 175 who made the decision. Despite his burning hatred of Germans, *all* Germans, he knew the wounded girl was honest. She obviously felt too seriously about things to be otherwise. Mackenzie, who was letting him do most of the talking in case his accent gave him away when speaking German, could see the younger man's clever brain working overtime. He'd use the girl and her as yet unknown father and when the time came for action, as it would, well ... Mackenzie, hard as he was, didn't like to think of that eventuality. For if the girl or her father guessed who they really were, there could be only one way to solve that particular dilemma. So when he heard Campbell say, '*Schon gut, junges Fraulein, wir kommen mit*,' laying it on with all the Rhenish charm of his youth in Cologne-on-Rhine, he let it happen. Besides a few elderly policemen were now beginning to arrive to help with the pathetic casualties. It was high time they took a dive.

So the three of them started off towards the little village in the shadow of the great sombre castle whose secret they had come to solve: a Jew with malice in his heart; a young girl shocked and vulnerable; and an older man, hard yet vulnerable too, who had not been happy for a long time now. It was a combination that couldn't survive for long...

Two

'Papa' Novak beamed at his guests, pushed his empty plate away from him and announced as if it were very important, 'There's nothing better than a simple "farmer's breakfast".'

Although it was evening and not breakfast time and neither the old German guard with his ill-fitting uniform and heavy belly nor they were farmers, Mackenzie and Campbell 175 had to agree with him. The simple meal of fried potatoes, mixed with smoked bacon and topped with a layer of milk mixed with a couple of eggs had been the best meal they had eaten for a long time.

'Everyone calls me "Papa",' the guard at Colditz Castle had explained after Irma Novak had introduced her father to them when he had come off duty, 'even the Tommy officers, and they are real snobs. Though I can't say I've been very good in the fathering business. As you can see, *meine Herren*, I've only produced one daughter.' His old eyes had moistened for a moment, as he had pressed Irma's hand. 'And I'm grateful to you for bringing her back to me. In the crazy world we live in these days, I didn't think I'd see her—' He hadn't finished the sentence and hastily she had kissed his white head and said, 'Silly old Papa.' She had had tears in her beautiful dark eyes too, and Mackenzie could see that both of them possessed more emotion than was usual in the dour Saxons, 'the Scots of Germany', as his old professor of German had called them. That explained perhaps, too, her broad Slavic cheekbones and un-German appearance, plus the old man's strangely accented German. Old Novak must have been one of those '*Wasserpolacks*', the 'Water Poles' of the German–Polish frontier who had come to Germany at the turn of the century to work in the Reich's booming new industries. That fact made him feel easier about his own German accent, though now and again he did catch Irma looking at him rather strangely when he mispronounced a word.

Still it was a happy little household, especially now that old Papa's daughter had returned safely to keep the old man company and to survive what was to come. As he described it, 'Better an end with terror than a terror without end. *Meine Herren*, it won't be long now – all hell is going to be let loose.' He pointed the stem of his evil-smelling pipe at the obligatory picture of

Hitler on the kitchen wall. 'That man's going to plunge us into damnation. Even here in our little Colditz trouble's brewing. It's a kettle boiling over, with the lid about to explode, especially in the Castle.'

'How do you mean, Papa?' Campbell 175 asked, as the girl placed wooden boards in front of them upon which they would cut their bread to eat the last of the tough smoked bacon.

'Well...' He drew slowly on his pipe in the fashion of old men, who still believe they have all the time in the world. 'They're packing ever more prisoners into the place. They're coming from all over the Reich. In February we had five thousand French prisoners. Last month it was Poles – again hundreds of them. We just don't have the guards to keep them in place. They're doing what they like. The Commandant is worried stiff that Berlin will find out that he's losing control. His head could be on the block.' The old man looked hard at them for a moment, levelling his pipe at his two guests, as if he were pointing a pistol at them. 'No one is safe really, *meine Herren*.'

Campbell 175 looked at Mackenzie significantly in the same moment that Irma Novak came in bearing the slabs of hard bacon on another board. Even in the weak light cast by the petroleum lamp, she caught the look and faltered a fraction of a second, as if she had realized that there was more going on in the tiny sitting room than just idle chat on the part of Papa and the strangers.

Mackenzie saw her expression and wondered for a moment. Had she picked up something? Could she be trusted? He hoped she could, for even in the brief time he had known her, he had felt an attraction towards the young girl with those flashing dark eyes, of a kind that he had not sensed for any woman since his wife had been so cruelly killed in what now seemed another age.

Then the moment passed and she was dividing out the remaining meat, while Campbell 175 asked more questions about the camp in the Castle in a seemingly casual fashion, as if it were merely a matter of passing the evening.

But that night as the two of them slept, muffled in a thick feather bed in the hay of the stall where Papa Novak kept his one remaining pig – 'pray God, gentlemen, that she'll keep us through this summer' – the steady drone of the RAF bomber squadrons heading for Leipzig once again woke them. That was followed by a fierce artillery duel somewhere to the east of Colditz where the German 25th Army was putting up a last-ditch defence against the advancing Yanks of the American 1st Army. Then they could sleep no longer.

They turned to a whispered discussion of what they could do now, based on the information they had received from Papa Novak and what they had seen of Colditz village itself, now packed with refugees from half a dozen nationalities, caught between the fronts and undecided whether to go east to the Russians or west to the Americans. 'It looks,' Mackenzie said, resting his head on one hand, the only light the silver spectral light of the sickle moon through the gaps in the wooden frame of the pigsty, 'as if it might not be as difficult to get into Colditz Castle as we thought it would.'

'But to do what?' Campbell 175 whispered back.

'To contact the Senior British Officer. He was the chap who had the original signal sent to MI9 about the murder of poor old Dalby. If anyone knows what's going on, it should be the SBO.'

Campbell considered for a moment before saying, 'But that was months ago now. If the Yanks were behind it all, and I think they might have been, wouldn't they – the killer – have long since vanished?'

'Probably. But the SBO still might give us a clue. We've got to try. The sooner that we can pin something on the Yanks, or those involved in Roosevelt's plot, the sooner we might be able to shame them, blackmail them, oh, I don't know–' he shrugged with irritation at his own inability to come up with the right solution to the problem – 'into backing off.'

'You mean for good?'

Mackenzie shook his head. 'No, I don't think so. Sooner or later they'll destroy the British Empire. It's on the cards.'

'Why should it be?' Campbell 175 snapped a little angrily. 'Why give up? There's always hope.'

'There you go – the paid barbarian defending the decadent Roman Empire once again.' He laughed softly.

Campbell joined him, saying, 'All right, *pace*. But how are we to get into the camp? Things might be falling apart, but not that much. There'll be plenty of suspicious guards up there still. The war's not over yet and they must know their own lives are on the line still, if they fuck up.'

'Agreed. But have you thought of old Papa? A nice harmless old bloke, don't you think?'

'For a German,' Campbell sniffed.

'Oh, all right. Didn't he say he got someone up there every day from the village when he's on duty to sneak out whatever pig swill there is from the German officers' mess – and if the prisoners leave anything, which won't be much I'm sure on the hunger rations they get.'

'Go on.'

'Well, we could be the two who go up there under *his* supervision to collect the swill. Who'd suspect anyone under his supervision? The old boy's been at the camp since the year dot. It would be an ideal way to get in – *and* out.'

Campbell 175 whistled softly. 'Right you are. We could be two Polacks he'd picked up from the village – it's packed with former forced labourers from the east and he's half Polish himself. It would stand up to a casual scrutiny.' His voice fell. 'But how could we convince your friend old Papa to do it? Why should he?'

'Perhaps the girl – she likes us. Irma might be the way...'

Outside, almost noiseless despite the wooden clogs all the locals wore around the house, Irma stopped at the faint mention of her name from the direction of the pigsty. She was on her way to the privy, with the usual heart cut in its green door, a shawl wrapped around her pretty shoulders against the night cold. Above her the purple sky sparkled icily in the light of the stars and the curved silver of the moon. It was the immensity of that night sky, broken only by the faint pink flashes of the guns to the west that had made her walk slowly so that she had heard her name mentioned.

She stopped, the urgency of her need abruptly forgotten. It was the older of the two men, Karl, who had mentioned her name. She turned her head into the faint night breeze to hear better. But she could make out nothing else, for she realized they were not speaking German, though she knew they both spoke her native language fluently. Why, then, were two Germans speaking a tongue she couldn't understand?

Of course she knew that the village was packed with foreigners, the whole of Central Germany was. There were supposed to be millions of them. Yet all the same, the farm labourers and foreign factory workers she had met since the great panic-stricken exodus had commenced didn't speak fluent German like these two did. What was going on?

For what seemed a long time she stood there, a pretty girl dressed in a shapeless nightdress with a shawl that had belonged to her dead mother wrapped around her thin shoulders, so that she looked more like a child than the young woman that she was. She was puzzled, but she was also a little afraid. Of what she didn't know exactly. All the same she felt that something bad was going to happen and it would include the two strangers, Papa and herself and that there was nothing she could do about it.

Suddenly in the trees that climbed up the height to the stark black silhouette of the Castle, an owl hooted. She jumped at the sound. Normally she liked the sound of owls when she was warmly tucked up in her childhood wooden bed with the crucifix on the wall above it and weighed down by the comforting folds of the enormous *Federdecke*. But not now. Somehow it frightened her. She waited no longer. Clutching the shawl more tightly about her shoulders, she fled towards the privy. Inside the pigsty the two Englishmen continued to talk, unaware that she had ever been there.

Three

President Roosevelt lit yet another cigarette. He slipped the end into the cigarette holder, a kind of trademark for him over the years since he had been first elected back in 1933. What had he proclaimed to a depressed America then with millions out of work? 'We have nothing to fear, but fear itself.' He tried to smile, that famous, big-toothed smile of his. But it didn't quite come off.

Opposite him in the big airy room, Madame Shoumatoff, who had been painting his portrait, continued to fill in the colours, waiting for the President to strike the suggested pose. But the President seemed to be finding the simple act difficult. He raised his left hand to his temple and squeezed his forehead. Suddenly the hand fell. His fingers twitched. It was as though he was fumbling for something. What, she didn't know. 'Did you drop anything?' she queried.

The President's speech was thick, hard to understand. She thought he said, 'I ... I have a terrific headache.' His arm fell. His great head dropped to one side. His chest slumped. His eyes closed. He was unconscious, his breathing harsh and gasping.

The President of the United States of America, the one who would break the power of the decadent European imperialists and their cruel, repressive empires, was dying.

Instantly there was mass hysteria in his household. His mistress, Lucy Rutherfurt, fled the place. The President's wife must never know that she had been there and shared the Great Man's last moments. A doctor – many doctors – were summoned to help out. Messages, some authorized, some not, were flashed to public and private figures all over the States to warn them what was about to happen. Vainly the doctors laboured to keep the President alive. Not that they thought he had a chance of surviving. No, they had to keep him going until the vital decisions for the future, to be made by others, were taken still under President Roosevelt's authority. That way, they reasoned, there would be less debate – and less criticism – afterwards.

Unknown to the nation that April day at Warm Springs, the President's holiday hideout, Franklin D. Roosevelt was in extremis, his clothing already being changed by his doctor and a black servant into new blue-striped pyjamas so that he'd be ready for the official photographers as soon as the men behind the throne allowed him to die. Not only the future of the United States hung in the balance this April day, but that of the British Empire did too, and perhaps ultimately two brave men quartered now in a remote Saxon village, where their lives might well be forfeited at any moment.

Vice-President Harry Truman was ostensibly presiding over the United States Senate that day. But as he sat there against a dramatic background of marble pillars and heavy blue velvet embellished with a gold-embroidered border, the bespectacled ex-haberdasher was scrawling a note to his wife and daughter Mary. 'Dear Mama and Mary,' he wrote, 'I am trying to write you a letter today from the desk of the President of the Senate while a windy senator ... is making a speech on a subject with which he is in no way familiar...' He finished the letter with: 'Write when you can.' But he was not fated to post it that day after the Senate closed or for many days to come for that matter.

Then two hours later when he was accepting his first drink of the day and had, unknown to him, been the thirty-third President of the United Stated for over an hour, he was informed President Roosevelt was dead and that he was the new president. For a while, it seemed, he was in a daze. But the little man with the glasses, virtually unknown outside Washington, started to take charge in a manner which surprised those who thought they could handle him. But the new President had a mind of his own. 'Harry won't rock the boat,' they intoned. 'He'll just sit out Roosevelt's fourth term and then disappear into obscurity again.'

But they were wrong. That Friday Truman told his cronies and advisers, 'Inside, Roosevelt was the coldest man I ever met. He didn't care about you or me or anyone else in the world on a personal level, as far as I can see.' He added a little hesitantly, 'But he was a great president. He brought this country into the twentieth century.'

All the same Truman was not prepared to hurry things up in the manner that Roosevelt had prescribed. He felt, as soon as he was informed of the great plot against the British Empire and the other European ones, that it had to be stopped. The war against Germany might be virtually won, but there were still the 'Nips' to be beaten. This was no time to antagonize the British. After all he had fought besides them in France in the Old War. He knew the limeys could be 'hard-nosed sons-of-bitches'. For the time being 'Project Venlo', as it had been code-named, had to be called off. 'Was that understood?'

It was. But already it was too late. The wheels had been set in motion. The orders had been given. The killer was about to strike again...

'The Whisperer', as they called him at Eisenhower's Shaef Headquarters in Paris, had started it all. Double agent as he already was, Philby had no hesitation in working for those backroom Americans at the great Versailles HQ, as long as it helped the cause of his secret Soviet masters. It wasn't much that he knew, but it was enough to raise the scent once more and begin the new operation. 'Mackenzie and Campbell had disappeared from London, but had re-appeared some time later dressed in the uniform of the Royal Air Force,' he had stuttered over the phone to his American contact, that crooked cynical grin on his face as he thought of how he was setting the cat among the pigeons yet again.

They had been so pathetically grateful, he told himself as he put down the phone in the shabby room of that backstreet Parisian MI6 headquarters. But then they were Yanks and even though they were involved in the 'Great Game', they were as innocent as the driven snow, save for one thing. Philby's jaw had hardened when he had thought of it, and when he spoke, the thought aloud in the manner of lonely men, the customary stutter had vanished: 'The Yanks don't have the slightest scruple about murder!'

Spatz's US Army Air Corps HQ in England, had produced the information about the missing Lancaster on the abortive raid on Jena and the strange fact that it had been carrying two extra air gunners. They had told themselves they didn't need a crystal ball to know who those gunners were – Mackenzie and Campbell. A week later and they had learned most of the plot, added to by the hot tip they had received from the colonel in the armoured corps who had overrun the *Oflag* in the other side of the River Elbe. That clinched it for the plotters at Versailles. They knew all they needed to know.

'So you see, Al,' the Colonel, with the dark glasses that made his eyes almost invisible said, mustering the German-American sitting before him in the office while outside the typewriters clattered and the phones rang incessantly with the latest information from the rapidly advancing front in Central Germany, 'we've got 'em virtually nailed – the limeys. Let's go for it, eh.' He feigned enthusiasm, hoping it might prove contagious for the younger man.

But he slumped there, twisting the brass class ring with its American eagle design, face revealing nothing. In fact he was hardly listening to the fat prick of a colonel. He was one of the usual crappy chairborne warriors who talked, but stayed on their soft keesters and did nothing. *He* was the guy who did the killing and he knew how to do that –

brother, did he know! Besides his mind was on the French broad of the night before. She had been something – and then some, especially when she brought her friend and suggested a threesome. Jesus H., his prick had nearly jumped out of the bed by itself when the other whore had come in, buck-assed naked with a frigging big dildo in her hand. *Brother*!

'So this is the deal,' the fat colonel with the concealed eyes was saying, 'we're flying you out to a field airfield just east of Magdeburg. A recon troop of armoured cars and half-tracks with infantry Joes will be waiting for you. You'll be in charge, of course.'

The killer smiled to himself. What was the fat-assed cunt saying? He was *always* in charge. He didn't comment aloud however. He waited. There ought to be some dough soon. Where was the mazuma?

It came, as he had expected. Wasn't he the best? The best had to be paid.

The fat colonel reached in his drawer. He drew out the bundle. 'I could give you Frog dough,' he said, counting the brand-new dollar bills swiftly. 'But I guess you, being you, would tell me to stick them.' He smiled, but there was no corresponding light in those hidden eyes. It was supposed to be a joke, but both of them knew it wasn't. The killer would have said just that – 'Stick the Frog dough, Colonel.' He handed over the twenty dollar bills. 'Count 'em, if you want.'

'No need to, Colonel.' The killer broke his silence for the first time during the whole briefing. 'I trust you.' Now he smiled. He was taunting the fat officer and the latter knew it. 'I always have.'

'Nice to know it,' the Colonel echoed, hating the murderous bastard ever more. ''Kay, you've got the dough. Why don't you enjoy yourself tonight in some of the local dives. You young guys ought to get the dirty water off'n ya chests before you go into action. Me, I'm getting too old for that kinda stuff.'

'Yeah, I guess you are,' the killer said, pocketing the bundle of notes.

The colonel felt himself flush. The cocky bastard was really rubbing it in. Still he consoled himself that the killer would soon be getting his. He reached out his hand. 'Remember, zero six hundred tomorrow morning at Orly.'

'Yessir, Colonel,' the killer said easily. He didn't take the hand. Another calculated insult. Without another word, he sauntered out and even the way he swaggered at the door appeared to his spymaster to be an affront. He could hardly wait till the bastard had closed the door behind him and he could then dare pick up the phone to the next room where the big ex-paratrooper from the 'Screaming Eagles' had been listening to their conversation through the open 'squawk box'.

'Did you hear everything, Bo-Bo?' he asked.

'Yeah,' the giant para answered, or at least the Colonel thought he answered in the affirmative. For you never knew with Bo-Bo, who grunted most of the time, it seemed to him. He guessed he'd been made punch-drunk by all his years in the ring before the 101st Airborne had claimed him (but only for long enough to find out that the ex-heavyweight was surprised to learn he was going to be given a parachute in order to jump out of planes; Bo-Bo was that dumb).

'Okay, the boys'll take you down to the field now. You understand?'

Again the giant para grunted.

'Good and you know what to do – *later*?'

'I tink so, 'Bo-Bo answered slowly, very slowly, for it was a real effort for him to utter more than a couple of words. Indeed the Colonel was surprised that he had managed a real sentence, even if it consisted only of three words. 'Kill?'

'Exactly, Bo-Bo, you kill.'

'I kill him,' the giant repeated like some terribly backward four-year-old who was having great difficulty in repeating his lesson.

The Colonel had had enough. He put

down the phone, idly wondering how long it would take Bo-Bo to realize that the apparatus had gone dead on him. But he supposed the boys would tell him eventually. He dismissed Bo-Bo and was abruptly pleased with himself. Everything was under control. That smart-arsed bastard would do his job and finish off the limeys. Then he'd get his. 'And you, dear friend,' he said aloud to the empty office, 'are going to the Sphinx* tonight – cost what it may – and you are going to get well and truly laid.' He beamed at himself in the mirror, well pleased with the afternoon's work.

In the outer room, the giant black allowed the 'boys' to guide him out of the door. 'Kill ... kill,' he seemed to be grunting to himself, or so they thought.

**A well-known Parisian brothel during WWII.* Transl.

Four

They became lovers almost by chance. All the night of the April Friday when President Roosevelt died in faraway Warm Springs, Colditz village was kept awake by constant alarms and excursions. Low-flying American spotter planes zoomed in time and time again, dropping flares and occasionally light bombs trying to identify any German forces occupying the place and the Castle towering above the village. In between the roar of the marauding light planes came the much heavier thunder of the RAF bombers, carrying out Bomber Harris's orders to wipe out the remaining German cities; for the head of Britain's Bomber Command wanted his hard-pressed crews, who had suffered horrific casualties in the last few months, to fight to the very end. The Supreme Commander Eisenhower was not going to squeeze Harris out of the war, even if there were no more real targets for his bombers.

But the really startling noises which kept the little household sheltering in the cellar of Papa Novak's little cottage in Colditz village awake that night of Friday/Saturday when it all came to a final head, were those of the tanks to the west. There was no mistaking that rusty creak of heavy tank tracks and the roar of their engines, as their drivers sped forward to meet the dug-in German 88mm anti-tank guns. Once, Campbell braved leaving the cellar to go to the privy outside and through the open door of the smelly thunderbox, he could see the white blur of anti-tank and armour-piercing shells zipping back and forth in a lethal Morse, followed seconds later by the hollow clang of steel striking steel.

As he told the others huddled in the cellar next to the last of Papa's potatoes and the very nervous pig (the old man's pride and joy which he comforted from time to time with *'Schön gut, schön gut, bald ist alles vorbei,'* as if it were a frightened child), 'There's a real ding-dong battle going on out there to the west. I don't know whether they–' and he meant the Germans – 'can hold the *Amis*. But it looks as if they are having a damn good try. Those 88mm guns must be murder.'

Mackenzie, squatting in the straw next to Irma, their faces hollowed out to yellow skulls in the crazily flickering light of the candle, nodded his understanding and hoped that Campbell 175 wouldn't give the game away by adding he hoped the Yanks would soon finish off the German anti-tank gun screen. But Campbell didn't and they settled down again, listening to the planes and the land battle and wondering what the morrow would bring.

It brought temporary calm. The planes had departed, hurrying back to their bases, for a splendid breakfast of bacon and eggs, perhaps. The tank battle had calmed too. As they ventured to the surface and peeped out expecting to see a devastated landscape, all that met their gaze was a few signal flares hissing into the dawn sky to the west and straggling columns of ragged, lousy German soldiers retreating eastwards. But as yet that retreat was orderly and controlled, Mackenzie noted with a professional eye as Irma hovered next to him, as if she wanted to be in his company all the time, and her father plucked more of the yellowing tobacco leaves from beneath the eaves to rub together in his horny palms prior to filling his old pipe with the noxious powerful mix.

Finally Irma left to prepare a poor breakfast of ersatz coffee made of acorns and a piece of dry bread, each covered with a thin layer of turnip syrup, giving Mackenzie time to issue orders to Campbell 175. They were hurried and whispered, for by now he had guessed Irma didn't take him for a German. He didn't want her to come out and hear him talking English to the younger man. He said, 'Things are coming to a head. My guess is that the Yanks won't take more than a day, perhaps even less, and they'll be here. The question is what the Germans will do. Will they defend the Castle? Will they use the prisoners as hostages? Some of the new ones at Colditz, as we've been told, are the relatives of big shots back home. I hear one of them is related to the King.'

'So, we've got to get cracking as soon as possible. This morning?' Campbell queried.

'Yes, this morning. The old man's typical Jerry. He's going to turn up for duty although everything is falling apart. He's changing into his uniform now. He's already kissed that bloody pig of his goodbye.' He smiled and Campbell chuckled. 'He'll need swill for it. I suggest we volunteer to go with him with the *Bollerwagen** and collect it.'

'We? What about only me, sir?' Campbell objected. 'I mean, I know you pass very well as a Jerry, but under very close scrutiny...' He shrugged and left the rest unsaid.

Mackenzie considered for a moment. He knew as the senior man he should go. Besides what would the POWs make of Campbell 175 when he attempted to contact the SBO in the camp? He didn't look very English and in this case, it would be Campbell who had the foreign accent. Still

**A German farmer's handcart. Transl.*

he was hesitant. Later he realized that it had been on account of Irma. Somehow, he didn't know exactly why, at that dawn, he felt he couldn't leave her.

So it was arranged. Campbell 175 would go up with the old man alone and try to contact the SBO. As soon as he found out the lie of the land, he'd return and it would be up to Mackenzie to act. At seven that morning, fine, bright, with spring in the air now, birds singing in the budding trees, a morning for renewal and hope instead of the destruction and death soon to come to Colditz, Papa and his new assistant, pulling the *Bollerwagen*, set off up the hill to Colditz Castle. They left behind an oddly nervous and somehow jittery Mackenzie and Irma watching them until they had disappeared around the bend. Then they returned to the little cottage that smelled of drying tobacco leaf, apples and animal waste, and waited in an awkward silence for what the day would bring...

' 'Kay, squirt,' the Killer snarled, 'go and peddle your papers. I'm the boss here, you do as I say.'

The young officer, with the gold bar of a second lieutenant on his shoulder, flushed. West Pointers, however young they were, weren't used to being talked to like that. Still, the Old Man at his briefing had told him that he had to obey this hard-faced man who wore no badges of rank on his uniform, to the letter; and there was one thing that four years at the Point had drilled into him. You never queried the orders of a superior officer.

Accordingly he took one glance at the terrain ahead, noting the black silhouettes of horsemen – cavalry? – on the ridge to his right and decided that he'd take the low road leading to Colditz. He pressed the throat mike to speak to the column of Staghound armoured cars and White half-tracks, packed with infantry, lined up on the track behind him. 'Move out,' he commanded. 'Watch your flanks. There's cavalry up there to the left. They could be Russian Cossacks. Don't fire unless ordered to. Okay, guys, *roll 'em!*'

He kicked the driver in the compartment below the turret on the right shoulder. The driver engaged the first of his many gears and the six-wheel armoured car started to move. He crouched a little in the turret. His gaze swung from left to right. He was a sitting duck, he knew, for any long-haired Hitler Youth armed with a *Panzerfaust*. The teenaged bastards were real fanatics.

Beside him in the turret of the Staghound, the Killer showed no fear; perhaps he didn't realize the danger lurking in the drainage ditches at both sides of the track. As he chain-smoked – against standing regulations

– he thought of his mission and his rewards thereafter, once he'd finally rubbed out the limeys.

He knew the limeys weren't in the Castle. So they had to be in the village. Accordingly he didn't want this West Point punk to get involved in the POW camp. He wanted him in the village. It didn't matter where. He hadn't the time to search for the limeys. The easy way was to get in and out like Flynn. (He grinned at the thought of what the handsome movie star Errol Flynn was getting in and out of at top speed.) Take the whole goddam place apart. They had the firepower. Then hightail it back to the Combat Command HQ. His grin broadened in anticipation. Then it would be back to the States tootsweet and it'd be frigging roses all the frigging way.

In the half-track filled with infantry from the 69th Infantry Division that followed the lead armoured car, a big man watched the Killer in its turret. He was unusual-looking, both his features – how did he get that twisted nose and a left ear from which it seemed a large chunk had been bitten off? – and his blackness. This was still a segregated army and black men had only begun appearing in the ranks of the infantry since December '44. But the big black still wore the 'Screaming Eagle' patch of the 101st Airborne Division, which had black paratroopers in its ranks, and besides, who'd dare call a black nearly seven foot tall with half an ear missing 'a nigger' or even worse 'a coon'? So the big black, who answered to the name of 'Bo-Bo', watched the Killer through his looted German field glasses and nobody said a word about it. After all, as Mike Dooley, the squad sergeant, said privately to his cronies when he thought Bo-Bo wasn't listening, 'He can call himself frigging Jo-Jo as far as I'm concerned – or Dwight D. Eisenhower. With the mitts that black guy has gotten on him, he can do frigging well what he likes, brother.'

Slowly the long column began their descent out of the hills, every man (save the big black) tense and nervous, wrapped up in a cocoon of their own thoughts and apprehension, knowing, even the dullest and most unimaginative among them, that soon they were to do battle...

Campbell had lost old Papa Novak. It hadn't been difficult. There was confusion everywhere. A party of SS were trying to take away some *Prominenten*, high-ranking prisoners or those with VIP relatives back in England, and they were refusing to go. They had scattered all over the Castle and there were flustered young SS troopers everywhere trying to winkle them out of their hiding places.

Then there were POWs of half a dozen

Allied nations having a final feast using up the last of their hoarded rations now that the Yanks were almost there and drinking their potent home-brews, made from raisins, potatoes, meths – anything that had an alcoholic kick. They were whooping and yelling, red-faced with booze and joy, like crazy Indians, ignoring the pleas .and commands of their superiors, trying to restore order.

Others were packing furiously. Some had been behind the wire since Dunkirk back in '40. In that time they had collected an enormous amount of worthless kit, which they were now trying to sort out, so that their barracks and the cobbled yard outside was littered knee-deep in old boots, darned socks, unrecognizable carved objects made from bed planks, stills constructed from powdered milk cans; the treasures of what had seemed a life-time 'inside' and which now were just more weight.

Watching it all, waiting to see the SBO, who was trying to deal with the SS colonel, Campbell thought of the doggerel he had just come across, carved on the wall of one of the towers: 'Here I lie ... In a great cold castle ... And wonder why ... And wonder why we are what we are ... And whither we are going...' Supreme realist that Campbell 175 was, momentarily, he wondered, too. What had been the purpose of it all, those many years spent by these young men confined in this awful place, cut off from their country, the ordinary pleasures of family and friends, sex? 'Whither we are going?' he said the words of the doggerel softly to himself and watched as one of the drunks dressed in some sort of tutu and wearing a blonde wig, probably from one of the theatrical entertainments put on at the Castle by the POWs, danced drunkenly up to one of the red-faced SS men and tried to kiss him. Could men like these ever settle down to a normal life again? He thought not.

Five minutes later he was speaking to a harassed, red-faced and somewhat suspicious SBO. The Colonel had managed to put the SS men off for a while and had ordered no one, even the drunks, should leave the camp. Now he said before finally turning to Campbell, 'Keep 'em together, it's the only way. There's all hell let loose out there.' As if to emphasize his words, the first shells from the advancing Americans on the other side of the ridge beyond the castle began to fall in and about the hill. 'All right, Campbell, make it quick. What can I do for you?' He mopped his face and Campbell noticed the hand holding the khaki handkerchief shook badly. The Colonel was about at the end of his tether.

Swiftly Campbell explained his mission

and why they were there.

The SBO looked irritated. 'Yes ... poor Dalby. But that's long ago. Still I'll tell you this. The swine who did it to him was some sort of German-American. We found that out from a young Yank POW whom he approached for food a few days later.'

'So he did hide in the Castle till the heat was off,' Campbell said.

The SBO was not listening. 'The Yank didn't like the business. Where had this chap been and why was he without rations? Besides he seemed to talk with a bit of an accent. To cut a long story—' Hastily the Colonel threw a glance over his shoulder. A shell had just burst next to the approach road and a thick black cloud was mushrooming to the April sky. Up at the gate, the guards were already slinging their rifles nervously as if they might make a run for it any minute now. 'The Yank was going to report the stranger as a German stooge, one of the goons dressed in US uniform, perhaps, to our Safety Officer when the bugger gave him a great whack over the head ... An old army sock filled with earth, it appears. Thereafter he did a bunk. That was the last we ever heard—'

The sudden heavy harsh rat-tat-tat of a heavy machine gun, followed by an urgent line of white tracer flying over the cobbled yard, drowned the rest of his words. At the gate the middle-aged guards shrank back. Angrily the SS troopers started to unsling their own weapons, glaring angrily at both POWs and guards. The situation was growing ugly.

'Oh, God save us,' the Colonel exclaimed. 'There's going to be a bloody massacre ... Sorry, Campbell, no more time for ancient history now. Got to think of the present.' And with that he was gone, loping across the courtyard with the aid of his stick with surprising speed for such an old man. Campbell 175 hesitated only a second more and then he was hurrying too, through the abandoned gate, pausing only to pick up one of the guards' dropped machine pistols before running down the hill towards the already burning village. Colditz's last hours as Germany's most feared prisoner-of-war camp had commenced...

Five

It had started with the first American shell landing in the village. It had slammed into the houses only a street away. Tiles and bricks had come roaring down in a sudden avalanche of stone. Next moment the blast had struck the two of them across the face like a blow from a damp palm. Instinctively they dropped to the ground as the cottage's little windows shattered and glass sliced through the rooms everywhere. She fell on top of him. For the first time Mackenzie felt the youthful softness of her body pressing into his. Almost automatically he put his arms around her in protection and held her to him tightly. Despite the danger, he felt a sudden urge – the first for a long time. Ashamed of himself, but unable to control the sexual desire, he kissed her.

Her mouth opened. His tongue penetrated its warm heat and he felt a satisfaction that was almost totally sexual in itself. Now the shells began to land more frequently. The cottage rocked under the impact. The noise was hellish. But the two of them didn't seem to notice. In that reeling world of high explosives and sudden violent death, they appeared isolated by desire, love, perhaps lust too.

He felt his hand slide under her skirt. She didn't object. Her legs parted almost automatically. He touched her there. She gasped slightly. Her loins rose as if she were only too eager to meet him. His finger slid into her. She was wet with desire. At the back of his mind a little voice said, 'This is mad!' He ignored the voice. What did reason matter now? He had let reason dominate his life. It had done no good. Let passion take over.

She knocked his hand away. Abruptly he felt she had come to *her* senses. But she hadn't. Raising herself slightly, she had begun undoing his flies. His erection sprang out of the opening. She sighed and lay back, legs spread as she removed her knickers and waited. It was all perfectly natural, as if it had been planned – no, *ordained* – a long time ago. He levered himself up on his elbows. He slid himself into that hot, wet nothingness. She wasn't a virgin. It didn't matter. She gasped – and it began...

Outside, the bombardment continued. Shells were landing all around the village and the rattle of tracks was becoming louder and louder. Up in the Castle, they were rigging up white flags and makeshift national ones – French, Polish, American, British.

Soon it was clear that the Americans would launch their all-out attack on Colditz. For the SS, the last of the *Wehrmacht* prepared to make a fight for it, nervous as they were, could see the spotter planes diving up and down among the fog of war, trying to spot the positions they were hastily digging into the fields around the Castle.

She lay in his arms. He could still feel her heart beating frantically and his own hand, as he stroked her hair, was shaking slightly with the excitement of that wild ride to culmination. 'You are not German,' she said softly, despite the thunder of the guns and snarl and roar of the spotter planes outside; it was as if she was unaware of the noise.

'No,' he answered quietly, without any attempt at subterfuge. 'I am English.'

'I thought so. Right from the start. Not the other one. But you. You have the English look.' She reached up and kissed him gently on the mouth, as if the matter was finished. She had found out all she needed to know.

Thus for a few minutes Mackenzie found happiness, a brief time detached from the war raging outside, not knowing, not caring what might – would – come: that happy feeling of contentment with the world that comes only in the arms of a woman whom one loves and who, a man knows implicitly, loves him. He knew nothing about Irma really. She came from a totally different world from his, he realized that, of course. She was a peasant girl of no education really. There'd be no classy chats about the cosmos with her. Yet she possessed what the Germans called in that untranslatable phrase of theirs – *Herzenswarme*. 'Warmth of the heart': that was it. What did all the sophistication, the intellectual knowledge, the tutored calm mean in comparison with *Herzenswarme*?

Thus they lay in each other's arms, happy and oblivious, or so it seemed, to the crazy war raging outside. It was a time out of war rarely given to young people in the last month of the great conflict. Naturally, it couldn't possibly last…

Papa Novak groaned and threw up his hands. He clawed the air, as if he were climbing the rungs of a ladder. The sudden scarlet patch on the front of his shabby tunic grew larger and larger. He mumbled something. It wasn't in German; Campbell 175 thought it might have been in Polish. 'Hold on,' he cried, grabbing the old man's rifle, as it fell from his suddenly nerveless fingers. But it was already too late. Without another sound, Papa Novak pitched to the churned, smoking earth, dead before he hit it.

'*Halt … was machst du da*?' a young voice, which was harsh, but trembly, challenged him.

He looked up.

A kid in the grey uniform of the SS was facing him, rifle in his hand. He looked about sixteen and he was scared. Campbell didn't hesitate. He dropped the old man's rifle, swung the machine pistol hanging from his chest round and fired in one and the same movement. The kid screamed. A series of blood-red buttonholes was now stitched across his skinny chest. He dropped and died, choking and gurgling in his own hot blood.

It didn't move Campbell 175. He had hated too long and too much. Yet before he left the bloody scene of sudden death, he bent and closed Papa Novak's eyelids Why, he didn't know. Perhaps it was a token of respect. Afterwards when everything went rotten, he didn't want to know. All that concerned him was that he now knew more about Major Dalby's killer and he thought it imperative to let Mackenzie know. He ran on, bent low, leaving the old man and the boy – some might have said the good German and the bad German – behind him...

The first American armoured cars were nosing their way over the hill, turrets swinging from left to right like the predatory snouts of some primeval monsters scenting out their intended prey. Behind him the covering Yank artillery barrage had ceased for fear of hitting its own men. Campbell breathed a sigh of relief. At least he was safe from the shells, though of course the Yanks might see him as fair game: just another Kraut civilian to be sent to his Nazi heaven.

A burst of machine-gun fire ripping up the earth in angry eruptions at his heels told him he wasn't safe. Someone had spotted him and had taken him for a 'Kraut civilian'.

'Bugger it,' he hissed to himself and flung himself in a ditch, just as an amoured car hove into sight, its turret machine gun blasting away furiously. Behind it came a small open-tracked vehicle, which made his heart miss a beat. He recognized it immediately for what it was: a British built Wasp, the most fearsome weapon at the command of the poor bloody infantry. If anything was calculated to send enemy infantry fleeing panic-stricken from a well-prepared defensive position it was the British tracked vehicle, towing behind it the two-wheeled trailer that contained the source of its frightening power.

The next instant he had frightening proof of the Wasp's effectiveness. There was a sudden hiss. It was like that of some fiery mythical dragon drawing a first fetid breath. There was a crack, like a rod slapping the side of a great tree. Next moment a stream of ugly red flame tinged with black smoke shot out of the front of the carrier, curved upwards slightly, sending a sudden heat wave towards his hiding place and making him gasp for breath, to slam against the nearest cottage.

In a flash it was ringed with flame. The house began to burn immediately. Windows cracked. The beams turned into flaming pillars and all the while there came terrible, inhuman screams from within, with a lone figure staggering out, already burning, its movements jerking as the flesh burned and charred until it fell to the ground, a blackened pygmy, the hands frozen for all time like leafless branches in winter.

Campbell 175 turned his head away in horror for a moment. Instinctively he knew what the Yanks were going to do now. They weren't going to risk their motorized infantry in house-to-house fighting inside Colditz village. They were going to burn the place down cruelly, house after house, and once that terrible little Wasp sighted and aimed there was no hope for the inhabitants of those houses. This wasn't war; it was a heartless bloody massacre.

Frightened as he was, Campbell 175 knew he had to do something. The Wasp, satisfied that it had burned out the house, was now beginning to roll down the hill again. Some two hundred yards away, Campbell saw to his horror, lay the Novak house where he had left the boss and the girl, Irma.

Mackenzie didn't even have a weapon to defend himself, he knew. God, they'd frizzle him and the girl to a cinder, without either of them having a snowball's chance in hell of doing anything to save themselves from that ghastly fate.

Campbell sprang up once more from the ditch. His heart was pounding like a trip hammer. He had never been so scared in the whole of his young life. But he knew he had to do something. On the turret of the lead armoured car, a yellow-haired American spotted him. Campbell yelled, 'Friend ... friend ... FOR FUCK'S SAKE ... F.R.I.E.N.D!'

The Yank grinned evilly. He raised his gun and took deliberate aim.

It would be like falling off a frigging log to kill the stupid Kraut, the murderer told himself. His sight filled with the wildly gesticulating Kraut...

Mackenzie had spotted the Wasp, too. He knew all about the fearsome little mobile weapon, based on the British Army's pre-war Bren gun carrier. With the hellish racket going on all around them, he realized, all the shouting and protesting in the world wouldn't stop the little monster from flaming the Novak house and the two of them in it. They had to get out now.

'*Schnell*,' he said, pulling Irma to her feet.

'*Was ist los?*' He didn't give her any time to ask questions. He tugged hard at her hand

and hurried her to the back door which led to the old man's potato patch with which he fed his beloved porker. 'We've got to get out. Is there a lane at the back of the houses?'

'Yes, but why? We should hide in the house ... it's safer,' she began to protest. The rest of her words were drowned by that horrific rearing whoosh of flame. A solid red of burnished gold and scarlet hit the cottage at the top of the little village street. She reeled back, face concerted with sudden fear, her left arm raised to shield her face from the terrific heat. *'Um Gotteswillen,'* she gasped as the house's straw roof ignited at once. Abruptly the whole place was burning fiercely, as the Wasp fired its terrible weapon yet again and the house was wreathed in fierce, crackling fire.

Mackenzie swallowed hard. What was he to do? The Wasp was swivelling round in the house's garden, churning up the flower beds in a wild wake of flying earth, positioning itself for one final burst of fire. But where would it go after that? Would it stick to the road? Or would it come down the track behind the row of little houses? It could flame them better from that position. After all, if the Wasp fired from too close a range, the fire might well engulf it, too. He told himself, it was a decision that no one should be forced to make. If he got it wrong, there'd be no second chance. *What was he to do?*

Bo-Bo, the giant black ex-boxer was confused. But then he was always confused. The years of having his shaven skull pounded in the ring had had their effect. But he did know two things – those he couldn't forget, confused as his mental processes were. They were: he was hated because he was black and he was feared because he was so big and powerful. Why, in his time he had snapped a couple of whiteys' necks with his bare hands. Yeah, the white guys were scared of him, that was for sure. Even the 'head shirt', who had just ordered him out of the half-track to cover the lead armoured car with his tommy gun just in case some Kraut kid sneaked up on it with one of those bazookas of theirs.

But now that he was alone on the ground trailing the Staghound, which was just behind the little limey vehicle with its flaming popgun, he had already forgotten what he was supposed to do. He knew from what the whitey colonel had told him back in Paris, France, that the yellow-haired guy in the turret of the armoured car had to be killed. He knew that all right. But – his dark face with the broken pug boxer's nose creased in a bewildered frown – *when* was he to be killed? Was it now? Or was it sometime afterwards? But when afterwards? He ran his tongue round his thick cracked lips and wished he could have a drink – that would help. He didn't want to screw up. If he did, the whitey colonel back in Paris, France, wouldn't look after him and these days he knew he needed someone to look after him. Holy shit, he didn't even know the way back to the States! He knew he'd come from there. In a big ship. But where he'd find that ship again, he hadn't an idea. He shook his big shaven head again like a boxer trying to ward off the count of ten. If he could only get rid of that goddam fog that seemed to wreath his mind these days!

'Hey you, you goddam coon!' The angry voice cut through the mist that dogged his brain processes. 'Get your black ass outa the way!'

It was the man in the turret. He was shouting through a loud-hailer, as the Wasp came rattling up, its trailer full of fuel, bouncing up and down as it entered the rough track behind the row of houses.

'Can't you see, boy, you're holding up the fuckin' war!' The Killer glared angrily at this great black man who had seemingly appeared out of nowhere and was standing there like a spare prick at a wedding, holding a tommy gun in a black hand that looked like a small steam shovel. He waved his hand impatiently at Bo-Bo, as if he wanted physically to remove him. 'Move it, goddamnit, you stupid S.O.B!'

Satisfied that the coon would move now – who dared disobey him? – the Killer turned back to the petrified Kraut civilian. He raised his tommy gun again. Why didn't the silly bastard make a run for it? he asked himself. It always gave him greater pleasure to plug someone who was cowering with fear or tried to make a run for it. He guessed that was sort of the thrill of the chase, as those upper-class fruits who went in for hunting called it.

An electric shock surged through Campbell 175. *Wach auf!* a voice cried within him in that harsh guttural language he hated. Wake up! If he didn't move in the next few seconds, he would be dead.

The Killer's merciless smile spread. His dreams were always full of killings like this. Death, sex and money were the only things that made his life worth living. Although all around him was noise, fire and chaos, he took his time. He squeezed the trigger slowly, taking first pressure, as if he were savouring the ritualistic moves – so slow, controlled, mechanical – which led to violent, hectic death.

Campbell acted. Without even looking down, he pressed the trigger of the Schmeisser hanging from his skinny chest. The Killer had overlooked it. After all, the muzzle was not pointing in his direction. The burst flashed by Campbell's chest in a blaze of hot excruciating pain. The burst ripped the length of the Wasp, manoeuvring just to his left and behind Bo-Bo.

For what seemed an age, the shock of that sudden burst caught both him and the Killer off guard. The latter faltered. He had no chance to recover. The little fuel tank exploded in a massive sheet of blinding searing flame. Like a giant blowtorch it ran the length of the Wasp immediately. Desperately the crew fought to get out. In vain. The flames consumed them in an instant, as the paint on the carrier's steel sides bubbled and burst under that terrific heat like the loathsome symptoms of some disgusting skin disease. Next second, the Wasp exploded and Campbell 175 found himself flung back into the ditch, all the breath dragged from his lungs as he fell so that he was gasping and choking like some chronic asthmatic in the throes of one final attack.

The Killer shielded his suddenly terrified face as great jagged fragments from the disintegrating carrier hissed lethally through the air, cutting down all in their path. Bo-Bo yelped with pain and looked down, as bewildered as ever, to find that a great chunk of flesh had been sliced off his leg to reveal the bone below shining in its gory-red setting like some prized piece of polished ivory. He staggered a few paces backwards, his black face appearing to be lathered in sweat in the flames which were rising higher and higher. Another man would have remained down, perhaps for good. Not Bo-Bo. In his time he had taken tremendous punishment in the ring and these whiteys who had made money from him (before they had abandoned him when he couldn't make money any more) had yelled, '*Go on, Bo-Bo, boy* ... Stay in there punching, *boy*, you've got the Wop, Hunkey, Polack (whatever nationality the other boxer was supposed to he) on the ropes, *boy* ... Knock the shit outa him, *boy*...' It had always been 'boy' and in a crazy way he had been proud of being called 'boy'. The whiteys were rooting for him, a black boy. That meant, his poor befuddled mind had told him, they liked him in a way; and he had been proud they had liked him, poor nigger trash from the south, and he had kept on going. Now he did the same. That whitey colonel back in Paris, France, who had actually sat with him and smoked a cigarette together and had arranged for him to have that white Frog girl in bed, a whore to be sure, but *white*, in bed with him before he had left Paris, France, expected him to keep on punching – and goddamnit, so he would.

He limped forward, face turned away from the flames. To his front the turret of the Staghound armoured car had begun to glow a dull red. Frantically, in his box below the turret, the driver was attempting to start the stalled engine. The Killer was shrieking at him, panicked now. Winded and shocked, seemingly unable to move, Campbell 175 watched the inevitable happen as he lay there in the ditch, shielded from that roaring inferno. Amazed, he saw the gigantic Negro, his uniform beginning to smoulder and smoke, too, now reach up one huge paw of a hand. The Killer shrank back. But there was no escape. Even as he watched, Campbell 175 knew that something terrible was going to happen to the two Americans, one black and one white.

The Killer attempted to fire at the man below him. He didn't get a chance. As the driver abandoned the stalled armoured car, slipping out of the escape hatch below the turret, the black man heaved. Campbell 175 imagined he could hear him grunt with the effort. Later he knew it had been in his imagination. Suddenly he had the Killer by the scruff of his neck, dragging him down, his legs kicking wildly and impotently, as he tried to free himself from the merciless grip.

In vain. The black's other hand fastened on the white man's throat. Campbell, awed and shaken by the spectacle, caught one last glimpse of them, as Bo-Bo held the Killer, his feet trampling uselessly like those of some puppet in the hands of a puppeteer who had suddenly gone mad, hands that were squeezing the life out of the man who had killed Major Dalby. Next moment the flames surged around the stalled armoured car. Its engine caught fire in a sheet of searing, violent flame. The air was abruptly filled with the cloying, sickly smell of escaping petrol. Just in time Campbell dropped once more into the cover of his ditch as the armoured car disintegrated with a great roar that seemed to go on for ever and ever...

ENVOI

'Your visitation shall receive such thanks
As fits a king's remembrance.'

Shakespeare

Outside, the bells of the village churches pealed for victory. It was the first time since the Battle of El Alamein two years before that the authorities had allowed them to be rung, to celebrate the German surrender and the end of the war in Europe. Now they rang out in a joyous, merry peal – a happy triumphant sound.

But there was nothing happy or triumphant in the mood of those gathered in the drawing room of the old house in the country. Their mood was sombre, pensive, even apprehensive, as if the peacetime future brought them no renewal of hope, only a continuation of the old fears and dreads. Even Campbell 175, the youngest and perhaps the most optimistic of those present, puffed his cigarette in an introspective way, as if he had serious problems on his mind. Occasionally he darted a glance at Mackenzie, his chief. But the Major's hard face revealed nothing and when Campbell tried to engage the older man in eye-to-eye contact, Mackenzie obstinately refused to respond. Again Campbell realized the boss had changed. Even the release of the overjoyed, almost hysterically happy POWs from Colditz Castle a week ago had not been enough to change his mood. He had carried the dead girl, struck in the very moment of triumph by a steel fragment from the disintegrating Wasp and killed outright, to the little village cemetery and had begun digging her grave personally. When he and others had offered to help, he had turned on them, eyes blazing, red and almost mad, and snarled, 'Keep away from her ... take your hands off her ... I'll bury her *alone*.' And he had. Kneeling beside the pile of fresh brown earth, ignoring the *feu de joie* and drunken whooping of the liberated POWs, he had broken down and wept, his shoulders heaving like those of some broken-hearted innocent child. Thereafter he had disappeared for twenty-four hours. Frantically Campbell had searched for him everywhere. He had feared the worst. But when Mackenzie had reappeared, he had been washed and shaved and had been completely in control of himself (though he had exuded a coldness that hadn't been there before). Since then he had never mentioned Irma Novak again and now Campbell, puffing moodily at his Player's, felt certain he never would in the future either.

Now the soft chatter of the others present

in the great timbered reception hall of Chequers began to die away. Important-looking senior officers started to look at their watches. It was getting near the time for the Great Man to make his appearance. They took their last puffs at their cigarettes and cigars and the VIPs, who had been offered drinks, finished them. A little wearily, Campbell 175, now supporting his new 'pips' as a lieutenant in the Intelligence Corps, did the same. It was an honour, he supposed, to be summoned here, but why they were there was beyond him.

A few minutes later the great door opened. The generals and important civilians tugged at their tunics, straightened their hair and went through the gestures of preparing to meet the Great Man. They were to be disappointed. Churchill sauntered in, his cherubic face wreathed in a warm smile, though the eyes didn't reflect a mood of good humour. He was dressed in his familiar 'rompers': a one-piece siren suit with zips, which he'd had tailored specially for him. In his hand he held a cigar the size of a small pole. He paused and surveyed the faces of the high-ranking men lined up respectfully before saying, 'Mackenzie and you – er – Lieutenant Campbell, please follow me. I have a few words to say to you.'

They squeezed their way to the front of the line. While the top brass looked on, puzzled or frustrated, the two lonely officers followed Churchill into the inner sanctum and the doors were closed firmly behind them. Churchill waited till the servant completed the action and then he said simply, 'I should like to thank you both.' He sat down suddenly and for an instant the smile vanished and he looked to Campbell abruptly like the Chinese God of Plenty suffering from bellyache. 'The matter to which I referred originally when we met last has come to a conclusion–' he took a puff at his cigar – 'or should I say has been deferred. The new President, Truman, is not so eager to destroy the British Empire as his late lamented predecessor.'

Campbell wondered whether Churchill was being ironic or not with his 'late lamented'. Mackenzie, for his part, remained grave but somehow absent. His gaze was set on some vista known only to him and Campbell guessed it was nothing to do with the global politics to which Churchill referred.

'However, we must take it,' Churchill continued, and now his bantering mood vanished to be replaced by one of grim-faced seriousness, 'that soon those who are the real power in that great country over the sea will take up Roosevelt's campaign once more. There are those in that place who have rapacious natures. They are interested in power, supremacy in our poor, stricken world, but they are more interested in – *money*.' He made a gesture that Campbell 175 was only too familiar with from his days as a young boy in Cologne: a flicking movement with thumb and forefinger as if one were counting coins.

Churchill shrugged eloquently. 'No matter,' he said softly, as if to himself. 'We shall attempt to survive.' His voice held little conviction. Then he was businesslike once more. 'You have done well, Major Mackenzie and you, Lieutenant Campbell, if that is really your name. I won't forget you, for perhaps I will need you again in the future.' He raised a finger, as if in warning. 'But remember this, *you* must forget all this. What you have learned and what you have done must remain for all time part of the secret history of the late great conflict. Promise me that.'

Numbly the two of them mumbled that they promised.

Churchill took out his old-fashioned pebble, half-spectacles, perched them on the end of his nose and peered at a paper on the eighteenth-century desk in front of him. The interview, if that was what it was supposed to be, was over.

They went out, Campbell, the foreign Jew, flushed with admiration for the man who had sworn he had not become the 'King's First Minister' to preside over the dissolution of the British Empire. England, Britain, needed people like Churchill.

They emerged into the damp English air. Mackenzie said nothing. Was he still thinking of that Irma of his? Campbell wondered. He felt he had to say something, as they walked to the waiting staff car. 'It's going to be all right, sir,' he ventured.

Mackenzie nodded curtly. The expression on his hard face didn't change. His gaze was still fixed on some private horizon known only to himself. 'It would be nice to think so,' he answered.

Campbell 175's mood of hope vanished as soon as it had come. In silence they walked the rest of the way to the car. The bells of victory continued to herald the start of the long road ahead, filling the abruptly grey sky…

1	26	51	76	101	126	151	220	310	460
2	27	52	77	102	127	152	227	312	461
3	28	53	78	103	128	153	233	317	478
4	29	54	79	104	129	154	234	324	479
5	30	55	80	105	130	155	237	331	486
6	31	56	81	106	131	156	238	341	488
7	32	57	82	107	132	157	241	355	499
8	33	58	83	108	133	160	242	357	500
9	34	59	84	109	134	164	243	363	509
10	35	60	85	110	135	166	244	375	511
11	36	61	86	111	136	167	249	380	517
12	37	62	87	112	137	168	250	383	519
13	38	63	88	113	138	172	252	393	523
14	39	64	89	114	139	174	257	396	529
15	40	65	90	115	140	175	259	400	534
16	41	66	91	116	141	180	262	403	538
17	42	67	92	117	142	182	268	405	544
18	43	68	93	118	143	183	269	413	552
19	44	69	94	119	144	188	272	417	565
20	45	70	95	120	145	189	273	435	570
21	46	71	96	121	146	192	274	440	575
22	[illegible]	72	97	122	147	195	279	447	583
23	[illegible]	73	98	123	148	203	285	451	595
24	4[illegible]	[illegible]	99	124	149	208	288	452	619
25	50	[illegible]	100	125	150	212	299	453	624